THE TRUTH ABOUT TRISTREM VARICK.
&
MR. INCOUL'S MISADVENTURE.

Two Novels

by
EDGAR SALTUS

UNDERWORLD AMUSEMENTS

"Saltus's first two novels bear the imprint of the kind of diffident, decadent pessimism *The Philosophy of Disenchantment* elaborates. Indeed, the sensitivity requisite for the recognition that life has no value informs *Mr. Incoul's Misadventure*, the first novel, while the delusion that life has value motivates the action of the obtuse hero of the second novel, *The Truth about Tristram Varick*."
—David Weir, *Decadent Culture in the United States*, 2008

This edition prepared by Kevin I. Slaughter
for Underworld Amusements.
www.UnderworldAmusements.com

ISBN: 978-0-9830314-1-3

THE TRUTH ABOUT TRISTREM VARICK.

I.

It is just as well to say at the onset that the tragedy in which Tristrem Varick was the central figure has not been rightly understood. The world in which he lived, as well as the newspaper public, have had but one theory between them to account for it, and that theory is that Tristrem Varick was insane. Tristrem Varick was not insane. He had, perhaps, a fibre more or a fibre less than the ordinary run of men; that something, in fact, which is the prime factor of individuality and differentiates the possessor from the herd; but to call him insane is nonsense. If he were, it is a pity that there are not more lunatics like him.

It may be that the course of conduct which he pursued in regard to his father's estate served as basis to the theory alluded to. At the time being, it created quite a little stir; it was looked upon as a piece of old-world folly, an eccentricity worthy of the red-heeled days of seigneurial France, and, as such, altogether out of place in a money-getting age like our own. But it was not until after the tragedy that his behavior in that particular was brought up in evidence against him.

The facts in the case were these: Tristrem's father, Erastus Varick, was a man of large wealth, who, when well on in the forties, married a girl young enough to be his daughter. The lady in question was the only child of a neighbor, Mr. Dirck Van Norden by name, and very pretty is she said to have been. Before the wedding Erastus Varick had his house, which was situated in Waverley Place, refurbished from cellar to garret; he had the parlor—there were parlors in those days—fitted up in white and gold, in the style known as that of the First Empire. The old Dutch furniture, black with age and hair-cloth, was banished. The walls were plastered with a lime cement of peculiar brilliance. The floors of the bedrooms were carpeted with rugs that extended under the beds, a novelty in New York, and the bedsteads themselves, which were vast enough to make coffins for ten people, were curtained with chintz patterns manufactured in Manchester to frighten children. In brief, Erastus Varick succeeded in making the house even less attractive than before, and altogether acted like a man in love.

After three years of marriage, Tristrem was born and Mrs. Varick died. The boy had the best of care and everything that money could procure. He was given that liberal education which usually unfits the recipient for making so much as his bread and butter, and at school, at college, and when he went abroad his supply of funds was of the amplest description. Shortly after his return from foreign lands Erastus Varick was gathered to his fathers. By his will he bequeathed to Tristrem a Panama hat and a bundle of letters. The rest and residue of his property he devised to the St. Nicholas Hospital. The value of that property amounted to seven million dollars.

Now Dirck Van Norden had not yet moved from the neighborhood to a better place. Tristrem was his only grandson, and when he learned of the tenor of the will, he shook his fist at himself in the looking-glass and swore, in a bountiful old-fashioned manner which was peculiar to him, that his grandson should not be divested of his rights. He set the lawyers to work, and the lawyers were not long in discovering a flaw which, through a wise provision of the legislature, rendered the will null and void. The Hospital made a bold fight. It was shown beyond peradventure that from the time of Tristrem's birth the intention of the testator—and the intention of a testator is what the court most considers—had been to leave his property to a charitable institution. It was proved that he had made other wills of a similar character, and that he had successively destroyed them as his mind changed in regard to minor details and distributions of the trust. But the wise law was there, and there too were the wise lawyers. The decision was made in accordance with the statute, and the estate reverted to Tristrem, who then succeeded in surprising New York. Of his own free will he made over the entire property to the account of the Hospital to which it had been originally devised, and it was in connection with that transfer that he was taxed with old-world folly. But the matter was misunderstood and afterward forgotten, and only raked up again when the press of two continents busied itself with his name. At that time he was in his twenty-fifth or twenty-sixth year.

He was slender, of medium height, blue of eye, and clear-featured. His hair, which was light in color, he wore brushed upward and back from the forehead. When he walked, it was with a slight stoop, which was the more noticeable in that, being nearsighted, he had a way of holding his chin out and raising his eyebrows as though he were peering at something which he could not quite discern. In his face there was a charm that grew and delighted and fastened on the beholder. At the age of twenty-six he would have been recognized by anyone who had known him as a boy. He had expanded, of course, and a stoop and dimness of vision had come with years; but in his face was the same unmistakable, almost childish, expression of sweet good-will.

His school-days were passed at Concord. When he first appeared there he looked so much like a pretty girl, in his manner was such gentleness, and his nature was found to be so vibrant and sensitive, that his baptismal name was promptly shortened into Trissy. But by the time he reached the fourth form it was lengthened back again to its rightful shape. This change was the result of an evolution of opinion. One day while some companions, with whom he happened to be loitering, scurried behind a fence, he stopped a runaway horse, clinging to the bridle though his arm had been dislocated in the earliest effort. Another time, when a comrade had been visited, unjustly it appeared, with some terrible punishment—five hundred lines, perhaps, or something equally direful—Tristrem made straight for the master, and argued with him to such effect that the punishment was remitted. And again, when a tutor asked how it was that there was no W in the French language, Tristrem answered, "Because of Waterloo."

Boys are generous in their enthusiasms; they like bravery, they are not deaf to wit, but perhaps of all other things they admire justice most. And Tristrem seemed to exhale it. It is said that everyone has a particular talent for some one thing, whether for good or evil, and the particular talent which was accorded to Tristrem Varick was that of appreciation. He was a born umpire. In disputes his school-fellows turned to him naturally, and accepted his verdict without question. When he reached the altitudes which the Upper School offers, no other boy at St. Paul's was better liked than he. At that time the form of which he was a member—and in which, parenthetically, he ranked rather low—was strengthened by a new-comer, a turbulent, precocious boy who had been expelled from two other schools, and with whom, so ran the gossip, it would go hard were he expelled again. His name was Royal Weldon, and on his watch, and on a seal ring which he wore on his little finger, he displayed an elaborate coat-of-arms under which for legend were the words, *Well done, Weldon*, words which it was reported an English king had bawled in battle, ennobling as he did so the earliest Weldon known to fame.

Between the two lads, and despite the dissimilarity of their natures, or perhaps precisely on that account, there sprang up a warm friendship which propinquity cemented, for chance or the master had given them a room in common. At first, Tristrem fairly blinked at Weldon's precocity, and Weldon, who was accustomed to be admired, took to Tristrem not unkindly on that account. But after a time Tristrem ceased to blink and began to lecture, not priggishly at all, but in a persuasive manner that was hard to resist. For Weldon was prone to get into difficulties, and equally prone to make the difficulties worse than they need have been. When cross-questioned he would decline to answer; it was a trick he had. Now Tristrem never got into difficulties, except with Latin prosody or a Greek root, and he was frank to a fault.

It so happened that one day the headmaster summoned Tristrem to him. "My dear," he said, "Royal is not acting quite as he should, is he?" To this Tristrem made no reply. "He is a motherless boy," the master continued, "a poor motherless boy. I wish, Tristrem, that you would use your influence with him. I see but one course open to me, unless he does better—" Tristrem was a motherless boy himself, but he answered bravely that he would do what he could. That evening, as he was battling with the platitudes of that Augustan bore who is called the Bard of Mantua, presumably because he was born in Andes—Weldon came in, smelling of tobacco and drink. It was evident that he had been to town.

Tristrem looked up from his task, and as he looked he heard the step of a tutor in the hall. He knew, if the tutor had speech with Weldon, that on the morrow Weldon would leave the school. In a second he had seated him before the open dictionary, and in another second he was kneeling at his own bedside. Hardly had he bowed his head when there came a rap at the door, the tutor entered, saw the kneeling figure, apologized in a whisper, and withdrew.

When Tristrem stood up again, Weldon was sobered and very pale. "Tristrem—" he began, but Tristrem interrupted him. "There, don't say anything, and don't do it again. To-morrow you had better talk it over with the doctor."

Weldon declined to talk it over with anyone, but after that he behaved himself with something approaching propriety. Two years later, in company with his friend, he entered Harvard, from which institution he was subsequently dropped.

Tristrem meanwhile struggled through the allotted four years. He was not brilliant in his studies, the memorizing of abstruse questions and recondite problems was not to his liking. He preferred modern tongues to dead languages, an intricate fugue was more to his taste than the simplest equation, and to his shame it must be noted that he read Petrarch at night. But, though the curriculum was not entirely to his fancy, he was conscientious and did his best. There are answers that he gave in class that are quoted still, tangential flights that startled the listeners into new conceptions of threadbare themes, totally different from the usual cut and dried response that is learned by rote. And at times he

THE TRUTH ABOUT TRISTREM VARICK.

would display an ignorance, a stupidity even, that was fathomless in its abysses.

After graduation, he went abroad. England seemed to him like a rose in bloom, but when autumn came and with it a succession of fogs, each more depressing than the last, he fled to Italy, and wandered among her ghosts and treasuries, and then drifted up again through Germany, to Paris, where he gave his mornings to the Sorbonne and his evenings to orchestra-stalls.

II.

It was after an absence of nearly five years that Tristrem Varick returned to the States. He had wearied of foreign lands, and for some time previous he had thought of New York in such wise that it had grown in his mind, and in the growing it had assumed a variety of attractive attributes. He was, therefore, much pleased at the prospect of renewing his acquaintance with Fifth Avenue, and during the homeward journey he pictured to himself the advantages which his native city possessed over any other which he had visited.

He had not, however, been many hours on shore before he found that Fifth Avenue had shrunk. In some unaccountable way the streets had lost their charm, the city seemed provincial. He was perplexed at the discovery that the uniform if depthless civility of older civilizations was rarely observable; he was chagrined to find that the *minutiæ* which, abroad, he had accepted as a matter of course, the thousand trifles which amount, after all, to nothing particularly indispensable, but which serve to make mere existence pleasant, were, when not overlooked, inhibited by statute or custom.

In the course of a week he was surprised into reflecting that, while no other country was more naturally and bountifully favored than his own, there was yet no other where the art of living was as vexatiously misunderstood.

Of these impressions he said nothing. His father asked him no questions, nor did he manifest a desire for any larger sociological information than that which he already possessed. His grandfather was too irascible for anyone to venture with in safety through the shallows of European refinements, and of other relatives Tristrem could not boast. Few of his former friends were at once discoverable, and of those that he encountered some had fallen into the rut and routine of business life, some had married and sent in their resignations to everything but the Humdrum, and some passed their days in an effort to catch a train.

For the moment, therefore, there was no one to whom Tristrem could confide his earliest impressions, and in a month's time the force of these impressions waned; the difference between New York and Paris lost much of its accent, and in its place came a growing admiration for the pluck and power of the nation, an expanding enthusiasm for the stretch and splendor of the land.

During the month that followed, an incident occurred which riveted his patriotism forever. First among the friends and acquaintances whom Tristrem sought on his return was Royal Weldon. Outwardly the handsome, turbulent boy had developed into an admirable specimen of manhood, he had become one on whom the feminine eye likes to linger, and in whose companionship men feel themselves refreshed. His face was beardless and unmustached, and into it had come that strength which the old prints give to Karl Martel. In the ample jaw and straight lips was a message which a physiognomist would interpret as a promise of successful enterprise, whether of good or evil. It was a face which a Crusader might have possessed, or a pirate of the Spanish main. In a word, he looked like a man who might be a hero to his valet.

Yet, despite this adventurous type of countenance, Weldon's mode of life was seemingly conventional. Shortly after the removal from Harvard, his father was mangled in a railway accident and left the planet and little behind him save debts and dislike. Promptly thereupon Royal Weldon set out to conquer the Stock Exchange. For three years he grit his teeth, and earned fifteen dollars a week. At the end of that period he had succeeded in two things. He had captured the confidence of a prominent financier, and the affection of the financier's daughter. In another twelvemonth he was partner of the one, husband of the other, and the taxpayer of a house in Gramercy Park.

Of these vicissitudes Tristrem had been necessarily informed. During the penury of his friend he had aided him to a not inconsiderable extent; though afar, he had followed his career with affectionate interest, and the day before Weldon's wedding he had caused Tiffany to send the bride a service of silver which was mentioned by the reporters as "elegant" and "chaste." On returning to New York, Tristrem naturally found the door of the house in Gramercy Park wide open, and it came about that it was in that house that his wavering patriotism was riveted.

This event, after the fashion of extraordinary occurrences, happened in a commonplace manner. One Sunday evening he was bidden there to dine. He had broken bread in the house many times before, but the bread breaking had been informal. On this particular occasion, however, other guests had been invited, and Tristrem was given to understand that he would meet some agreeable people.

When he entered the drawing-room, he discovered that of the guests of the evening he was the first to arrive. Even Weldon was not visible; but Mrs. Weldon was, and, as Tristrem entered, she rose from a straight-backed chair in which

THE TRUTH ABOUT TRISTREM VARICK.

she had been seated, and greeted him with a smile which she had copied from a chromo.

Mrs. Weldon was exceedingly pretty. She was probably twenty-two or twenty-three years of age, and her intellect was that of a girl of twelve. Her manner was arch and noticeably affected. She had an enervating way of asking unnecessary questions, and of laughing as though it hurt her. On the subject of dress she was very voluble; in brief, she was prettiness and insipidity personified—the sort of woman that ought to be gagged and kept in bed with a doll.

She gave Tristrem a little hand gloved with *suède*, and asked him had he been at church that morning. Tristrem found a seat, and replied that he had not. "But don't you like to go?" she inquired, emphasizing each word of the question, and ending up with her irritating laugh.

"He does," came a voice from the door and Weldon entered. "He does, but he can resist the temptation." Then there was more conversation of the before-dinner kind, and during its progress the door opened again, and a young girl crossed the room.

She was dressed in a gown of canary, draped with madeira and fluttered with lace. Her arms and neck were bare, and unjewelled. Her hair was Cimmerian, the black of basalt that knows no shade more dark, and it was arranged in such wise that it fell on either side of the forehead, circling a little space above the ear, and then wound into a coil on the neck. This arrangement was not modish, but it was becoming— the only arrangement, in fact, that would have befitted her features, which resembled those of the Cleopatra unearthed by Lieutenant Gorringe. Her eyes were not oval, but round, and they were amber as those of leopards, the yellow of living gold. The corners of her mouth drooped a little, and the mouth itself was rather large than small. When she laughed one could see her tongue; it was like an inner cut of water-melon, and sometimes, when she was silent, the point of it caressed her under lip. Her skin was of that quality which artificial light makes radiant, and yet of which the real delicacy is only apparent by day. She just lacked being tall, and in her face and about her bare arms and neck was the perfume of health. She moved indolently, with a grace of her own. She was not yet twenty, a festival of beauty in the festival of life.

At the rustle of her dress Tristrem had arisen. As the girl crossed the room he bethought him of a garden of lilies; though why, for the life of him, he could not have explained. He heard his name mentioned, and saw the girl incline her head, but he made little, if any, acknowledgment; he stood quite still, looking at her and through her, and over her and beyond. For some moments he neither moved nor spoke. He was unconscious even that other guests had come.

He gave his hand absently to a popular novelist, Mr. A. B. Fenwick Chisholm-Jones by name, more familiarly known as Alphabet, whom Weldon brought to him, and kept his eyes on the yellow bodice. A fair young woman in pink had taken a position near to where he stood, and was complaining to someone that she had been obliged to give up cigarettes. And when the someone asked whether the abandonment of that pleasure was due to parental interference, the young woman laughed shortly, and explained that she was in training for a tennis tournament. Meanwhile the little group in which Tristrem stood was re-enforced by a new-comer, who attempted to condole with the novelist on the subject of an excoriating attack that one of the critics had recently made on his books, and suggested that he

THE TRUTH ABOUT TRISTREM VARICK.

ought to do something about it. But of condolence or advice Mr. Jones would have none.

"Bah!" he exclaimed, "if the beggar doesn't like what I write let him try and do better. I don't care what any of them say. My books sell, and that's the *hauptsache*. Besides, what's the use in arguing with a newspaper? It's like talking metaphysics to a bull; the first you know, you get a horn in your navel." And while the novelist was expressing his disdain of all adverse criticism, and quoting Emerson to the effect that the average reviewer had the eyes of a bug and the heart of a cat, Tristrem discovered Mrs. Weldon's arm in his own, and presently found himself seated next to her at table.

At the extreme end, to the right of the host, was the girl with the amber eyes. The novelist was at her side. Evidently he had said something amusing, for they were both laughing; he with the complacency of one who has said a good thing, and she with the appreciation of one accustomed to wit. But Tristrem was not permitted to watch her undisturbed. Mrs. Weldon had a right to his attention, and she exercised that right with the pertinacity of a fly that has to be killed to be got rid of. "What do you think of Miss Finch?" she asked, with her stealthy giggle.

"Her name isn't Finch," Tristrem answered, indignantly.

"Yes it is, too—Flossy Finch, her name is; as if I oughtn't to know! Why, we were at Mrs. Garret and Mlle. de l'Entresol's school together for years and years. What makes you say her name isn't Finch? I had you here on purpose to meet her. Did you ever see such hair? There's only one girl in New York——"

"It *is* black," Tristrem assented.

"Black! Why, you must be crazy; it's orange, and that dress of hers——"

Tristrem looked down the table and saw a young lady whom he had not noticed before. Her hair, as Mrs. Weldon had said, was indeed the color of orange, though of an orange not over-ripe. "I thought you meant that girl next to Royal," he said.

"That! Oh! that's Miss Raritan."

Mrs. Weldon's voice had changed. Evidently Miss Raritan did not arouse in her the same enthusiasm as did Miss Finch. For a moment her lips lost their chromo smile, but presently it returned again, and she piped away anew on the subject of the charms of Flossy Finch, and after an interlude, of which Tristrem heard not one word, she turned and cross-questioned the man on her left.

The conversation had become very animated. From Royal's end of the table came intermittent shrieks of laughter. The novelist was evidently in his finest form. "Do you mean to tell me," Miss Finch asked him across the table, "do you mean to say that you don't believe in platonic affection?"

"I never uttered such a heresy in my life," the novelist replied. "Of course I believe in it; I believe in it thoroughly— between husband and wife."

At this everyone laughed again, except Tristrem, who had not heard, and Mrs. Weldon, who had not understood. The latter, however, felt that Miss Finch was distinguishing herself, and she turned to Tristrem anew.

"I want you to make yourself very agreeable to her," she said. "She is just the girl for you. Don't you think so? Now promise that you will talk to her after dinner."

"Talk metaphysics to a bull, and the first thing you know—the first thing you know—I beg your pardon, Mrs. Weldon, I didn't mean to say that—I don't know how the stupid phrase got in my head or why I said it." He hesitated

THE TRUTH ABOUT TRISTREM VARICK.

a moment, and seemed to think. "H'm," he went on, "I am a trifle tired, I fancy."

Mrs. Weldon looked suspiciously at the glasses at his side, but apparently they had not been so much as tasted; they were full to the rim. She turned again to the guest at her left. The dinner was almost done. She asked a few more questions, and then presently, in a general lull, she gave a glance about her. At that signal the women-folk rose in a body, the men rising also, to let them pass.

Tristrem had risen mechanically with the others, and when the ultimate flounce had disappeared he sat down again and busied himself with a cup of coffee. The other men had drawn their chairs together near him, and over the liqueurs were discussing topics of masculine interest and flavor. Tristrem was about to make some effort to join in the conversation, when from beyond there came the running scale that is the prelude to the cabaletta, *Non più mesta*, from Cenerentola. Then, abruptly, a voice rang out as though it vibrated through labyrinths of gold—a voice that charged the air with resonant accords—a voice prodigious and dominating, grave and fluid; a voice that descended into the caverns of sound, soared to the uttermost heights, scattering notes like showers of stars, evoking visions of flesh and dazzling steel, and in its precipitate flights and vertiginous descents disclosing landscapes riotous with flowers, rich with perfume, sentient with beauty, articulate with love; a voice voluptuous as an organ and languorous as the consonance of citherns and guitars.

Tristrem, as one led in leash, moved from the table and passed into the outer room. Miss Raritan was at the piano. Beyond, a group of women sat hushed and mute; and still the resilient waves of song continued. One by one the men issued noiselessly from the inner room. And then, soon, the voice sank and died away like a chorus entering a crypt.

Miss Raritan rose from the piano. As she did so, Weldon, as it becomes a host, hastened to her. There was a confused hum, a murmur of applause, and above it rose a discreet and prolonged *brava* that must have come from the novelist. Weldon, seemingly, was urging her to sing again. The women had taken up anew some broken thread of gossip, but the men were at the piano, insisting too. Presently Miss Raritan resumed her seat, and the men moved back. Her fingers rippled over the keys like rain. She stayed them a second, and then, in a voice so low that it seemed hardly human, and yet so insistent that it would have filled a cathedral and scaled the dome, she began a ballad that breathed of Provence:

"*O Magali, ma bien aimée, Fuyons tous deux sous la ramée Au fond du bois silencieux....*"

When she had finished, Tristrem started. The earliest notes had sent the blood pulsing through his veins, thrilling him from finger-tips to the end of the spine, and then a lethargy enveloped him and he ceased to hear, and it was not until Miss Raritan stood up again from the piano that he was conscious that he had not been listening. He had sat near the entrance to the dining-room, and when the applause began afresh he passed out into the hall, found his coat and hat, and left the house.

As he walked down Irving Place he fell to wondering who it was that he had heard complain of being obliged to give up cigarettes, not on account of parental interference but because of a tournament. Yet, after all, what matter did it make? Certainly, he told himself, the Weldons seemed to live very well. Royal must be making money. Mrs. Weldon—Nanny, as Royal called her—was a nice little thing, somewhat—h'm, somewhat—well, not quite up to Royal. She looked like that girl in Munich, the girl that lived over the way, only Mrs. Weldon was prettier and dressed better, much better. *Du hast die schönsten Augen.* Munich wasn't a bad place, but what a hole Innsprück was. There was that Victoria Cross fellow; whatever became of him? He drank like a fish; it must have caught him by this time. H'm, he *would* give me the address of his shoemaker. I ought to have taken more from that man in Paris. Odd that the Cenerentola was the last thing I should have heard there. The buffo was good, so was the contralto. *She* sings much better. What a voice! what a voice! Now, which was the more perfect, the voice or the girl? Let me see, which is the better fulfilled, the odor of the lily or the lily itself? Tulips I never cared for.... That is it, then. I wonder, though——

Tristrem had reached the house in Waverley Place. He let himself in with a latch-key, and went to his room. There he sat a while, companioned only by his thoughts. Before he fell asleep, his patriotism was riveted. A land that could produce such a specimen of girlhood outvalued Europe, Asia, and Africa combined—aye, a thousand times—and topped and exceeded creation.

III.

Among the effects and symptoms of love, there is an involuntary action of the mind which, since the days of Stendhal, has been known as crystallization. When a man becomes interested in a woman, when he pictures her not as she really is, but as she seems to him—as she ought to be, in fact—he experiences, first, admiration; second, desire; third, hope; and, behold, love or its counterfeit is born.

This crystallization affects the individual according to his nature. If that nature be inexperienced, unworn—in a word, if it be virginal, its earliest effects are those of a malady. On the other hand, if the nature on which it operates has received the baptism of fire, its effect is that of a tonic. To the one it is a fever, to the other a bugle-call. In the first instance, admiration is pursued by self-depreciation, desire is pinioned before conventional obstacles, and hope falters beneath a weight of doubt. In the second, admiration, desire, and hope are fused into one sentiment, the charm of the chase, the delight of the prospective quarry. As an example, there is Werther, and there is also Don Juan.

Now Tristrem Varick had never known a mother, sisters he had none, the feminine had been absent from his life, but in his nature there was an untarnishable refinement. During his student-days at Harvard, and throughout his residence abroad, there had been nothing of that which the French have agreed to denominate as *bonnes fortunes*. Such things may have been in his path, waiting only to be gathered, but, in that case, certain it is that he had passed them by unheeded. To use the figurative phrase, he was incapable of stretching his hand to any woman who had not the power of awakening a lasting affection; and during his wanderings, and despite, too, the example and easy morals of his comrades, no such woman having crossed his horizon, he had been innocent of even the most fugitive liaison. Nevertheless, the morning after the dinner in Gramercy Park, crystallization had done its work. He awoke with the surprise and wonder of an inexperienced sensation; he awoke with the consciousness of being in love, wholly, turbulently, absurdly in love with a girl to whom he had not addressed a single word.

The general opinion to the contrary notwithstanding, there are, after all, very few people who know what love really is. And among those that know, fewer there are that tell. A lexicographer, deservedly forgotten, has defined it as an exchange of fancies, the contact of two epiderms. Another, wiser if less epigrammatic, announced it as a something that no one knew what, coming no one knew whence, and ending no one knew how. But in whatever fashion it may be described, one thing is certain, it has been largely over-rated.

In the case of Tristrem Varick it appeared in its most perfect form. The superlative is used advisedly. Love has a hundred aspects, a thousand toilets. It may come at first sight, in which event, if it be enduring, it is, as Balzac has put it, a resultant of that prescience which is known as second sight. Or, it may come of the gradual fusion of two natures. It may come of propinquity, of curiosity, of sympathy, of hatred. It may come of the tremors of adolescence, the mutual attraction of one sex for the other; and, again, it may come of natural selection, of the discernment which leads a man through mazes of women to one in particular, to the woman who to him is the one woman in the world and manacles him at her feet. If Tristrem Varick had not met Miss Raritan, it is more than probable that he never would have known the meaning of the word.

When the first surprise at the discovery waned, delight took its place. He saw her amber eyes, he recalled as she had crossed the room the indolent undulation of her hips, he breathed the atmosphere of health which she exhaled, and in his ears her voice still rang. The *Non più mesta* of her song seemed almost a promise, and the *O Magali* an invitation. He recalled the movement of her lips, and fell to wondering what her name might be. At first he fancied that it might be Stella; but that, for some occult reason which only a lover would understand, he abandoned for Thyra, a name which pleasured him awhile and which he repeated aloud until it became sonorous as were it set in titles. But presently some defect presented itself, it sounded less apt, more suited to a blue-eyed daughter of a viking than to one so *brune* as she. Decidedly, Thyra did not suit her. And yet her name might be something utterly commonplace, such as Fanny, for instance, or Agnes, or Gertrude. But that was a possibility which he declined to entertain. When a girl is baptized, the mother, in choosing the name, should, he told himself, think of the lover who will one day pronounce it. And what had her mother chosen? It would be forethought indeed if she had selected Undine or even Iseult; but what mother was ever clairvoyant enough for that?

He thought this over awhile and was about to give the query up, when suddenly, without an effort on his part, he was visited by a name that announced her as the perfume announces the rose, a name that pictured and painted her, a name that suited her as did her gown of canary, a name that crowned her beauty and explained the melancholy of her lips. "It is Madeleine," he said, "it can be nothing else."

And into the syllables he threw the waving inflection of the French.

"It is Madeleine," he continued, "and when I see her I will tell in what way I divined it."

The possibility that she might be indifferent to such homage did not, for the moment, occur to him. He was loitering in the enchanted gardens of the imagination, which have been visited by us all. It was the improbable that fluttered his pulse.

Hitherto the life of Tristrem Varick had been that of a dilettante. There had been no reason why he should work. His education had unfitted him for labor, and his tastes, if artistic, were not sufficiently pronounced to act as incentives. He handled the brush well enough to know that he could never be a painter; he had a natural understanding of music, its value was clear to him, yet its composition was barred. The one talent that he possessed—a talent that grows rarer with the days—was that of appreciation, he could admire the masterpieces of others, but creation was not his. A few centuries ago he would have made an admirable knight-errant. In a material age like our own, his *raison dêtre* was not obvious. In a word, he was just such an one as his father had intended he should be, one whose normal condition was that of chronic pluperfect subjunctive, and who, if thrown on his own resources, would be helpless indeed.

In some dim way he had been conscious of this before, and hitherto he had accepted it, as he had accepted his father's attitude, as one accepts the inevitable, and put it aside again as something against which, like death, or like life, it is useless to rebel. After all, there was nothing particularly dreadful about it. An inability to be Somebody was not a matter of which the District Attorney is obliged to take cognizance. At least he need do no harm, and he would have wealth enough to do much good. It was in thoughts like these that hitherto he had found consolation. But on this particular morning he looked for them anew, and the search was fruitless. Not one of the old consolations disclosed the slightest worth. He stood before himself naked in his nothingness. The true knowledge of his incompetence had never come home to him before—but now it closed round him in serried arguments, and in the closing shut out all hope of her. Who was he, indeed, to pretend to such a girl?

To win her, he told himself, one must needs be a conqueror, one who has coped with dangers and could flaunt new triumphs as his lady's due. Some soldier bearing a marshal's baton back from war, some hero that had liberated an empire or stolen a republic for himself, some prince of literature or satrap of song, someone, in fact, who, booted and spurred, had entered the Temple of Fame, and claimed the dome as his. But he! What had he to offer? His name, however historical and respected, was an accident of birth. Of the wealth which he would one day possess he had not earned a groat. And, were it lost, the quadrature of the circle would not be more difficult than its restoration. And yet, and yet—though any man she could meet might be better and wiser and stronger than he, not one would care for her more. At least there was something in that, a tangible value, if ever there were one. There was every reason why she should turn her back, and that one reason, and that one only, why she should not. But that one reason, he told himself, was a force in itself. The resuscitation of hope was so

THE TRUTH ABOUT TRISTREM VARICK.

sudden that the blood mounted to his temples and pulsated through his veins.

He left the bed in which his meditations had been passed. "They say everything comes to him who waits," he muttered, and then proceeded to dress. He took a tub and got himself, absent-mindedly, into a morning suit. "I don't believe it," he exclaimed, at last, "the world belongs to the impatient, and I am impatient of her."

Tristrem was in no sense a diplomatist. In his ways there was a candor that was as unusual as it is delightful; yet such is the power of love that, in its first assault, the victim is transformed. The miser turns prodigal, the coward brave, the genius becomes a simpleton, and in the simpleton there awakes a Machiavelli. Tristrem passed a forenoon in trying to unravel as cruel a problem as has ever been given a lover to solve—how, in a city like New York, to meet a girl of whom he knew absolutely nothing, and who was probably unaware of his own existence. He might have waited, it is true—chance holds many an odd trick—but he had decided to be impatient, and in his impatience he went to Gramercy Park and drank tea there, not once, but four afternoons in succession, an excess of civility which surprised Mrs. Weldon not a little.

That he should make an early visit of digestion was quite in the order of things, but when that visit was repeated again and again, Mrs. Weldon, with a commingling of complacency and alarm, told herself that, in her quality of married woman, such persistence should be discouraged. But the opportunity for such discouragement did not present itself, or rather, when it did the need of discouragement had passed. Tristrem drank tea with her several times, and then disappeared abruptly. "He must have known it was hopeless," she

reflected, when a week went by unmarked by further enterprise on his part. And then, the intended discouragement
notwithstanding, she felt vaguely vexed.

In the tea-drinking Tristrem's object, if not apparent
to Mrs. Weldon, was perfectly clear to himself. He desired
to learn something of Miss Raritan, and he knew, if the
tea-drinking was continued with sufficient endurance, not
only would he acquire, from a talkative lady like his hostess,
information of the amplest kind, which after all was second-
ary, but that in the course of a week the girl herself must
put in an appearance. A dinner call, if not obligatory to him,
was obligatory to her, and on that obligation he counted.

To those who agree to be bound by what the Western
press calls etiquette, there is nothing more inexorable than a
social debt. A woman may contest her mantua-maker's bill
with impunity, her antenuptial promises may go to protest
and she remain unestopped; but let her leave a dinner-call
overdue and unpaid, then is she shameless indeed. In this
code Tristrem was necessarily learned. On returning to
Fifth Avenue he had marvelled somewhat at noting that
laws which applied to one sex did not always extend to the
other, that civility was not exacted of men, that politeness
was relegated to the tape-counter and out of place in a drawing-room; in a word, that it was not good form to be courteous, and not ill-bred to be rude.

While the tea-drinking was in progress he managed
without much difficulty to get Mrs. Weldon on the desired
topic. There were spacious digressions in her information
and abrupt excursions into irrelevant matter, and there were
also interruptions by other visitors, and the consequent and
tedious exchange of platitude and small-talk. But after the
fourth visit Tristrem found himself in possession of a store

of knowledge, the sum and substance of which amounted to this: Miss Raritan lived with her mother in the shady part of the Thirties, near Madison Avenue. Her father was dead. It had been rumored, but with what truth Mrs. Weldon was not prepared to affirm, that the girl had some intention of appearing on the lyric stage, which, if she carried out, would of course be the end of her socially. She had been very much run after on account of her voice, and at the Wainwarings the President had said that he had never heard anything like it, and asked her to come to Washington and be present at one of the diplomatic dinners. Personally Mrs. Weldon knew her very slightly, but she intimated that, inasmuch as the government had once sent Raritan *père* abroad as minister—in order probably to be rid of him—his daughter was inclined to look down on those whose fathers held less exalted positions—on Mrs. Weldon herself, for example.

It was with this little store of information that Tristrem left her on the Thursday succeeding the dinner. It was meagre indeed, and yet ample enough to afford him food for reflection. During the gleaning many people had come and gone, but of Miss Raritan he had as yet seen nothing. The next afternoon, however, as he was about to ascend Mrs. Weldon's stoop for the fifth time in five days, the door opened and the girl on whom his thoughts were centred was before him.

Throughout the week he had lived in the expectation of meeting her, it was the one thing that had brought zest to the day and dreams to the night; there was even a little speech which he had rehearsed, but for the moment he was dumb. He plucked absently at his cuff, to the palms of his hands there came a sudden moisture. In the vestibule above, a servant stood waiting for Miss Raritan to reach the pavement before closing the door, and abruptly, from a barrel-organ at the corner, a waltz was thrown out in jolts.

The girl descended the steps before Tristrem was able to master his emotion.

"Miss Raritan," he began, hastily, "I don't suppose you remember me. I am Mr. Varick. I heard you sing the other night. I have come here every day since in the hope of——; you see, I wanted to ask if I might not have the privilege of hearing you sing again?"

"If you consider it a privilege, certainly. On Sunday evening, though, I thought you seemed rather bored." She made this answer very graciously, with her head held like a bird's, a trifle to one side.

Tristrem gazed at her in a manner that would have mollified a tigress. "I was not bored. I had never heard anyone sing before."

"Yet your friend, Mr. Weldon, tells me that you are very fond of music."

"That is exactly what I mean."

At this speech of his she looked at him, musingly. "I wish I deserved that," she said.

Tristrem began again with new courage. "It is like anything else, I fancy. I doubt if anyone, ignorant of difficulties overcome, ever appreciates a masterpiece. A sonnet, if perfect, is only perfect to a sonneteer. The gallery may applaud a drama, it is the playwright who judges it at its worth. It is the sculptor that appreciates a Canova——"

They had reached the corner where the barrel-organ was in ambush. A woman dragging a child with Italy and dirt in its face followed them, her hand outstretched. Tristrem had an artful way of being rid of a beggar, and after the fumble of a moment he gave her some coin.

"—And the artist who appreciates rags," added Miss Raritan.

"Perhaps. I am not fond of rags myself, but I have often caught myself envying the simplicity which they sometimes conceal. That woman, now, she may be as pleased with my little gift as I am to be walking with you."

"I thought it was my voice you liked," Miss Raritan answered, demurely.

Tristrem experienced a mental start. A suspicion entered his mind which he chased indignantly. There was about the girl an aroma that was incompatible with coquetry.

"You would not, I am sure, have me think of you in the *vox et præterea nihil* style," he replied. "To be candid, I thought that very matter over the other night." He hesitated, as though waiting for some question, but she did not so much as look at him, and he continued unassisted. "I thought of a flower and its perfume, I wondered which was the more admirable, and—and—I decided that I did not care for tulips."

"But that you did care for me, I suppose?"

"Yes, I decided that."

Miss Raritan threw back her head with a movement indicative of impatience.

"I didn't mean to tell you," he added—"that is, not yet."

They had crossed Broadway and were entering Fifth Avenue. There the stream of carriages kept them a moment on the curb.

"I hope," Tristrem began again, "I hope you are not vexed."

"Vexed at what? No, I am not vexed. I am tired; every other man I meet—There, we can cross now. Besides, I am married. Don't get run over. I am going in that shop."

"You are *not* married!"

"Yes, I am; if I were a Harvard graduate I would say to Euterpe. As it is, Scales is more definite." She had led him to the door of a milliner, a portal which Tristrem knew was closed to him. "If you care to come and see me," she added, by way of *congé*, "my husband will probably be at home." And with that she opened the door and passed into the shop.

"I can imagine a husband," thought Tristrem, with a glimmer of that spirit of belated repartee which Thackeray called cab-wit, the brilliancy which comes to us when we are going home, "I can imagine a husband whose greatest merit is his wife."

IV.

The fact that few days elapsed before Tristrem Varick availed himself of Miss Raritan's invitation, and that thereafter he continued to avail himself of it with frequence and constancy, should surprise no one. During the earliest of these visits he met Miss Raritan's mother, and was unaccountably annoyed when he heard that lady address her daughter as Viola. He had been so sure that her baptismal name was Madeleine that the one by which he found she was called sounded false as an alias, and continued so to sound until he accustomed himself to the syllables and ended by preferring it to the Madeleine of his fancy. This, however, by the way. Mrs. Raritan was a woman who, in her youth, must have been very beautiful, and traces of that beauty she still preserved. When she spoke her voice endeared her to you, and in her manner there was that something which made you feel that she might be calumniated, as good women often are, but yet that she could never be the subject of gossip. She did not seem resolute, but she did seem warm of heart, and Tristrem felt at ease with her at once.

Of her he saw at first but little. In a city like New York it is difficult for anyone to become suddenly intimate in a household, however cordial and well-intentioned that household may be. And during those hours of the winter days when Miss Raritan was at home it was seldom that her mother was visible. But it was not long before Tristrem became an occasional guest at dinner, and it was in the process of breaking bread that a semblance of intimacy was established. And at last, when winter had gone and the green afternoons opposed the dusk, Tristrem now and then would drop in of an evening, and in the absence of Miss Raritan pass an hour with her mother. Truly she was not the rose, but did she not dwell at her side?

Meanwhile, Miss Raritan's attitude differed but little from the one which she had first adopted. She treated Tristrem with exasperating familiarity, and kept him at arm's length. She declined to see him when the seeing would have been easy, and summoned him when the summons was least to be expected. He was useful to her as a piece of furniture, and she utilized him as such. In the matter of flowers and theatres he was a convenience. And at routs and assemblies the attention of an heir apparent to seven million was a homage and a tribute which Miss Raritan saw no reason to forego.

In this Tristrem had no one but himself to blame. He had been, and was, almost canine in his demeanor to her. She saw it, knew it, felt it, and treated him accordingly. And he, with the cowardice of love, made little effort at revolt. Now and then he protested to Mrs. Raritan, to whom he had made no secret of his admiration for her daughter, and who consoled him as best she might; but that was all. And so the winter passed and the green afternoons turned sultry, and Tristrem was not a step further advanced than on the day when he had left the girl at the milliner's. On the infrequent occasions when he had ventured to say some word of that which was nearest his heart, she had listened with tantalizing composure, and when he had paused for encouragement or rebuke, she would make a remark of such inappositeness that anyone else would have planted her there and gone. But Tristrem was none other than himself; his nature commanded and he obeyed.

It so happened that one May morning a note was brought him, in which Miss Raritan said that her mother and herself were to leave in a day or two for the country, and could he not get her something to read on the way. Tristrem passed an hour selecting, with infinite and affectionate care, a small bundle of foreign literature. In the package he found room for Balzac's "Pierrette" and the "Curé de Tours," one of Mme. Craven's stupidities, a volume of platitude in rhyme by François Coppée, a copy of De Amicis' futile wanderings in Spain—a few samples, in fact, of the *pueris virginibusque* school. And that evening, with the bundle under his arm, he sought Miss Raritan.

The girl glanced at the titles and put the books aside. "When we get in order at Narragansett," she said, "I wish you would come up."

Had she kissed him, Tristrem could not have revelled more. "There are any number of hotels," she added, by way of douche.

"Certainly, if you wish it, but—but——"

"Well, but what?"

"I don't know. You see—well, it's this way: You know that I love you, and you know also that you care for me as for the snows of yester-year. There is no reason why you should do otherwise. I don't mean to complain. If I am unable to make you care, the fault is mine. I did think—h'm—no matter. What I wanted to say is this: there is no reason why you should care, and yet——. See here; take two slips of paper, write on one, I will marry you, and, on the other, Put a bullet through your head, and let me draw. I would take the chance so gladly. But that chance, of course, you will not give. Why should you, after all? Why should I give everything I own to the first beggar I meet? But why should you have any other feeling for me than that which you have? And yet, sometimes I think you don't understand. Any man you meet could be more attractive than I, and very easy he would find it to be so; but no one could care for you more— no one——"

Miss Raritan was sitting opposite to him, her feet crossed, her head thrown back, her eyes fixed on the ceiling. One arm lay along the back of the lounge which she occupied, the other was pendant at her side. And while he still addressed her, she arose with the indolence of a panther, crossed the room, picked up a miniature from a table, eyed it as though she had never seen it before and did not particularly care to see it again, and then, seating herself at the piano, she attacked the *Il segreto per esser felice*, the brindisi from "Lucrezia Borgia."

In the wonder of her voice Tristrem forgot the discourtesy of the action. He listened devoutly. And, as he listened, each note was an electric shock. *Il segreto per esser felice*, indeed! The secret of happiness was one which she alone of all others in the world could impart. And, as the measures of the song rose and fell, they brought him a transient exhilaration like to that which comes of champagne, dowering him with factitious force wherewith to strive anew. And so it happened that, when the ultimate note had rung out and the girl's fingers loitered on the keys, he went over to her with a face so eloquent that she needed but a glance at it to know what he was seeking to say.

With a gesture coercive as a bit, she lifted one hand from the keys and stayed his lips. Then, she stood up and faced him. "Tristrem," she began, "when I first saw you I told you that I was married to my art. And in an art such as mine there is no divorce. It may be that I shall go on the stage. After all, why should I not? Is society so alluring that I should sacrifice for it that which is to me infinitely preferable? If I have not done so already it is because of my mother. But should I decide to do so, there are years of study before me yet. In which case I could not marry, that is self-evident, not only because I would not marry a man who would suffer me to sing in public—don't interrupt—but also because—well, you told me that you understood the possibilities of the human voice, and you must know what the result would be. But even independent of that, you said a moment ago that I did not love you. Well, I don't. I don't love you. Tristrem, listen to me. I don't love you as you would have me. I wish I did. But I like you. I like you as I can like few other men. Tristrem, except my mother, I have not a friend in the world. Women never care for me, and men—well, save in the case of yourself, when their friendship has been worth the having, it belonged to someone else. Give me yours."

"It will be hard, very hard."

Miss Raritan moved from where she had been standing and glanced at the clock. "You must go now," she said, "but promise that you will try."

She held her hand to him, and Tristrem raised it to his lips and kissed the wrist. "You might as well ask me to increase my stature," he answered. And presently he dropped the hand which he held and left the house.

It was a perfect night. The moon hung like a yellow feather in the sky, and in the air was a balm that might have come from fields of tamaris and of thyme. The street itself was quiet, and as Tristrem walked on, something of the enchantment of the hour fell upon him. On leaving Miss Raritan, he had been irritated at himself. It seemed to him that when with her he was at his worst; that he stood before her dumb for love, awkward, embarrassed, and ineffectual of speech. It seemed to him that he lacked the tact of other men, and that, could she see him as he really was when unemotionalized by her presence, if the eloquence which came to him in solitude would visit him once at her side, if he could plead to her with the fervor with which he addressed the walls, full surely her answer would be other. She would make no proffer then of friendship, or if she did, it would be of that friendship which is born of love, and is better than love itself. But as he walked on the enchantment of the night encircled him. He declined to accept her reply; he told himself that in his eagerness he had been abrupt; that a girl who was worth the winning was slow of capture; that he had expected months to give him what only years could afford, and that Time, in which all things unroll, might yet hold this gift for him. He resolved to put his impatience aside like an unbecoming coat. He would pretend to be but a friend. As a friend he would be privileged to see her, and then, some day the force and persistence of his affection would do the rest. He smiled at his own cunning. It was puerile as a jackstraw, but it seemed shrewdness itself to him. Yes, that was the way. He had done wrong; he had unmasked his batteries too soon. And such batteries! But no matter, of his patience he was now assured. On the morrow he would go to her and begin the campaign anew.

He had reached the corner and was on the point of turning down the avenue, when a hansom rattled up and wheeled so suddenly into the street through which he had come, that he stepped back a little to let it pass. As he did so he looked

THE TRUTH ABOUT TRISTREM VARICK.

in at the fare. The cab was beyond him in a second, but in the momentary glimpse which he caught of the occupant, he recognized Royal Weldon. And as he continued his way, he wondered where Royal Weldon could be going.

The following evening he went to dine at the Athenæum Club. The house in Waverley Place affected him as might an empty bier in a tomb. The bread that he broke there choked him. His father was as congenial as a spectre. He only appeared when dinner was announced, and after he had seated himself at the table he asked grace of God in a low, determined fashion, and that was the end of the conversation. Tristrem remembered that in the infrequent vacations of his school and college days, that was the way it always had been, and being tolerably convinced that that was the way it always would be, he preferred, when not expected elsewhere, to dine at the club.

On entering the Athenæum on this particular evening, he put his hat and coat in the vestiary and was about to order dinner, when he was accosted by Alphabet Jones.

"I say, Varick," the novelist exclaimed—(during the winter they had seen much of each other), "do you know who was the originator of the cloak-room? Of course you don't—I'll tell you; who do you suppose now? Give it up? Mrs. Potiphar! How's that? Good enough for Theodore Hook, eh? Let's dine together, and I'll tell you some more."

"Let's dine together" was a formula which Mr. Jones had adopted. Literally, it meant, I'll order and you pay. Tristrem was aware in what light the invitation should be viewed, he had heard it before; but, though the novelist was of the genus *spongia*, he was seldom tiresome, often entertaining, and moreover, Tristrem was one who would rather pay than not. As there were few of that category in the club,

Mr. Jones made a special prey of him, and on this particular evening, when the ordering had been done and the dinner announced, he led him in triumph to the lift.

As they were about to step in, Weldon stepped out. He seemed hurried and would have passed on with a nod, but Tristrem caught him by the arm. Of late he had seen little of him, and it had seemed to Tristrem that the fault, if fault there were, must be his own.

"I caught a glimpse of you last night, didn't I, Royal?" he asked.

Weldon raised his eyebrows for all response. Evidently he was not in a conversational mood. But at once an idea seemed to strike him. "I dare say," he answered, "I roam about now and then like anyone else. By the way, where are you going to-night? Why not look in on my wife? She says you neglect her."

"I would like it, Royal, but the fact is I am going to make a call."

"In Thirty-ninth Street?"

Tristrem looked at him much as a yokel at a fair might look at a wizard. He was so astonished at Weldon's pre-science that he merely nodded.

"You can save yourself the trouble then—I happened to meet Miss Raritan this afternoon. She is dining at the Wainwarings. Look in at Gramercy Park." And with that he turned on his heel and disappeared into the smoking-room.

"Didn't I hear Weldon mention Miss Raritan?" Jones asked, when he and Tristrem had finished the roast. "There's a girl I'd like to put in a book. She has hell in her eyes and heaven in her voice. What a heroine she would make!" he exclaimed, enthusiastically; and then in a complete change of key, in a tone that was pregnant with suggestion, he added, "and what a wife!"

"I don't understand you," said Tristrem, in a manner which, for him, was defiant.

Whether or not Jones was a good sailor is a matter of small moment. In any event he tacked at once.

"Bah! I am speaking in the first person. I don't believe in matrimony myself, I am too poor. And besides, I never heard of but one happy marriage, and that was between a blind man and a deaf-mute. Though even then it must have been difficult to know what the woman thought. Now, in regard to Miss Raritan, half the men in the city are after her, *pour le bon motif, s'entend*; but when a girl has had the *dessus du panier* at her feet, no fellow can afford to ask her to take a promenade with him down the aisle of Grace Church, unless he has the Chemical Bank in one pocket and the United States Trust Company in the other. *Et avec ça!*" And Jones waved his head as though not over-sure that the coffers of those institutions would suffice.

"I don't see what that has to do with it," Tristrem indignantly interjected.

"Isn't that odd now?" was Jones' sarcastic reply. "Dr. Holmes says that no fellow can be a thorough-going swell unless he has three generations in oil. And mind you, daguerreotypes won't do. There are any number of your ancestors strung along the walls of the Historical Society, and how many more you may have in that crypt of yours in Waverley Place, heaven only knows. Imprimis, if you accept Dr. Holmes as an authority, you are a thorough-going swell. In the second place, you look like a Greek shepherd. Third, you are the biggest catch in polite society. Certainly it's odd that with such possibilities you should see no reason for not marrying a girl who will want higher-stepping horses than

Elisha's, and who, while there is a bandit of a dressmaker in Paris, will decline to imitate the lilies of the field. Certainly——"

"I never said anything about it, I never said anything about marrying or not marrying——"

"Oh, didn't you? I thought you did." And Jones leaned back in his chair and summoned a waiter with an upward movement of the chin. "Bring another pint of this, will you."

"I think I won't take anything more," said Tristrem, rising from the table as he spoke. "It's hot in here. I may see you down-stairs." And with that he left the room.

Mr. Alphabet Jones looked after him a second and nodded sagaciously to himself. "Another man overboard," he muttered, as he toyed with his empty glass. "*Ah! jeunesse, jeunesse!*"

V.

Tristrem descended the stair and hesitated a moment at the door of the smoking-room. Near-by, at a small table, two men were drinking brandy. He caught a fragment of their speech: it was about a woman. Beyond, another group was listening to that story of the eternal feminine which is everlastingly the same. Within, the air was lifeless and heavy with the odor of cigars, but in the hall there came through the wide portals of the entrance the irresistible breath of a night in May.

Tristrem turned and presently sauntered aimlessly out of the club and up the avenue. Before him, a man was loitering with a girl; his arm was in hers, and he was whispering in her ear. A cab passed, bearing a couple that sat waist-encircled devouring each other with insatiate eyes. And at Twenty-third Street, a few shop-girls, young and very pretty, that were laughing conspicuously together, were joined by some clerks, with whom they paired off and disappeared. At the corner, through the intersecting thoroughfares came couple after couple, silent for the most part, as though oppressed by the invitations of the night. Beyond, in the shadows of the Square, the benches were filled with youths and maidens, who sat hand-in-hand, oblivious to the crowd that circled in indolent coils about them. The moon had not yet risen, but a leash of stars that night had loosed glowed and trembled with desire. The air was sentient with murmurs, redolent

43

with promise. The avenues and the adjacent streets seemed to have forgotten their toil and to swoon unhushed in the bewitchments of a dream of love.

Tristrem found himself straying through its mazes and convolutions. Whichever way he turned there was some monition of its presence. From a street-car which had stayed his passage he saw the conductor blow a kiss to a hurrying form, and through an open window of Delmonico's he saw a girl with summer in her eyes reach across the table at which she sat and give her companion's hand an abrupt yet deliberate caress.

Tristrem continued his way, oppressed. He was beset by an insidious duscholia. He felt as one does who witnesses a festival in which there is no part for him. The town reeked with love as a brewery reeks with beer. The stars, the air, the very pavements told of it. It was omnipresent, and yet there was none for him.

He tried to put it from him and think of other things. Of Jones, for instance. Why had he spoken of Viola? And then, in the flight of fancies which surged through his mind, there was one that he stayed and detained. It was that he must see her again before she left town. He looked at his watch: it lacked twenty minutes to ten, and on the impulse of the moment he hailed a passing 'bus. It was inexplicable to him that the night before she should have let him go without a word as to her movements. It seemed to be understood that he was to come again to wish her a pleasant journey. And when was he to come if not that very evening? Surely at the time she had forgotten this engagement with the Wainwarings, and some note had been left for him at the door. And if no note had been left, then why should he not ask for her mother or wait till she returned? A bell rang sharply through the vehicle and aroused him from his reverie. He glanced up, and saw the driver eyeing him through the machicoulis of glass. It was the fare he wanted, and as Tristrem deposited it in the box he noticed that the familiar street was reached.

In a few moments he was at the house. On the stoop a servant was occupied with the mat.

"Is, eh, did——"

"Yes, sir," the man answered, promptly. "Miss Raritan is in the parlor."

In the surprise at the unexpected, Tristrem left his hat and coat, and pushing aside the portière, he entered the room unannounced. At first he fancied that the servant had been mistaken. Miss Raritan was not at her accustomed place, and he stood at the door-way gazing about in uncertainty. But in an instant, echoing from the room beyond, he caught the sound of her voice; yet in the voice was a tone which he had never heard before—a tone of smothered anger that carried with it the accent of hate.

Moved by unconscious springs, he left the door-way and looked into the adjoining room. A man whom at first he did not recognize was standing by a lounge from which he had presumably arisen. And before him, with both her small hands clinched and pendent, and in her exquisite face an expression of relentless indignation, stood Miss Raritan. Another might have thought them rehearsing a tableau for some theatricals of the melodramatic order, but not Tristrem. He felt vaguely alarmed: there came to him that premonition without which no misfortune ever occurs; and suddenly the alarm changed to bewilderment. The man had turned: it was Royal Weldon. Tristrem could not credit his senses. He raised his hand to his head: it did not seem possible that a felon could have told a more wanton lie than he had been told but little over an hour before; and yet the teller of that lie was his nearest friend. And still he did not understand; surely there was some mistake. He would have spoken, but Weldon crossed the room to where he stood, and with set teeth and contracted muscles fronted him a second's space, and into his eyes he looked a defiance that was the more hideous in that it was mute. Then, with a gesture that almost tore the portière from its rings, he passed out into the hall and let the curtain fall behind him.

As he passed on Tristrem turned with the obedience of a subject under the influence of a mesmerist; and when the curtain fell again he started as subjects do when they awake from their trance.

The fairest, truest, and best may be stricken in the flush of health; yet after the grave has opened and closed again does not memory still subsist, and to the mourner may not the old dreams return? However acute the grief may be, is it not often better to know that affection is safe in the keeping of the dead than to feel it at the mercy of the living? We may prate as we will, but there are many things less endurable than the funeral of the best-beloved. Death is by no means the worst that can come. Whoso discovers that affection reposed has been given to an illusory representation; to one not as he is, but as fancy pictured him; to a trickster that has cheated the heart—in fact, to a phantom that has no real existence outside of the imagination, must experience a sinking more sickening than any corpse can convey. At the moment, the crack of doom that is to herald an eternal silence cannot more appal.

Tristrem still stood gazing at the portière through which Weldon had disappeared. He heard the front door close, and the sound of feet on the pavement. And presently he was back at St. Paul's, hurrying from the Upper School to intercede with the master. It was bitterly cold that morning, but in the afternoon the weather had moderated, and they had both gone to skate. And then the day he first came. He remembered his good looks, his patronizing, precocious ways; everything, even to the shirt he wore—blue, striped with white—and the watch with the crest and the motto *Well done, Weldon*. No, it was ill done, Weldon, and the lie was ignoble. And why had he told it? Their friendship, seemingly, had been so stanch, so unmarred by disagreement, that this lie was as a dash of blood on a white wall—an ineffaceable stain.

If there are years that count double, there are moments in which the hour-glass is transfixed. The entire scene, from Tristrem's entrance to Weldon's departure, was compassed in less than a minute, yet during that fragment of time there had been enacted a drama in epitome—a drama humdrum and ordinary indeed, but in which Tristrem found himself bidding farewell to one whom he had never known.

He was broken in spirit, overwhelmed by the suddenness of the disaster, and presently, as though in search of sympathy, he turned to Miss Raritan. The girl had thrown herself in a chair, and sat, her face hidden in her hands. As Tristrem approached her she looked up. Her cheeks were blanched.

"He told me you were at the Wainwaring's," Tristrem began. "I don't see," he added, after a moment—"I don't understand why he should have done so. He knew you were here, yet he said——"

"Did you hear what he said to me?"

Tristrem for all response shook his head wonderingly.

The girl's cheeks from white had turned flame.

"He has not been to you the friend you think," she said, and raising her arm to her face, she made a gesture as though to brush from her some distasteful thing.

"But what has he done? What did he say?"

"Don't ask me. Don't mention him to me." She buried her face again in her hands and was silent.

Tristrem turned uneasily and walked into the other room, and then back again to where she sat; but still she hid her face and was silent. And Tristrem left her and continued his walk, this time to the dining-room and then back to the parlor which he had first entered. And after a while Miss Raritan stood up from her seat and as though impelled by the nervousness of her companion, she, too, began to pace the rooms, but in the contrary direction to that which Tristrem had chosen. At last she stopped, and when Tristrem approached her she beckoned him to her side.

"What did you say to me last night?" she asked.

"What did I say? I said—you asked me—I said it would be difficult."

"Do you think so still?"

"Always."

"Tristrem, I will be your wife."

A Cimmerian led out of darkness into sudden light could not marvel more at multicolored vistas than did Tristrem, at this promise. Truly they are most hopeless who have hoped the most. And Tristrem, as he paced the rooms, had told himself it was done. His hopes had scattered before him like last year's leaves. He had groped in shadows and had been conscious only of a blind alley, with a dead wall, somewhere, near at hand. But now, abruptly, the shadows had gone, the blind alley had changed into a radiant avenue, the dead wall had parted like a curtain, and beyond was a new horizon, gold-barred and blue, and landscapes of asphodels and beckoning palms. He was as one who, overtaken by sleep on the banks of the Styx, awakes in Arcadia.

His face was so eloquent with the bewitchments through which he roamed that, for the first time that evening, Miss Raritan smiled. She raised a finger warningly.

"Now, Tristrem, if you say anything ridiculous I will take it back."

But the warning was needless. Tristrem caught the finger, and kissed her hand with old-fashioned grace.

"Viola," he said, at last, "I thank you. I do not know what I can do to show how I appreciate this gift of gifts. But yet, if it is anything, if it can bring any happiness to a girl to know that she fills a heart to fulfilment itself, that she dwells in thought as the substance of thought, that she animates each fibre of another's being, that she enriches a life with living springs, and feels that it will be never otherwise, then you will be happy, for so you will always be to me."

The speech, if pardonably incoherent, was not awkwardly made, and it was delivered with a seriousness that befitted the occasion. In a tone as serious as his own, she answered:

"I will be true to you, Tristrem." That was all. But she looked in his face as she spoke.

They had been standing, but now they found seats near to each other. Tristrem would not release her hand, and she let it lie unrebellious in his own. And in this fashion they sat and mapped the chartless future. Had Tristrem been allowed his way the marriage would have been an immediate one. But to this, of course, Miss Raritan would not listen.

"Not before November," she said, with becoming decision.

"Why, that is five months off!"

"And months are short, and then——"

"But, Viola, think! Five months! It is a kalpa of time. And besides," he added, with the cogent egotism of an accepted lover, "what shall I do with myself in the meantime?"

"If you are good you may come to the Pier, and there we will talk edelweiss and myosotis, as all engaged people do." She said this so prettily that the sarcasm, if sarcasm there were, was lost.

To this programme Tristrem was obliged to subscribe.

"Well, then, afterward we will go abroad."

"Don't you like this country?" the girl asked, all the stars and stripes fluttering in her voice, and in a tone which one might use in reciting, "Breathes there the man, with soul so dead?"

"I think," he answered, apologetically, "that I do like this country. It is a great country. But New York is not a great city, at least not to my thinking. Collectively it is great, I admit, but individually not, and that is to me the precise difference between it and Paris. Collectively the French amount to little, individually it is otherwise."

"But you told me once that Paris was tiresome."

"I was not there with you. And should it become so when we are there together, we have the whole world to choose from. In Germany we can have the middle ages over again. In London we can get the flush of the nineteenth century. There is all of Italy, from the lakes to Naples. We can take a doge's palace in Venice, or a Cæsar's villa on the Baia. With a dahabieh we could float down into the dawn of history. You would look well in a dahabieh, Viola."

"As Aida?"

"Better. And that reminds me, Viola; tell me, you will

give up all thought of the stage, will you not?"

"How foolish you are. Fancy Mrs. Tristrem Varick before the footlights. There are careers open to a girl that the acceptance of another's name must close. And the stage is one of them. I should have adopted it long ago, had it not been for mother. She seems to think that a Raritan—but there, you know what mothers are. Now, of course, I shall give it up. Besides, Italian opera is out of fashion. And even if it were otherwise, have I not now a lord, a master, whom I must obey?"

Her eyes looked anything but obedience, yet her voice was melodious with caresses.

And so they sat and talked and made their plans, until it was long past the conventional hour, and Tristrem felt that he should go. He had been afloat in unnavigated seas of happiness, but still in his heart he felt the burn of a red, round wound. The lie that Weldon had told smarted still, yet with serener spirit he thought there might be some unexplained excuse.

"Tell me," he asked, as he was about to leave, "what was it Weldon said?"

Miss Raritan looked at him, and hesitated before she spoke. Then catching his face in her two hands she drew it to her own.

"He said you were a goose," she whispered, and touched her lips to his.

With this answer Tristrem was fain to be content. And presently, when he left the house, he reeled as though he had drunk beaker after flagon of the headiest wine.

VI.

After a ten-mile pull on the river, a shandygaff of Bass and champagne is comforting to the oarsman. It is accounted pleasant to pay a patient creditor an outlawed debt. But a poet has held that the most pleasurable thing imaginable is to awake on a summer morning with the consciousness of being in love. Even in winter the sensation ought not to be disagreeable; yet when to the consciousness of being in love is added the belief that the love is returned, then the bleakest day of all the year must seem like a rose of June.

Tristrem passed the night in dreams that told of Her. He strayed through imperishable beauties, through dawns surrounded by candors of hope. The breath of brooks caressed him, he was enveloped in the sorceries of a sempiternal spring. The winds, articulate with song, choired to the skies ululations and messages of praise. Each vista held a promise. The horizon was a prayer fulfilled. He saw grief collapse and joy enthroned. From bird and blossom he caught the incommunicable words of love. And when from some new witchery he at last awoke, he smiled—the real was fairer than the dream.

For some time he loitered in the gardens which his fancy disclosed, spectacular-wise, for his own delight, until at last he bethought him of the new duties of his position and of the accompanying necessity of making those duties known to those to whom he was related. Then, after a breakfast of sliced oranges and coffee, he rang for the servant and told him to ask his father whether he could spare a moment that morning. In a few minutes the servant returned. "Mr. Varick will be happy to see you, sir," he said.

"What did he say?" Tristrem asked; "what were his exact words?"

"Well, sir, I said as how you presented your compliments, and could you see him, and he didn't say nothing; he was feeding the bird. But I could tell, sir; when Mr. Varick doesn't like a thing, he looks at you and if he does, he doesn't."

"And he didn't look at you?"

"No, sir, he didn't turn his 'ead."

"H'm," said Tristrem to himself, as he descended the stairs, "I wonder, when I tell him, whether he will look at me." And the memory of his father's stare cast a shadow on his buoyant spirits.

On entering the room in which Mr. Varick passed his mornings, Tristrem found that gentleman seated at a table. In one hand he held a bronze-colored magazine, and in the other a silver knife. In the window was a gilt cage in which a bird was singing, and on the table was a profusion of roses—the room itself was vast and chill. One wall was lined, the entire length, with well-filled book-shelves. In a corner was a square pile of volumes, bound in pale sheep, which a lawyer would have recognized as belonging to the pleasant literature of his profession. And over the book-shelves was a row of Varicks, standing in the upright idleness which is peculiar to portraits in oil. It was many years since Tristrem had entered this room; yet now, save for the scent of flowers and the bird-cage, it was practically unchanged.

"Father," he began at once, "I would not have ventured to disturb you if—if—that is, unless I had something important to say." He was looking at his father, but his father was not looking at him. "It is this," he continued, irritated in spite of himself by the complete disinterestedness of one whose son he was; "I am engaged to be married."

At this announcement Mr. Varick fluttered the paper-knife, but said nothing.

"The young lady is Miss Raritan," he added, and then paused, amazed at the expression of his father's face. It was as though unseen hands were torturing it at will. The mouth, cheeks, and eyelids quivered and twitched, and then abruptly Mr. Varick raised the bronze-colored magazine, held it before his tormented features, and when he lowered it again his expression was as apathetic as before.

"You are ill!" Tristrem exclaimed, advancing to him.

But Mr. Varick shook his head, and motioned him back. "It is nothing," he answered. "Let me see, you were saying——?"

"I am engaged to Miss Raritan."

"The daughter of——"

"Her father was Roanoke Raritan. He was minister somewhere—to England or to France, I believe."

While Tristrem was giving this information Mr. Varick went to the window. He looked at the occupant of the gilt cage, and ran a thumb through the wires. The bird ruffled its feathers, cocked its head, and edged gingerly along the perch, reproving the intrusive finger with the scorn and glitter of two eyes of bead. But the anger of the canary was brief. In a moment Mr. Varick left the cage, and turned again to his son.

"Nothing you could do," he said, "would please me better."

"Thank you," Tristrem answered, "I——"

"Are you to be married at once?"

"Not before November, sir."

"I wish it were sooner. I do not approve of protracted engagements. But, of course, you know your own business best. If I remember rightly, the father of this young lady did not leave much of a fortune, did he?"

"Nothing to speak of, I believe."

"You have my best wishes. The match is very suitable, very suitable. I wish you would say as much, with my compliments, to the young lady's mother. I would do so myself, but, as you know, I am something of an invalid. You might add that, too—and—er—I don't mean to advise you, but I would endeavor to hasten the ceremony. In such matters, it is usual for the young lady to be coy, but it is for the man to be pressing and resolute. I only regret that her father could not know of it. In regard to money, your allowance will have to be increased—well, I will attend to that. There is nothing else, is there? Oh, do me the favor not to omit to say that I am much pleased. I knew Miss Raritan's father." Mr. Varick looked up at the ceiling, and put his hand to his mouth. It was difficult to say whether he was concealing a smile or a yawn. "He would be pleased, I know." And with that Mr. Varick resumed his former position, and took up again the magazine.

"It is very good of you," Tristrem began; "I didn't know, of course—you see, I knew that if you saw the young lady— but what am I calling her a young lady for?" he asked, in an aside, of himself—"Miss Raritan, I mean," he continued aloud, "you would think me fortunate as a king's cousin." He paused. "I am sure," he reflected, "I don't know what I am talking about. What I say—is sheer imbecility. However," he continued, again, "I want to thank you. You have seen so little of me that I did not expect you would be particularly interested, I—I——"

He hesitated again, and then ceased speaking. He had been looking at his father, and something in his father's stare fascinated and disturbed his train of thought. For the moment he was puzzled. From his childhood he had felt that his father disliked him, though the reason of that dislike he had never understood. It was one of those things that you get so accustomed to that it is accepted, like baldness, as a matter of course, as a thing which had to be and could not be otherwise. To his grandfather, who was at once the most irascible and gentlest of men, and whom he had loved instinctively, from the first, with the unreasoning faith that children have—to him he had, in earlier days, spoken more than once of the singularity of his father's attitude. The old gentleman, however, had no explanation to give. Or, if he had one, he preferred to keep it to himself. But he petted the boy outrageously, with some idea of making up for it all, and of showing that he at least had love enough for two.

And now, as Tristrem gazed in his father's face, he seemed to decipher something that was not dislike—rather the contented look of one who learns of an enemy's disgrace, a compound of malice and of glee.

"That was all I had to say," Tristrem added, with his winning smile, as though apologizing for the lameness of the conclusion. And thereupon he left the room and went out to consult a jeweller and bear the tidings to other ears.

For some time he was absurdly happy. His grandfather received the announcement of the coming marriage with proper enthusiasm. He laughed sagaciously at Tristrem's glowing descriptions of the bride that was to be, and was for going to call on the mother and daughter at once, and was

THE TRUTH ABOUT TRISTREM VARICK.

only prevented on learning that they had both left town.

"But I must write," he said, and write he did, two elaborate letters, couched in that phraseology at once recondite and simple which made our ancestors the delightful correspondents that they were. The letters were old-fashioned indeed. Some of the sentences were enlivened with the eccentricities of orthography which were in vogue in the days of the *Spectator*. The handwriting was infamous, and the signature on each was adorned with an enormous flourish. They were not models for a Perfect Letter Writer, but they were heartfelt and honest, and they served their purpose very well.

"And, Tristrem," the old gentleman said, when the addresses had been dried with a shower of sand and the letters despatched, "you must take her this, with my love. I gave it to your mother on her wedding day, and now it should go to her." From a little red case he took a diamond brooch, set in silver, which he polished reflectively on his sleeve. "She was very sweet, Tristrem, your mother was—a good girl, and a pretty one. Did I ever tell you about the time——"

And the old gentleman ran on with some anecdote of the dear dead days in which his heart was tombed. Tristrem listened with the interest of those that love. He had heard the story, and many others of a similar tenor, again and again, but, somehow, he never heard them too often. There was nothing wearisome to him in such chronicles; and as he sat listening, and now and then prompting with some forgotten detail, anyone who had happened on the scene would have accounted it pleasant to watch the young fellow and the old man talking together over the youth of her who had been mother to one and daughter to the other.

"See!" said Tristrem at last, when his grandfather had

given the brooch into his keeping. "See! I have something for her too." And with that he displayed a ruby, unset, that was like a clot of blood. "I shall have it put in a ring," he explained, "but this might do for a bonnet-pin;" and then he produced a green stone, white-filmed, that had a heart of oscillating flame.

Mr. Van Norden had taken the ruby in his hand and held it off at arm's length, and then between two fingers, to the light, that he might the better judge of its beauty. But at the mention of the bonnet-pin he turned to look:

"Surely, Tristrem, you would not give her that; it's an opal."

"And what if it is?"

"But it is not lucky."

Tristrem smiled blithely, with the bravery that comes of nineteenth-century culture.

"It's a pearl with a soul," he answered, "that's what it is. And if Viola doesn't like it I'll send it to you."

"God forbid," Mr. Van Norden replied; "if anyone sent me an opal I would swear so hard that if the devil heard me he'd go in a corner and cross himself."

At this threat Tristrem burst out laughing, and the old gentleman, amused in spite of himself at the fantasy of his own speech, burst out laughing too.

Then there was more chat, and more reminiscences, and much planning as to how Tristrem should best assume the rank and appanages of the married state. Tristrem dined with his grandfather that evening, and when Mr. Van Norden started out to his club for a game of whist, Tristrem accompanied him as far as the club door.

When they parted, Tristrem was in such spirits that he could have run up to Central Park and back again. "Divinities of Pindar," he kept exclaiming—a phrase that he had caught somewhere—"divinities of Pindar, she is mine."

Thereafter, for several days, he lived, as all true lovers do, on air and the best tenderloins he could obtain.

VII.

One morning Tristrem found the sliced oranges companied by a note from Her. It was not long, but he read it so often that it became lengthy in spite of the writer. The cottage, it informed him, which had been taken for the summer, was becoming habitable. As yet but one of the hotels, and that the worst, was prepared for guests. In a fortnight, however, the others would begin to open their doors, and meanwhile if, in the course of the week, he care to run up, there was a room in the cottage at his disposal.

"In the course of the week," soliloquized Tristrem; "h'm—well, this afternoon is in the course of it, and this afternoon will I go."

Pleasured by the artfulness of his own sophistry, he procured a provision of *langues dorées*, a comestible of which she was fond, found at Tiffany's the ruby and opal set in accordance with orders already given, and at two o'clock boarded the Newport express.

The train reached New London before Tristrem had so much as glanced at a volume which he held in his hand. He had little need of anything to occupy his thoughts. His mind was a scenario in which he followed the changes and convolutions of an entertainment more alluring than any that romancer or playwright could convey. He was in that mood which we all of us have experienced, in which life seems not only worth living, but a fountain of delight as well. Were ever fields more green or sky more fair? And such a promise as the future held! In his hearing was a choir of thrushes, and on his spirit had been thrown a mantle so subtle, yet of texture so insistent, that no thought not wholly pure could pierce the woof or find a vantage-ground therein. He was in that mood in which one feels an ascension of virtues, the companionship of unviolated illusions, the pomp and purple of worship, a communion with all that is best, a repulsion of all that is base—that mood in which hymns mount unsummoned from the heart.

He was far away, but the Ideal was at his side. The past was a mirror, mirroring nothing save his own preparation and the dream of the coming of her. And now she had come, fairer than the fairest vision and desire that ever visited a poet starving in a garret. To be worthy of her, even in the slightest measure, what was there that he would leave undone? And as the train brought him to his journey's end, he repeated to himself, gravely and decorously, and with the earnestness and sincerity of the untried, the grave covenants of the marriage pact.

On descending at the station he remembered, for the first time, that he had omitted to send Miss Raritan an avant-courier in the shape of a telegram. It is one of the oddities of hazard that, in turning down one street instead of turning up another, a man's existence, and not his own alone, but that of others also, may seem to be wholly changed thereby. The term *seem* is used advisedly, for, with a better understanding of the interconnection of cause and effect, chance has been outlawed by science, and in the operations of consistent laws the axiom, "Whatever will be, Is," has passed to the kindergarten. Tristrem thought of this months afterward. He remembered then, that that morning he had started out with the intention of sending a telegram from the club, but on the way there he had thought of the chocolate which Viola preferred, and, after turning into Broadway to purchase it, he had drifted into Tiffany's, and from there he had returned to Waverley Place, the message unsent and forgotten. He recalled these incidents months later, but for the moment he merely felt a vague annoyance at his own neglect.

There was a negro at the station, the driver of a coach in whose care Tristrem placed himself, and presently the coach rattled over a road that skirted the sea, and drew up at the gate of a tiny villa. On the porch Mrs. Raritan was seated, and when she recognized her visitor she came down the path, exclaiming her pleasure and welcome. It was evident at once that she had been gratified by her daughter's choice.

"But we didn't expect you," she said. "Viola told me you would not come before Saturday. I am glad you did, though; as yet there's hardly a soul in the place. Viola has gone riding. It's after seven, isn't it? She ought to be back now. Why didn't you send us word? We would have met you at the train."

They had found seats on the porch. Tristrem explained his haste, apologizing for the neglect to wire. The haste seemed pardonable to Mrs. Raritan, and the attendant absent-mindedness easily understood. And so for some moments they talked together. Tristrem delivered his father's message, and learned that Mr. Van Norden's letters had been received. Some word was even said of the possibility of a September wedding. And then a little plot was concocted. Dinner would be served almost immediately, so soon, in fact, as Viola returned. Meanwhile, Tristrem would go to his room, Mrs. Raritan would say nothing of his arrival, but, when dinner was announced, a servant would come to his door, and then he was to appear and give Viola the treat and pleasure of a genuine surprise.

This plan was acted on at once. Tristrem was shown to the room which he was to occupy, and proceeded to get his things in order. From his shirt-box, which, with his valise, had already been brought upstairs, he took the ring, the brooch, the pin, and placed them on the mantel. Then he found other garments, and began to dress. In five minutes he was in readiness, but as yet he heard nothing indicative of Viola's return. He went to the window and looked out. Above the trees, in an adjacent property, there loomed a tower. The window was at the back of the house; he could not see the ocean, but he heard its resilient sibilants, and from the garden came the hum of insects. It had grown quite dark, but still there was no sign of Viola's return.

He took up the volume which he had brought with him in the cars. It was the *Rime Nuove* of Carducci, and with the fancies of that concettist of modern Rome he stayed his impatience for a while. There was one octave that had appealed to him before. He read it twice, and was about to endeavor to repeat the lines from memory, when through the open window he heard the clatter of horses' hoofs, the roll of wheels; it was evident that some conveyance had stopped at the gate of the villa. Then came the sound of hurrying feet, a murmur of voices, and abruptly the night was cut with the anguish of a woman's cry.

Tristrem rushed from the room and down the stairs. Through the open door beyond a trembling star was visible, and in the road a group of undistinguished forms.

"She's only fainted," someone was saying; "she was right enough a minute ago."

Before the sentence was completed, Tristrem was at the gate. Hatless, with one hand ungloved and the other clutching a broken whip, the habit rent from hem to girdle, dust-covered and dishevelled, the eyes closed, and in the face the pallor and contraction of mortal pain, Viola Raritan lay, waist-supported, in her mother's arms.

"Help me with her to the house," the mother moaned. Then noticing Tristrem at her side, "She's been thrown," she added; "I knew she would be—I knew it——"

And as Tristrem reached to aid her with the burden, the girl's eyes opened, "It's nothing." She raised her ungloved hand, "I—" and swooned again.

They bore her into a little sitting-room, and laid her down. Mrs. Raritan followed, distraught with fright. In her helplessness, words came from her unsequenced and obscure. But soon she seemed to feel the need of action. One servant she despatched for a physician, from another a restorative was obtained. And Tristrem, meanwhile, knelt at the girl's side, beating her hand with his. It had been scratched, he noticed, as by a briar, and under the nails were stains such as might come from plucking berries that are red.

As he tried to take from her the whip, that he might rub the hand that held it too, the girl recovered consciousness again. The swoon had lasted but a moment or so, yet to him who watched it had been unmeasured time. She drew away the hand he held, and raising herself she looked at him; to her lips there came a tremulousness and her eyes filled.

"My darling," Mrs. Raritan sobbed, "are you hurt? Tell me. How did it happen? Did the horse run away with you. Oh, Viola, I knew there would be an accident. Where are you hurt? Did the horse drag you?"

The girl turned to her mother almost wonderingly. It

seemed to Tristrem that she was not yet wholly herself.

"Yes," she answered; "no, I mean—no, he didn't, it was an accident, he shied. *Do* get me upstairs." And with that her head fell again on the cushion.

Tristrem sought to raise her, but she motioned him back and caught her mother's hand, and rising with its assistance she let the arm circle her waist, and thus supported she suffered herself to be led away.

Tristrem followed them to the hall. On the porch a man loitered, hat in hand; as Tristrem approached he rubbed the brim reflectively.

"I saw the horse as good as an hour ago," he said, "I was going to Caswell's." And with this information he crooked his arm and made a backward gesture. "It's down yonder on the way to the Point," he explained. "As I passed Hazard's I looked in the cross-road—I call it a road, but after you get on a bit it's nothing more than a cow-path, all bushes and suchlike. But just up the road I see'd the horse. He was nibbling grass as quiet as you please. I didn't pay no attention, I thought he was tied. Well, when I was coming back I looked again; he wasn't there, but just as I got to the turn I heard somebody holloaing, and I stopped. A man ran up and says to me, 'There's a lady hurt herself, can't you give her a lift?' 'Where?' says I. 'Down there,' he says, 'back of Hazard's; she's been thrown.' So I turned round, and sure enough there she was, by the fence, sort of dazed like. I says, 'Are you hurt, miss?' and she says, 'No,' but could I bring her here, and then I see'd that her dress was torn. She got in, and I asked her where her hat was, and she said it was back there, but it didn't make no difference, she wanted to get home. And when we were driving on here I told her as how I see'd the horse, and I asked if it wasn't one of White's, and she said, 'Yes, it was,' and I was a-going to ask where she was thrown, but she seemed sort of faint, and, sure enough, just as we got here away she went. I always says women-folk ought not to be let on horse-back, she might have broke her neck; like as not——"

"You have been very kind," Tristrem answered, "very kind, indeed."

During the entire scene he had not said a word. The spectacle of Viola fainting on the roadside, the fear that she might be maimed, the trouble at her pallor—these things had tied his tongue; and even now, as he spoke, his voice was not assured, and a hand with which he fumbled in his waistcoat trembled so that the roll of bills which he drew out fell on the porch at his feet. He stooped and picked it up.

"If Mrs. Raritan were here, she would thank you as I do," he continued. "I wish—" and he was about to make some present, but the man drew back.

"That's all right, I don't want no pay for that."

"I beg your pardon," Tristrem answered, "I know you do not. Tell me, are you married?"

The man laughed.

"Yes, I am, and I got the biggest boy you ever see. He's going on four years and he weighs a ton."

"I wish you would do me a favor. Let me make him a little present."

But even to this the man would not listen. He was reluctant to accept so much as thanks. Having done what good he could, he was anxious to go his way—the sort of man that one has to visit the seashore to find, and who, when found, is as refreshing as the breeze.

As he left the porch, he looked back. "Here's the doctor,"

he said, and passed on into the night.

While the physician visited the patient, Tristrem paced the sitting-room counting the minutes till he could have speech with him, himself. And when at last he heard the stairs creak, he was out in the hall, prepared to question and intercept. The physician was most reassuring. There was nothing at all the matter. By morning Miss Raritan would be up and about. She had had a shock, no doubt. She was upset, and a trifle nervous, but all she needed was a good night's rest, with a chop and a glass of claret to help her to it. If sleep were elusive, then a bromide. But that was all. If she had been seventy a tumble like that might have done for her, but at nineteen! And the doctor left the house, reflecting that were not educated people the most timorous of all, the emoluments of his profession would be slight.

Whether or not Miss Raritan found the chop and claret sufficient, or whether she partook of a bromide as well, is not a part of history. In a little while after the physician's departure a servant brought word to Tristrem that for the moment Mrs. Raritan was unable to leave her daughter, but if he would have his dinner then, Mrs. Raritan would see him later. Such was the revulsion of feeling that Tristrem, to whom, ten minutes before, the mere mention of food would have been distasteful, sat down, and ate like a wolf. The meal finished, he went out on the porch. There was no moon as yet, but the sky was brilliant with the lights of other worlds. Before him was the infinite, in the air was the scent of sea-weed, and beyond, the waves leaped up and fawned upon the bluffs. And as he stood and watched it all, the servant came to him with Mrs. Raritan's apologies. She thought it better, the maid explained, not to leave Miss Raritan just yet, and would Mr. Varick be good enough to excuse her for that evening?

"Wait a second," he answered, and went to his room. He found the jewels, and brought them down-stairs. "Take these to Miss Raritan," he said, and on a card he wrote some word of love, which he gave with the trinkets to the maid. "*La parlate d'amor,*" he murmured, as the servant left to do his bidding, and then he went again to his room, and sat down at the window companioned only by the stars. From beyond, the boom and retreating wash of waves was still audible, and below in the garden he caught, now and then, the spark and glitter of a firefly gyrating in loops of gold, but the tower which he had noticed on arriving was lost in the night.

It was in that direction, he told himself, that the accident must have occurred. And what was it, after all? As yet he had not fully understood. Had the horse stumbled, or had he bolted and thrown her? If he had only been there! And as his fancy evoked the possibilities of that ride, he saw a terrified brute tearing along a deserted road, carrying the exquisite girl straight to some sudden death, and, just when the end was imminent, his own muscles hardened into steel, he had him by the bit and, though dragged by the impetus, at last he held him, and she was safe. She was in his arms, her own about his neck, and were he a knight-errant and she some gracious princess, what sweeter guerdon could he claim?

But one thing preoccupied him. In the vertiginous flight she had lost something—her whip, no, her hat—and it was incumbent on him to restore it to her. Very softly, then, that he might not disturb her, he opened the door. The house was hushed, and in a moment he was on the road. He could see the tower now; it was illuminated, and it seemed to him odd that he had not noticed the illumination before. It was that way, he knew, back of Hazard's, and he hurried along in the direction which the man had indicated. The insects had stilled their murmur, and the sky was more obscure, but the road was clear.

He hurried on, and as he hurried he heard steps behind him, hurrying too. He turned his head; behind him was a woman running, and who, as she ran, cast a shadow that was monstrous. In the glimpse that he caught of her he saw that she was bare of foot and that her breast was uncovered. Her skirt was tattered and her hair was loose. He turned again, the face was hideous. The eyes squinted, lustreless and opaque, the nose was squat, the chin retreated, the forehead was seamed with scars, and the mouth, that stretched to the ears, was extended with laughter. As she ran she took her teeth out one by one, replacing them with either hand. And still she laughed, a silent laughter, her thin lips distorted as though she mocked the world.

Tristrem, overcome by the horror of that laughter, felt as agonized as a child pursued. There was a fence at hand, a vacant lot, and across it a light glimmered. Away he sped. In the field his foot caught in a bramble; he fell, and could not rise, but he heard her coming and, with a great effort just as she was on him, he was up again, distancing her with ever-increasing space. The light was just beyond. He saw now it came from the tower; there was another fence, he was over it; the door was barred; no, it opened; he was safe!

In the middle of the room, circular as befits a tower, was a cradle, and in the cradle was a little boy. As Tristrem looked at him he smiled; it was, he knew, the child of the man to whom he had spoken that evening. One hand was under the pillow, but the other, that lay on the coverlid, held

Viola's hat. He bent over to examine it; the fingers that held it were grimy and large, and, as he looked closer, he saw that it was not a child, but the man himself. Before he had an opportunity to account for the delusion he heard the gallop of feet and a thunder at the door. It was she! He wheeled like a rat surprised. There was a lateral exit, through which he fled, and presently he found himself in a corridor that seemed endless in extension. The man evidently had left the cradle and preceded him, for Tristrem saw him putting on a greatcoat some distance ahead. In his feverish fright he thought, could he but disguise himself with that, he might pass out unobserved, and he ran on to supplicate for an exchange of costume; but when he reached the place where the man had stood he had gone, vanished through a dead wall, and down the corridor he heard her come. He could hear her bare feet patter on the stones. Oh, God, what did she wish of him? And no escape, not one. He was in her power, immured with her forevermore. He called for help, and beat at the walls, and ever nearer she came, swifter than disease, and more appalling than death. His nails sank in his flesh, he raised a hand to stay the beating of his heart, and then at once she was upon him, felling him to the ground as a ruffian fells his mistress, her knees were on his arms, he was powerless, dumb with dread, and in his face was the fetor of her breath. Her eyes were no longer lustreless, they glittered like twin stars, and still she laughed, her naked breast heaving with the convulsions of her mirth. "I am Truth," she bawled, and laughed again. And with that Tristrem awoke, suffocating, quivering, and outwearied as though he had run a race and lost it.

He sat awhile, broken by the horror of the dream. The palms of his hands were not yet dry. But soon he bestirred himself, and went to the door; the lights had been extinguished; he closed it again, and, with the aid of some candles, he prepared for bed. He would have read a little, but he was fatigued, tired by the emotions of the day, and when at last he lay down it was an effort to rise again and put out the candle. How long he lay in darkness, a second, an hour, he could not afterward recall; it seemed to him that he had drowsed off at once, but suddenly he started, trembling from head to foot. He had heard Viola's voice soaring to its uttermost tension. "Coward," she had called. And then all was still. He listened, he even went to the door, but the house was wrapped in silence.

"Bah!" he muttered, "I am entertaining a procession of nightmares." And in a few moments he was again asleep.

VIII.

At dawn he awoke refreshed. The sun rose from the ocean like an indolent girl from a bath. Before the house was astir he was out of doors exploring the land. He strolled past the row of hotels that front the sea, and pausing a moment at the Casino, fragrant then, and free of the stench of drink that is the outcome of the later season, he wondered how it was that, given money, and possibly brains, it was necessary to make a building as awkward as was that. And then he strayed to the shore, past the tenantless bath-houses, and on through the glories of the morning to the untrodden beach beyond.

As he walked, the village faded in the haze. The tide was low and the sand firm and hard. The waves broke leisurely in films and fringes of white, gurgling an invitation to their roomy embrace. And when the hotels were lost in the distance and the solitude was murmurous with nature alone, Tristrem, captivated by the allurements of the sea, went down into the waves and clasped them to him as lovers clasp those they love.

The sun was well on its amble to the zenith before he returned to the cottage. His hostess, he found, had not yet appeared, and as breakfast seemed to be served in that pleasant fashion which necessitates nothing, not even an appetite, Tristrem drank his coffee in solitude. And as he idled over the meal he recalled the horrors of the night, and smiled.

The air of the morning, the long and quiet stroll, the plunge in the sea, and the after-bath of sunlight that he had taken stretched full length on the sand, had dissipated the enervating emotions of dream and brought him in their stead a new invigoration. He was about to begin the dithyrambs of the day before, when the servant appeared, bearing a yellow envelope, and a book in which he was to put his name. He gave the receipt and opened the message, wonderingly.

"*Please come to town*," it ran, "*your father is dying.—Robert Harris.*"

"Your father is dying," he repeated. "H'm. Robert Harris. I never knew before what the butler's first name was. But what has that to do with it? There are times when I am utterly imbecile. Your father is dying. Yes, of course, I must go at once. But it isn't possible. H'm. I remember. He looked ghastly when I saw him. I suppose—I ought to—good God, why should I attempt to feign a sorrow that I do not feel? It is his own fault. I would have—But there, what is the use?"

He bit his nail; he was perplexed at his absence of sensibility. "And yet," he mused, "in his way he has been kind to me. He has been kind; that is, if it be kindness in a father to let a son absolutely alone. After all, filial affection must be like patriotism, ingrained as an obligation, a thing to blush at if not possessed. Yet then, again, if a country acts like a step-mother to its children, if a father treats a son as a guardian might treat a ward, the ties are conventional; and on what shall affection subsist? It was he who called me into being, and, having done so, he assumed duties which he should not have shirked. It was not for him to make himself a stranger to me; it was for him to teach me to honor him so much, to love him so well that at his death my head would be bowed in prostrations of grief. I used to try to school myself to think that it was only his way; that, outwardly cold and undemonstrative, his heart was warm as another's. But—well, it may have been, it may have been. After all, if I can't grieve, I would cross the continent to spare him a moment's pain. It was he, I suppose, who told Harris to wire. Yes, I must hurry."

He called the servant to him. "Can you tell me, please, when the next train goes?" But the servant had no knowledge whereon to base a reply. She suggested, however, that information might be obtained at an inn which stood a short distance up the road. He scribbled a few lines on a card, and gave it to the woman. "Take that to Miss Raritan, please, will you?" he said, and left the house.

At the inn a very large individual sat on the stoop, coatless, a straw covering of a remoter summer far back on his head, and his feet turned in. He listened to Tristrem with surly indifference, and spat profusely. He didn't know; he reckoned the morning train had gone.

"Hay, Alf," he called out to the negro who had taken Tristrem from the station the night before, and who was then driving by, "when's the next train go?"

"'Bout ten minutes; I just took a party from Taylor's."

"Thank you," said Tristrem to the innkeeper, who spat again by way of acknowledgment. "Can you take me to the station?" he asked the negro; and on receiving an affirmative reply, he told him to stop at Mrs. Raritan's for his traps.

As Tristrem entered the gate he saw Viola's assistant of the preceding evening drive up, waving a hat.

"I got it," the man cried out, "here it is. First time it ever passed a night out of doors, I'll bet. And none the worse for it, either." He handed it over to Tristrem. "I dreamt about you last night," he added.

"That's odd," Tristrem answered, "I dreamed about you." The man laughed at this as had he never heard anything so droll. "Well, I swan!" he exclaimed, and cracked his whip with delight. His horse started. "Here," he said, "I near forgot. Whoa, there, can't you. This goes with the hat." And he crumpled a handkerchief in his hand, and tossing it to Tristrem, he let the horse continue his way unchecked.

The hat which the man had found did not indeed look as though it had passed a night on the roadside. Save for an incidental speck or two it might have come fresh from a bandbox. Tristrem carried it into the cottage, and was placing it on the hall-table when Mrs. Raritan appeared.

"I am so sorry," she began, "Viola has told me——"

"How is she? May I not see her?"

"She scarcely slept last night."

Tristrem looked in the lady's face. The lids of her eyes were red and swollen.

"But may I not see her? May I not, merely for a moment."

"She is sleeping now," Mrs. Raritan answered; "perhaps," she added, "it is better that you should not. The doctor has been here. He says that she should be quiet. But you will come back, will you not? Truly I sympathize with you."

Mrs. Raritan's eyes filled with tears, but to what they were due, who shall say? She seemed to Tristrem unaccountably nervous and distressed.

"There is nothing serious the matter, is there?" he asked, anxiously. And at the question, Mrs. Raritan almost choked. She shook her head, however, but Tristrem was not assured. "I *must* see her," he said, and he made as would he mount the stair.

"Mr. Varick! she is asleep. She has had a wretched night. When you are able to come back, it will be different. But if you care for her, let her be."

The protest was almost incoherent. Mrs. Raritan appeared beside herself with anxiety.

"Forgive me," said Tristrem, "I did not mean to vex you. Nor would I disturb her." He paused a second, dumbly and vaguely afflicted. "You will tell her, will you not?" he added; "tell her this, that I wanted to see her. Mrs. Raritan, my whole life is wrapped up in her." He hesitated again. "You are tired too, I can see. You were up with her last night, were you not?"

Mrs. Raritan bowed her head.

"You must forgive me," he repeated, "I did not understand. Tell me," he continued, "last night I awoke thinking that I heard her calling. Did she call?"

"Call what?"

"I thought—you see I was half, perhaps wholly asleep, but I thought I heard her voice. I was mistaken, was I not?"

"Yes, you must have been."

The negro had brought down the luggage, and stood waiting at the gate.

"You will tell her—Mrs. Raritan—I love her with all my heart and soul."

The lady's lips quivered. "She knows it, and so do I."

"You will ask her to write."

"Yes, I will do so."

Tristrem took her hand in his. "Tell her from me," he began, but words failed him, it was his face that completed the message. In a moment more he was in the coach on his way to the station.

There was a brisk drive along the sea, a curve was rounded, and the station stood in sight. And just as the turn was made Tristrem caught the shriek of a whistle.

"There she goes," the negro exclaimed, "you ought to have been spryer."

"Has the train gone?" Tristrem asked.

"Can't you see her? I knew you'd be late." The man was insolent in his familiarity, but Tristrem did not seem to notice it.

"I would have given much not to be," he said.

At this the negro became a trifle less uncivil. "Would you ree-ly like to catch that train?" he asked.

"I would indeed."

"Is it worth twenty-five dollars to you?"

Tristrem nodded.

"Well, boss, I tell you. That train stops at Peacedale, and at Wakefield she shunts off till the mail passes. Like as not the express is late. If I get you to Kingston before the Newport passes, will you give me twenty-five?"

"If I make the connection I will give you fifty."

"That's talking. You'll get there, boss. Just lay back and count your thumbs."

The negro snapped his whip, and soon Tristrem was jolted over one of the worst and fairest roads of New England, through a country for which nature has done her best, and where only the legislator is vile. One hamlet after another was passed, and still the coach rolled on.

"We'll get there," the negro repeated from time to time, and to encourage his fare he lashed the horses to their utmost speed. Peacedale was in the distance; Wakefield was passed, and in a cloud of dust they tore through Kingston and reached the station just as the express steamed up.

"I told you I'd do it," the negro exclaimed, exultingly. "I'll get checks for your trunks."

A minute or two more, and the checks were obtained;

the negro was counting a roll of bills, and in a drawing-room car Tristrem was being whirled to New York.

For several hours he sat looking out at the retreating uplands, villages, and valleys. But after a while he remembered the scantiness of his breakfast, and, summoning the porter, he obtained from him some food and drink. By this time the train had reached New Haven, and there Tristrem alighted to smoke a cigarette. He was, however, unable to finish it before the whistle warned him that he should be aboard again. The porter, who had been gratified by a tip, then told him that there was a smoking compartment in the car beyond the one in which he had sat, and, as the train moved on, Tristrem went forward in the direction indicated.

The compartment was small, with seats for two on one side, and for three, or for four at most, on the other. As Tristrem entered it he saw that the larger sofa was occupied by one man, who lay out on it, full length, his face turned to the partition. Tristrem took a seat opposite him, and lit a fresh cigarette. As he smoked he looked at the reclining form of his *vis-à-vis*. About the man's neck a silk handkerchief had been rolled, but one end had come undone and hung loosely on the cushion, and as Tristrem looked he noticed that on the neck was a wound, unhealed and fresh, a line of excoriation, that neither steel nor shot could have caused, but which might have come from a scratch. But, after all, what business was it of his? And he turned his attention again to the retreating uplands and to the villages that starred the route.

When the cigarette was done, he stood up to leave the compartment. But however quietly he had moved, he seemed to arouse his neighbor, who turned heavily, as though to change his position. As he did so, Tristrem saw that it was Royal Weldon, and that on his face was a bruise. He would have spoken, for Weldon was looking at him, but he recalled the wanton lie of the week before, and as he hesitated whether to speak or pass on, Weldon half rose. "Damn you," he said, "you are everywhere." Then he lay down, turning his face again to the wall, and Tristrem, without a word, went to the other car and found his former seat.

Two hours later he reached his home. He let himself in with a latch-key, and rang the bell. But when Harris appeared he knew at once, by the expression which the butler assumed, that he had come too late.

"When did it happen?" he asked.

"It was last evening, sir; he came in from his drive and inquired for you, sir. I said that you had gone out of town, and showed him the address you left. When I went to hannounce dinner, sir, he was sitting in his arm-chair with his hat on. I thought he was asleep. I sent for Dr. McMasters, sir, but it was no use. Dr. McMasters said it was the 'art, sir."

"You have notified my grandfather, have you not?"

"Yes, sir, I did, sir; Mr. Van Norden came in this morning, and left word as how he would like to see you when you got back, sir."

"Very good. Call Davis, and get my things from the cabman."

"Yes, sir; thank you, sir. I beg pardon, sir," he added, "would you wish some dinner? There's a nice fillet and a savory."

IX.

The morning after the funeral Tristrem received a letter from Mrs. Raritan, and a little later a small package by express. The letter was not long, and its transcription is unnecessary. It was to the effect that on maturer consideration Viola had decided that the engagement into which she had entered was untenable. To this decision Mrs. Raritan felt herself reluctantly obliged to concur. It was not that Mr. Varick was one whom she would be unwilling to welcome as her daughter's husband. On the contrary, he was in many respects precisely what she most desired. But Viola was young; she felt that she had a vocation to which marriage would be an obstacle, and in the circumstances Viola was the better judge. In any event, Mr. Varick was requested to consider the decision as irrevocable. Then followed a few words of sympathy and a line of condolence expressive of Mrs. Raritan's regret that the breaking of the engagement should occur at a time when Tristrem was in grievous affliction.

In the package were the jewels.

Tristrem read the letter as though he were reading some accusation of felony levelled at him in the public press. If it had been a meteor which had fallen at his feet he could not have wondered more. Indeed, it was surprise that he felt. It was not anger or indignation; they were after-comers. For the moment he was merely bewildered. It seemed to him incredible that such a thing could be. He read the letter again,

and even examined the post-mark. At first he was for starting at once for Narragansett. If he could but see Viola! The
excuse about a vocation was nonsense. Had he not told her
that if she insisted on going on the stage, he would sit in the
stalls and applaud. No, it was not that; it was because—After all, it was his own fault; if he had been unable to make
himself beloved, why should the engagement continue? But
had an opportunity been given him? He had not had speech
with her since that evening when she had drawn his face to
hers. No, it could not be that.

He bowed his head, and then Anger came and sat at his
side. What had he done to Destiny that he should be to it
the play-thing that he was? But she; she was more voracious
even than Fate. No, it was damnable. Why should she take
his heart and torment it? Why, having given love, should
she take it away? He was contented enough until he saw
her. Why had she come to him as the one woman in the
world, luring him on; yes, for she had lured him on? Why
had she made him love her as he could never love again, and
just when she placed her hand in his,—a mist, a phantom,
a reproach? Why had she done so? Why was the engagement untenable? Untenable, indeed, why was it untenable?
Why—why—why? And in the increasing exasperation of
the moment, Tristrem did a thing that, with him, was unusual. He rang the bell, and bade the servant bring him drink.

It was on the afternoon of that day that he learned the
tenor of his father's will. It affected him as a chill affects a
man smitten with fever. He accepted it as a matter of course.
It was not even the last drop; the cup was full as it stood.
What was it to him that he had missed being one of the richest men in New York in comparison to the knowledge that
even had he the mines of Ormuz and of Ind, the revenue

would be as useless to him as the hands of the dead? Was she to be bought? Had she not taken herself away before the contents of the will were reported? He might be able to call the world his own, and it would avail him nothing.

The will left him strangely insensible, though, after all, one may wonder whether winter is severer than autumn to a flower once dead.

But if the will affected Tristrem but little, it stirred Dirck Van Norden to paroxysms of wrath. "He ought to have his ghost kicked," he said, in confidential allusion to Erastus Varick. "It's a thing that cries out to heaven. And don't you tell me, sir, that nothing can be done."

The lawyer with whom he happened to be in consultation said there were many things that could be done. Indeed, he was reassuringly fecund in resources. In the first place, the will was holographic. That, of course, mattered nothing; it only pointed a moral. Laymen should not draw up their own wills. For that matter, even professionals should be as wary of so doing as physicians are of doctoring themselves. And the lawyer instanced legal luminaries, judges whose *obiter dicta* and opinions *in banco* were cited and received with the greatest respect, and yet through whose wills, drawn up, mark you, by their own skilled hands, coaches and tandems had been driven full speed. In regard to the will of the deceased there was this to be said, it would not hold water. Chapter 360, Laws of 1860, declares that no person having a husband, wife, child, or parent, shall by his or her last will and testament, devise or bequeath to any benevolent, charitable, scientific, literary, religious, or missionary society, association, or corporation, in trust or otherwise, more than one-half part of his or her estate.

"But he devised the whole."

"Yes, so he did; but in devising it he overlooked that very wise law. My opinion in the matter is this. When, may I ask, was your grandson born?"

"He was born on the 10th of June, 1859."

"Exactly. The late Mr. Varick determined, on the birth of your grandson, that the property should go over. His reasons for so determining are immaterial. Rufus K. Taintor, the ablest man, sir, that ever sat on the bench or addressed it, drew up the will at that time in accordance with instructions received. Some years later, Taintor died of apoplexy, and he died, too, as you doubtless remember, after the delivery of that famous speech in the Besalul divorce case. Well, sir, what I make of the matter is this. The late Mr. Varick, relying on Taintor's ability, and possessing possibly some smattering of law of his own, recopied the will every time the fancy took him to make minor alterations in the general distribution of the trust. Consequently his last will and testament, having been made since the passage of the law of 1860, is nugatory and void as to one-half the bequest, and your grandson may still come in for a very pretty sum."

"He ought to have it all," said Mr. Van Norden, decidedly.

"I don't dispute that, sir, in the least—and my opinion is that he will get it. This will is dated five days previous to Mr. Varick's demise. Now, according to the law of 1848, Chapter 319, and, if I remember rightly, Section 6, no such bequest as the deceased's is valid in any will which shall not have been made and executed at least two months before the death of the testator. That, sir, I consider an extremely wise bit of legislation. The law of 1860, which I quoted, vitiates the will as to one-half the bequest; the law of 1848 does away with the will altogether. Practically speaking, your son-in-law might just as well have died intestate. Though, between ourselves, if Mr. Varick had not been ignorant of these laws, and had not, in consequence of his ignorance, made a disposition of certain private documents the contents of which are easily guessed, your grandson would have merely a *prima facie* right to have the will set aside; for, if you remember, these laws were passed only to provide for the possible interests of a surviving husband, wife, or *child*."

He emphasized the last word, and, as his meaning grew clear to Mr. Van Norden, that gentleman got very red in the face. He rang the bell.

"Thank you, sir," he said. "I shall be indebted if you will send me your account. And I shall be particularly indebted if you will send it at your very earliest convenience. Henry, get this—this—get this gentleman his hat and see him to the street."

Unfortunately for those that practise, there are a great many more lawyers in New York than one. And before the last will and testament of Erastus Varick came up for probate, Mr. Van Norden experienced slight difficulty in retaining another attorney to defend Tristrem's interests. The matter, of course, was set down for a hearing, and came up on the calendar three months later.

Of the result of that hearing the reader has been already informed, and then it was that Tristrem was taxed with old-world folly.

X.

In years gone by it had been Mr. Van Norden's custom to pass the heated term at Rockaway. But when Rockaway became a popular resort, Mr. Van Norden, like the sensible man that he was, discovered that his own house was more comfortable than a crowded hotel. This particular summer, therefore, he passed as usual in New York, and Tristrem, who had moved to his house, kept him company. June was not altogether disagreeable, but in July the city was visited by a heat at once insistent and enervating. In August it was cooler, as our Augusts are apt to be; yet the air was lifeless, and New York was not a nosegay. During these months Tristrem was as lifeless as the air. In his first need of sympathy he had gone to the irascible and kind-hearted old gentleman and told him of the breaking of the engagement, and, he might have added, of his heart, though in the telling he sought, with a lover's fealty, to palliate the grievousness of the cruelty to which he had been subjected.

"It is this way," he said; "Viola, I think, feels that she does not know me sufficiently well. After all, we have seen but little of each other, and if she accepted me, it was on the spur of the moment. Since then she has thought of it more seriously. It is for me to win her, not for her to throw herself in my arms. That is what she has thought. She may seem capricious; and what if she does? Your knowledge of women has, I am sure, made you indulgent."

"Not in the least," Mr. Van Norden answered. And then, for the time being, the subject was dropped.

It was this semi-consolatory view which Tristrem took of the matter after the effect of the first shock had lost its force. But when he received the bundle of letters, together with the Panama hat, which, through some splendid irony, had been devised to him in the only clause of the will in which his name was mentioned, it was as though a flash had rent the darkness and revealed in one quick glare an answer to the enigma in which he groped.

The letters were few in number—a dozen at most—and they were tied together with a bit of faded ribbon. They were all in the same hand, one and all contained protestations of passionate love, and each was signed in full, Roanoke Raritan. The envelope which held them was addressed to Mrs. Erastus Varick.

It was then that he saw the reason of his disinheritance, and it was then that he understood the cause of Viola's withdrawal. It was evident to him that Mrs. Raritan possessed either thorough knowledge of the facts, or else that she had some inkling of them which her feminine instinct had supplemented into evidence, and which had compelled her to forbid the banns. There were, however, certain things which he could not make clear to his mind. Why had Mrs. Raritan treated him with such consideration? She had known from the first that he loved her daughter. And after the engagement, if she wished it broken, why had she allowed Viola to invite him to the Pier?

These things were at first inexplicable to him. Afterward he fancied that it might be that Mrs. Raritan, originally uninformed, had become so only through the man whom he had believed was his father, after the announcement of the engagement had been made to him, and possibly through some communication which had only reached her after his sudden death. This explanation he was inclined to accept, and he was particularly inclined to do so on recalling the spasm which had agitated the deceased when he had come to him with the intelligence of the engagement, and the nervous excitement which Mrs. Raritan displayed on the morning when he left for town.

This explanation he accepted later—but in the horror of the situation in which he first found himself his mind declined to act. He had never known his mother, but her fame he had cherished as one cherishes that which is best and most perfect of all. And abruptly that fame was tarnished, as some fair picture might be sullied by a splash and splatter of mud. And as though that were insufficient, the letters which devastated his mother's honor brought him a hideous suspicion, and one which developed into certainty, that his father and the father of the girl whom he loved were one and the same.

It is not surprising, then, that during the summer months Tristrem was as lifeless as the air he breathed. His grandfather noticed the change—he would have been blind indeed had he not—and he urged him to leave New York. But at each remonstrance Tristrem shook his head with persistent apathy. What did it matter to him where he was? If New York, instead of being merely hot and uncomfortable, had been cholera-smitten, and the prey of pest, Tristrem's demeanor would not have altered. There are people whom calamity affects like a tonic, who rise from misfortune refreshed; there are others on whom disaster acts like a soporific, and he was one of the latter. For three months he did not open a book, the daily papers were taken from him unread, and if during that time he had lost his reason, it is probable that his insanity would have consisted in sitting always with eyes fixed, without laughing, weeping, or changing place.

But after the hearing in the Surrogate's Court there was a change of scene. The will was set aside, and the estate, of which Tristrem had taken absolutely no thought whatever, reverted to him. It was then that he made it over in its entirety to the institution to which it had been originally devised; and it was in connection with the disposal of the property, a disposal which he effected as a matter of course, and as the only right and proper thing for him to do, that he enjoyed a memorable interview with his grandfather.

He had not spoken to Mr. Van Norden about the letters, and the old gentleman, through some restraining sense of delicacy, had hesitated to question. Besides, he was confident that the estate would be Tristrem's, and thus assured, it seemed unnecessary to him to touch on a matter to which Tristrem had not alluded, and which was presumably distasteful to him. But when he learned what Tristrem had done, he looked upon the matter in a different light, and attacked him very aggressively the next day.

"I can understand perfectly," he said, "that you should decline to hold property on what you seem to regard as a legal quibble. But I should be very much gratified to learn in what your judgment is superior to that of the Legislature, and why you should refuse that to which you had as clear and indefeasible a claim as I have to this fob on my waistcoat. I should be really very much gratified to learn——"

Tristrem looked at his grandfather very much as though he had been asked to open a wound. But he answered nothing. He got the letters and placed them in the old gentleman's hand.

The Truth About Tristrem Varick.

Mr. Van Norden glanced at one, and then turned to Tristrem. It was evident that he was in the currents of conflicting and retroacting emotions. He made as though he would speak, yet for the time being the intensity of his feelings prevented him. He took up the letters again and eyed them, shaking his head as he did so with the anger of one enraged at the irreparable, and conscious of the futility of the wrath.

In the lives of most men and women there are moments in which they are pregnant with words. The necessity of speech is so great that until the parturition is accomplished they experience the throes of suffocation. If no listener be at hand, there are at least the walls. Mr. Van Norden was standing near to Tristrem, but that he might be the better assured of his attention, he caught him by the arm, and addressed him in abrupt, disjointed sentences, in a torrent of phrases, unconnected, as though others than himself beat their vocables from his mouth. His words were so tumultuous that they assailed the gates of speech, as spectators at the sight of flame crowd the exits of a hall, and issue, some as were they hurled from catapults, others, maimed, in disarray.

He was possessed of anger, and as sometimes happens off the stage, his anger was splendid and glorious to behold. And Tristrem, with the thirst of one who has drunk of thirst itself, caught the cascade of words, and found in them the waters and fountains of life.

"These letters——But how is it possible? God in Heaven——! But can't you see?—the bare idea is an infamy. Your mother was as interested in Raritan as—as——It's enough to make a mad dog blush. It was just a few months before you were born——Bah! the imbecility of Erastus Varick would unnerve a pirate. I know he was always running there, Raritan was, but anyone with the brain of a wooden Indian would have understood——Why, they were here—they came to me, all three of them, and because I knew her father——And precious little thanks I got for my pains. He said he would see the girl in her grave first. He would have it that Raritan was after her for her money. It's true he hadn't a penny—but—what's that got to do with it? The mischief's done. She must have sent these letters to your mother to return to Raritan just before she married that idiot Wainwaring. Your mother was her most intimate friend—they were at school together at Pelham Priory. Raritan, I suppose, was away. Before he got back, your mother—you were born, you know, and she died. She had no chance to return them. That imbecile of a father of yours must have found the letters, and thought——But how is such a thing possible? Good God! he ought to be dug up and cowhided. And it was for this he left you a Panama hat! And it was for this you have turned over millions to an institution for the shelter of vice! It was for this——See here, since Christ was crucified, a greater stupidity, or one more iniquitous, has never been committed."

In the magnificence of his indignation, Mr. Van Norden stormed on until he lacked the strength to continue. But he stormed to ravished and indulgent ears. And when at last he did stop, Tristrem, who meanwhile had been silent as a mouse, went over to the arm-chair into which, in his exhaustion, he had thrown himself, and touched his shoulder.

"If he did not wish me to have the money," he said, "how could I keep it? How could I?" And before the honesty that was in his face the old man lowered his eyes to the ground. "I am gladder," Tristrem continued, "to know myself his son than to be the possessor of all New York. But when I thought that I was not his son, was that a reason why I should cease to be a gentleman. Though I lost everything else, what did it matter if I kept my self-respect?"

He waited a moment for an answer, and then a very singular thing happened. From Dirck Van Norden's lowered eyes first one tear and then a second rolled down into the furrows of his cheek. From his throat came a sound that did not wholly resemble a sob and yet was not like to laughter, his mouth twitched, and he turned his head aside. "It's the first time since your mother died," he said at last, but what he meant by that absurd remark, who shall say?

For some time Tristrem lingered, lost in thought. It was indeed as he had said. He was gladder to feel again that he was free to love and free to be loved in return than he would have been at holding all New York in fee. As he rose from the nightmare in which he suffocated he did not so much as pay the lost estate the compliment of a regret. It was not that which had debarred him from her, nor was it for that that she had once placed her hand in his. He was well rid of it all, since in the riddance the doors of his prison-house were unlocked. For three months his heart had been not dead but haunted, and now it was instinct with life and fluttered by the beckonings of hope. He had fronted sorrow. Pain had claimed him for its own, and in its intensity it had absorbed his tears. He had sunk to the uttermost depths of grief, and, unbereft of reason, he had explored the horrors of the abyss. And now in the magic of the unforeseen he was transported to dazzling altitudes, to landscapes from which happiness, like the despot that it is, had routed sorrow and banished pain. He was like one who, overtaken by years and disease, suddenly finds his youth restored.

His plans were quickly made. He would go to Narragansett at once, and not leave until the engagement was renewed. He had even the cruelty to determine that his grandfather should come to the Pier himself, and argue with Mrs. Raritan, if argument were necessary.

"I have so much to say," he presently exclaimed, "that I don't know where to begin."

"Begin at the end," his grandfather suggested.

But Tristrem found it more convenient to begin in the middle. He led the old gentleman into the rhyme and reason of the rupture, he carried him forward and backward from old fancies to newer hopes. He explained how imperative it was that with the demolition of the obstacle which his father had erected the engagement should be at once renewed; he blamed himself for having even suggested that Viola was capricious; he mourned over the position in which she had been placed; he pictured Mrs. Raritan's relief when she learned of the error into which she had wandered; and after countless digressions wound up by commanding his grandfather to write an explanation which would serve him as a passport to renewed and uninterruptable favor.

"Certainly—certainly," Mr. Van Norden cried, with the impatience of one battling against a stream. "But even granting that your father wrote to Mrs. Raritan, which I doubt—although, to be sure, he was capable of anything—don't you see that you are in a very different position to-day than you would have been had you not—had you not——"

"You mean about the money?"

"Why, most assuredly I mean about the money," the old gentleman cried, aroused to new indignation by the wantonness of the question.

At this Tristrem, with the blithe confidence of a lover, shook his head. "You don't know Viola," he answered. "Besides, I can work. Other men do—why shouldn't I?"

"And be able to marry when you are ready for the grave. That's nonsense. Unless the young lady is a simpleton, and her mother a fit subject for Bedlam, don't tell them that you are going to work. And what would you work at, pray? No, no—that won't do. You are as fitted to go into business as I am to open a bake-shop."

"I might try stocks," said Tristrem, bravely.

"So you might, if you had the St. Nicholas money to start with. And even then you would have to lose two fortunes before you could learn how to make one. No, if you have not six or seven millions, you will, one of these days—and the later the day the better for me—you will have a few hundred thousand. It is paltry enough in comparison to the property which you threw out of the window, but, paltry or not, it's more than you deserve. Meanwhile, I will——There, don't begin your nonsense again, sir. For the last three months you have done nothing but bother the soul out of me. Meanwhile, if you don't accept what I care to give, and accept it, what's more, with a devilish good grace, I'll—I'll disinherit you myself—begad I will. I'll leave everything I have to the St. Nicholas. It's a game that two can play at. You have set the fashion, and you can abide by it. And now I would be very much indebted if you would let me get some rest."

Therewith the fierce old gentleman looked Tristrem in the eyes, and grasping him by the shoulder, he held him to him for a second's space.

XI.

When Tristrem reached Narragansett he had himself driv-
en to an hotel, where he removed the incidental traces of
travel before venturing to present himself at the villa. It was
a glorious forenoon, and as he dressed, the tonic that was
blown to him through the open window affected his spirits
like wine. The breeze promised victory. He had been idle
and dilatory, he told himself; but he was older, the present
was his, and he felt the strength to make it wholly to his use.
The past would be forgotten and put aside; no, but utterly,
as Nature forgets—and in the future, what things might be!

"O Magali, ma bien aimée, Fuyons tous deux, tous de—
ux——"

The old song came back to him, and as he set out for the
villa he hummed it gayly to himself. The villa was but the
throw of a stone from the hotel, and in a moment he would
be there. He was just a little bit nervous, and he walked
rapidly. As he reached the gate his excitement increased. In
his breast was a tightening sensation. And then at once he
stopped short. On the door of the cottage hung a sign, bearing for legend, "To Let—Furnished."

"But it is impossible," he exclaimed, "they were to be here
till October."

He went up and rang the bell. The front windows were
closed and barred. The porch on which he stood was chair-
less. He listened, and heard no sound. He tried the door—it

was locked.

"But it is impossible," he kept repeating. "H'm! 'To let—furnished; for particulars apply to J. F. Brown, at the Casino.' Most certainly, I will—most certainly," and monologuing in the fashion that was peculiar to him, he went down the road again, mindful only of his own perplexity.

On reaching the Casino he found that he would have no difficulty in seeing the agent. Mr. Brown, the door-keeper told him, was "right in there," and as he gave this information he pointed to a cramped little office which stood to the left of the entrance.

"Is this Mr. Brown?" Tristrem began. "Mr. Brown, I am sorry to trouble you. Would you be good enough to tell me about Mrs. Raritan's cottage. I——"

"For next summer? Nine hundred, payable in advance."

"I didn't mean about the price. I meant—I was told that Mrs. Raritan had taken it until October——"

"So she did. You can sublet for the balance of the season."

"Thank you—yes—but Mrs. Raritan hasn't gone away, has she?"

"She went weeks ago. There's nothing the matter with the cottage, however. Drainage excellent."

"I have no doubt. But can you tell me where Mrs. Raritan went to?"

"I haven't the remotest idea. Lenox, perhaps. If you want to look at the cottage I'll give you the key."

"I should think——Really, I must apologize for troubling you. Didn't Mrs. Raritan leave her address?"

"If she did, it wasn't with me. When do you want the cottage for?"

Tristrem had not the courage to question more. He turned despondently from Mr. Brown, and passing on through the vestibule, reached the veranda that fronts the sea. In an angle a group of violinists were strumming an inanity of Strauss with perfect independence of one another. Beyond, on the narrow piazza, and on a division of the lawn that leaned to the road, were a number of small tables close-packed with girls in bright costumes and men in loose flannels and coats of diverting hues. At the open windows of the restaurant other groups were seated, dividing their attention between the food before them and the throng without. And through the crowd a number of Alsatians pushed their way, bearing concoctions to the thirstless. The hubbub was enervating, and in the air was a stench of liquor with which the sea-breeze coped in vain.

Tristrem hesitated a second, and would have fled. He was in one of those moods in which the noise and joviality of pleasure-seekers are jarring even to the best-disposed. While he hesitated he saw a figure rising and beckoning from a table on the lawn. And as he stood, uncertain whether or no the signals were intended for him, the figure crossed the intervening space, and he recognized Alphabet Jones.

"Come and have a drink," said that engaging individual. "You're as solemn as a comedian. I give you my word, I believe you are the only sober man in the place."

"Thank you," Tristrem answered; "I believe I do not care for anything. I only came to ask——By the way, have you been here long?"

"Off and on all summer. It's a good place for points. You got my card, didn't you? I wanted to express my sympathy at your bereavement."

"You are very kind; I——"

"But what's this I hear about you? You've bloomed out into a celebrity. Everybody is talking about you—everybody, men, women, and children, particularly the girls. When a fellow gives away a fortune like that! *Mais, tu sais, mon cher, c'est beau, c'est bien beau, ça.*" And to himself he added, "*Et bien bête.*"

Already certain members of immediate groups had become interested in the new arrival, and it seemed to Tristrem that he heard his name circulating above the jangle of the waltz.

"I am going to the hotel," he said. "I wish you would walk back with me. I haven't spoken to a soul in an age. It would be an act of charity to tell me the gossip." Tristrem, as he made this invitation, marvelled at his own duplicity. For the time being, he cared for the society of Alphabet Jones as he cared for the companionship of a bum-bailiff. Yet still he lured him from the Casino and led him up the road, in the hope that perhaps without direct questioning he might gain some knowledge of Her.

As they walked on Jones descanted in the arbitrary didactic manner which is the privilege of men of letters whose letters are not in capitals, and moralized on a variety of topics, not with any covert intention of boring Tristrem, but merely from a habit he had of rehearsing ready-made phrases and noting their effect on a particular listener. This exercise he found beneficial. In airing his views he sometimes stumbled on a good thing which he had not thought of in private. And as he talked Tristrem listened, in the hope that he might say something which would permit him to lead up to the subject that was foremost in his mind. But nothing of such a nature was touched upon, and it was not until the cottage was reached that Tristrem spoke at all.

"The Raritans have gone, I see," he remarked, nodding at the cottage as he did so.

"Yes, I see by the papers that they sailed yesterday."

"You don't mean to say they have gone to Europe. I thought—I heard they were going to Lenox."

"If they were, they changed their plans. Miss Raritan didn't seem up to the mark when she was here. In some way she reminded me of a realized ideal—the charm had departed. She used to be enigmatical in her beauty, but this summer, though the beauty was still there, it was no longer enigmatical, it was like a problem solved. After all, it's the way with our girls. A winter or two in New York would take the color out of the cheeks of a Red Indian. *Apropos de bottes*, weren't you rather smitten in that direction?"

"And you say they have gone abroad?" Tristrem repeated, utterly unimpressed by the ornateness of the novelist's remarks.

"Yes, sir; and were it not that our beastly Government declines to give me the benefit of an international copyright, I should be able to go and do likewise. It's enough to turn an author into an anarchist. Why, you would be surprised——"

Jones rambled on, but Tristrem no longer listened. The position in which he found himself was more irritating than a dream. He was dumbly exasperated. It was his own inaction that was the cause of it all. If he had but bestirred himself sooner! Instead of struggling against that which every throb of his heart convinced him was false, he had dawdled with the impossible and toyed with apostils of grief. At the first obstacle he had turned aside. Where he should have been resolute, he had been weak. He had taken mists for barriers. A child frightened at its own shadow was never more absurd than he. And Viola—it was not surprising that the color had deserted her cheeks. It was no wonder that in his imbecile silence she had gone away. It was only surprising that she had not gone before. And if she had waited, might it not be that she waited expectant of some effort from him, hoping against hope, and when he had made no sign had believed in his defeat, and left him to it. There was no blame for her. And now, if he were free again, that very liberty was due not to his own persistence, but to chance. Surely she was right to go. Yet—yet—but, after all, *it was not too late*. Wherever she had gone he could follow. He would find her, and tell her, and hold her to him.

Already he smiled in scenes forecast. The exasperation had left him. Whether he came to Narragansett or journeyed to Paris, what matter did it make? The errand was identical, and the result would be the same. How foolish of him to be annoyed because he had not found her, in garlands of orange-blossoms, waiting on a balcony to greet his coming. The very fact of her absence added new weight to the import of his message. Yes, he would return to town at once, and the next steamer would bear him to her.

And then, unconsciously, through some obscure channel of memory, he was back where he had once been, in a *Gasthof* in the Bavarian Mountains. It was not yet dusk. Through the window came a choir of birds, and he could see the tender asparagus-green of neighborly trees. He was seated at a great, bare table of oak, and as he raised from it to his lips a stone measure of beer, his eyes rested on an engraving that hung on the wall. It represented a huntsman, galloping like mad, one steadying hand on the bridle and the other stretched forward to grasp a phantom that sped on before. Under the picture, in quaint German text, was the legend, *The Chase after Happiness*. "H'm;" he mused, "I don't see why I should think of that."

"That's the gist of it all," Jones was saying. "It's the fashion to rail against critics. I remember telling one of the guild the other day not to read my books—they might prejudice him in my favor; but in comparison to certain publishers the average reviewer stands as a misdemeanant does to a burglar. No, I have said it before and I say it again, until that copyright law is passed, the Government is guilty of nothing less than compounding a felony."

Of what had gone before Tristrem had not heard a single word, and these ultimate phrases which reached him were as meaningless as church-steeples. He started as one does from a nap, with that shake of the head which is peculiar to the absent-minded. He was standing, he discovered, at the entrance to the hotel at which he lodged.

"Don't you agree with me?" Jones asked. "Come and lunch at the Casino. You will get nothing here. Narragansett cookery is as iniquitous as the legislature. Besides, at this hour they give you dinner. It is tragic, on my word, it is."

"Thank you," Tristrem answered, elusively. "I have an appointment with—with a train." And with this excuse he entered the hotel, and as soon after as was practicable he returned to town.

It was, he learned, as Jones had said. Mrs. Raritan and Miss Raritan were passengers on a steamer which had sailed two days before. It was then Friday. One of the swiftest Cunarders was to sail the following morning, and it seemed not improbable to Tristrem that he might reach the other side, if not simultaneously with, at least but a few hours after the arrival of the Wednesday boat. Such preparations, therefore, as were necessary he made without delay. As incidental thereto, he went to the house in Thirty-ninth Street. There he learned, from a squat little Irishwoman who came out from the area and eyed him with unmollifiable suspicion, that, like the Narragansett cottage, the house was to let. The only address which he could obtain from her was that of a real-estate agent in the lower part of the city. Thither he posted at once. Yet even there the information which he gleaned was meagre. The house was offered for a year. During that period, the agent understood, Mrs. Raritan proposed to complete her daughter's musical education abroad; where, the agent did not know. The rental accruing from the lease of the house was to be paid over to the East and West Trust Co. Further than that he could say nothing. Thereupon Tristrem trudged hopefully to Wall Street; but the secretary of the East and West was vaguer even than the agent. He knew nothing whatever on the subject of Mrs. Raritan's whereabouts, and from his tone it was apparent that he cared less. There is, however, an emollient in courtesy which has softened greater oafs than he, and that emollient Tristrem possessed. There was in his manner a penetrating and pervasive refinement, and at the gruffness with which he was received there came to his face an expression of such perplexity that the secretary, disarmed in spite of himself, turned from his busy idleness and told Tristrem that if Mrs. Raritan had not left her address with him she must certainly have given it to the lawyer who held the power of attorney to collect the rents and profits of her estate. The name of that lawyer was Meggs, and his office was in the Mills Building.

In the Mills Building Tristrem's success was little better. Mr. Meggs, the managing clerk announced, had left town an hour before and would not return until Monday. However, if there was anything *he* could do, he was entirely at Tristrem's disposal. And then Tristrem explained his errand anew, adding that he sailed on the morrow, and that it was important for him to have Mrs. Raritan's address before he left. The clerk regretted, but he did not know it. Could not Mr. Meggs send it to him?

"He might cable it, might he not?" Tristrem suggested. And as this plan seemed feasible, he gave the clerk a card with a London address scrawled on it, and therewith some coin. "I should be extremely indebted if you would beg Mr. Meggs to send me the address at once," he added; and the clerk, who had read the name on the card and knew it to be that of the claimant and renouncer of a great estate, assured him that Mr. Meggs would take great pleasure in so doing.

After that there was nothing for Tristrem to do but to return to his grandfather's house and complete his preparations. He dined with Mr. Van Norden that evening, and a very pleasant dinner it was. Together they talked of those matters and memories that were most congenial to them; Mr. Van Norden looking steadily in the past, and Tristrem straight into the future. And at last, at midnight, when the carriage came to take Tristrem to the wharf—for the ship was to sail at so early an hour in the morning that it was deemed expedient for the passengers to sleep on board—as Tristrem took leave of his grandfather, "Bring her back soon," the old gentleman said, "bring her back as soon as you can. And, Tristrem, you must take this to her once more, with an old man's love and blessing."

Whereupon he gave Tristrem again the diamond brooch that had belonged to his daughter.

XII.

The journey over was precisely like any other, except in this, that, the tide of travel being in the contrary direction, the number of cabin passengers was limited. Among them there was no one whom Tristrem had met before; yet, after the second day out, there were few whom his appearance and manner had not attracted and coerced into some overture to better acquaintance. Of these his attention was particularly claimed by an Englishman who sat next to him at table, and a young lady who occupied the seat opposite to his own. In the eyes of the latter was the mischievous look of a precocious boy. She was extremely pretty; blonde, fair, with a mouth that said Kiss me—what the French call a *frimousse frottée de champagne*; and her speech was marked by great vivacity. She was accompanied by an elderly person who appeared at table but once, and who during the rest of the voyage remained bundled in shawls in the ladies' cabin, where refreshments were presumably brought her.

It was rumored that this young lady was an ex-star of the Gaiety, and more recently a member of a burlesque troupe that had disbanded in the States. It was added—but then, are not ill-natured things said about everybody? You, sir, and you, madam, who happen to read this page, have never, of course, been spoken of other than with the greatest respect, but what is said of your neighbor? and what have you said yourself?

Tristrem, unaffected by the gossip of the smoking-room, to which, indeed, he lent but an inattentive ear, allowed the young lady to march him up and down the deck and, as was his wont, permitted himself to be generally made use of. Yet if the elderly person in the ladies' cabin had exacted of him similar attentions, the attentions would have been rendered with the same prompt and diligent willingness. He was not a good listener, although he seemed one, but there was a breeziness in the young lady's conversation which helped him not a little to forget the discomforts of ocean travel. He walked with her, in consequence, mile after mile, and when she wearied of that amusement, he got her comfortably seated and, until she needed him again, passed the time in the smoking-room.

It was there that he became acquainted with the Englishman who sat next to him at table. His name, he learned, was Ledyard Yorke. He was an artist by profession, and in the course of a symposium or two Tristrem discovered that he was a very cultivated fellow besides. He seemed to be well on in the thirties, and it was evident that there were few quarters of the globe with which he was not familiar. He was enthusiastic on the subject of French literature, but the manufactures of the pupils of the Beaux Arts he professed to abominate.

"The last time I was at the Salon," he said, one evening, "there were in those interminable halls over three thousand pictures. Of these, there were barely fifty worth looking at. The others were interesting as colored lithographs on a dead wall. There was a Manet or two, a Moreau, and a dozen or more excellent landscapes, but the rest represented the apotheosis of mediocrity. The pictures which Gérôme, Cabanel, Bouguereau, and the acolytes of those pastry-cooks

THE TRUTH ABOUT TRISTREM VARICK.

exposed were stupid and sterile as church doors. What is art, after all, if it be not an imitation of nature? To my thinking, the greater the illusion, the nearer does the counterfeit approach the model. And look at the nymphs and dryads which those hair-dressers present. In the first place, nymphs and dryads are as overdone as the assumption of Virgins and the loves of Leda. Besides they were not modern, but even if they were, fancy a girl who lives in the open air in her birthday costume, and who, exposed to the sun, to say nothing of the wind, still preserves the pink and white skin of a baby—and a skin, mind you, that looks as though it had been polished and pinched by a masseur; however, place a dozen of them lolling in conventional attitudes in a glade, or represent them bathing in a pond, and although the sun shines on them through the foliage, be careful not to get so much as the criss-cross of a shadow on their bodies, smear the whole thing with cold cream, label one 'Arcadia,' and the other 'Nymphs surprised,' and you have what they call in France the *faire distingué.*"

There was nothing particularly new in what Mr. Yorke had to say, and if, like the majority of men whose thoughts run in a particular channel, he was apt to be dogmatic in his views, he yet possessed that saving quality, which consists in treating the subject in hand not as were it a matter of life and death, but rather as one which is as unimportant as the gout of a distant relative. And it was in the companionship of this gentleman, and that of the young lady alluded to, that Tristrem passed the six days which separated him from the Irish coast.

On the day preceding the debarcation he was in great and expectant spirits, but as the sun sank in the ocean his light-heartedness sank with it. During dinner his charming *vis-à-vis* rallied him as best she might, but he remained unresponsive, answering only when civility made it necessary for him to do so. It is just possible that the young lady may have entertained original ideas of her own on the subject of his taciturnity, but, however that may be, it so happened that before the meal was done Tristrem went up on deck, and seeking the stern of the ship, leaned over the gunwale.

So far in the distance as his eyes could reach was a trail of glistening white. On either side were impenetrable wastes of black. In his ears was the sob of water displaced, the moan of tireless discontent, and therewith the flash and shimmer of phosphorus seemed to invite and tell of realms of enchanted rest beneath. And, as Tristrem watched and listened, the sibilants of the sea gurgled in sympathy with his thoughts, accompanying and accentuating them with murmurs of its own. Its breast was bared to him, it lay at his feet, open-armed as though waiting his coming, and conjuring him to haste. "There is nothing sweeter," it seemed to say, "nothing swifter, and naught more still. I feed my lovers on lotus and Lethe. There is no fairer couch in the world than mine. A sister's kiss is not more chaste. I am better than fame, serener than hope; I am more than love, I am peace. I am unforsakable, and I never forsake."

And as the great ship sped on in fright, it almost seemed to Tristrem that the sea, like an affianced bride, was rising up to claim and take him as her own. Many months later, he thought of the sensation that he then experienced, the query that came to his mind, he knew not how or whence, whether it were not better perhaps—and then the after-shudder as he started back, wondering could it be that for the moment he was mad, and telling himself that in a few hours, a few days at most, he would be with Her. And what had the sea to do with him? Many months after he thought of it.

And as he still gazed at the tempting waters, he felt a hand touch his own, rest on, and nestle in it. He looked around; it was his charming *vis-à-vis* who had sought him out and was now looking in his face. She did not speak; her eyes had lost their mischief, but her mouth framed its message as before. Awkwardly as men do such things, Tristrem disengaged his hand. The girl made one little effort to detain it, and for a moment her lips moved; but she said nothing, and when the hand had gone from her, she turned with a toss of the head and disappeared in the night.

Soon after, Tristrem turned, too, and found his way to the smoking-room. In some way the caress which he had eluded had left a balm. He was as hopeful as before, and he smiled in silent amusement at the ups and downs of his needless fears. In a corner of the room was Yorke.

"I have been looking at the sea," he said, as he took a seat at his side; "it is captious as wine."

"You are a poet, are you not?" Yorke spoke not as though he were paying a compliment, but in the matter-of-fact fashion in which one drummer will say "Dry goods?" to another.

"No; I wish I were. I have never written."

"It's a popular prejudice to suppose that a poet must write. The greatest of all never put pen to paper. What is there left to us of Linus and Musæus? Siddartha did not write, Valmiki did not know how. The parables of the Christ were voiced, not written. Besides, the poet feels—he does not spend a year, like Mallarmé, in polishing a sonnet. De Musset is certainly the best example of the poet that France has to offer; with him you always catch the foot-fall of the Muse—you feel, as he felt, the inspiration. And all the more clearly in that his verses limp. He never would have had time to express himself if he had tried to sand-paper his thoughts. Don't you suppose that Murillo was a poet? Don't you suppose that Guido was? Don't you think that anyone who is in love with beauty must be? I say beauty where I might say the ideal. That is the reason I thought you a poet. You have in your face that constant preoccupation which is distinctive of those who pursue the intangible."

"I am not pursuing the intangible, though," Tristrem answered, with a little sententious nod.

"Ah, who shall say? We all do. I am pursuing it myself, though not in the sense that I attribute to you. Did you ever read Flaubert's *Tentation*? No? Well, fancy the Sphinx crouching at sunset in the encroaching sand. In the background is a riot of color, and overhead a tender blue fading into salmon and the discreetest gray. Then add to that the impression of solitude and the most absolute silence. In the foreground flutters a Chimera, a bird with a dragon's tail and the rainbow wings of a giant butterfly. The Sphinx is staring at you, and yet through and beyond, as though her eyes rested on some inaccessible horizon. Cities crumble, nations rise and subside, and still that undeviating stare! And in her face the unroutable calm of fabulous beauty. I want those eyes, I want that face. You never heard the duo which Flaubert gives, did you? It runs somewhat this way: The motionless Sphinx calls: 'Here, Chimera, rest a while.'

"The Chimera answers: 'Rest? Not I.'

"*The Sphinx.* Whither goest thou in such haste?

"*The Chimera.* I gallop in the corridors of the labyrinth. I soar to the mountain-tops. I skim the waves. I yelp at the foot of precipices. I cling to the skirt of clouds. With my training tail I sweep the shores. The hills have taken their curve from the form of my shoulders. But thou—I find thee

THE TRUTH ABOUT TRISTREM VARICK.

perpetually immobile, or else with the end of thy claw drawing alphabets in the sand.

"*The Sphinx.* I am guarding my secret, I calculate and I dream.

"*The Chimera.* I—I am joyous and light of heart. I discover to man resplendent perspectives, Utopias in the skies, and distant felicities. Into his soul I pour the eternal follies, projects of happiness, plans for the future, dreams of fame, and the vows of love and virtuous resolutions. I incite to perilous journeys, to great undertakings. It is I that chiselled the marvels of architecture. It is I that hung bells on the tomb of Porsenna, and surrounded with an orchalc wall the quays of the Atlantides. I seek new perfumes, larger flowers, and pleasures unenjoyed. If anywhere I perceive a man whose mind rests in wisdom, I drop from space and strangle him.

"*The Sphinx.* All those whom the desire of God torments, I have devoured."

Yorke had repeated these snatches from the duo in French. He had repeated them well, bringing out the harmony of the words in a manner which in our harsher tongue would have been impossible. And now he felt parched, and ordered some drink of the steward.

"It is the face of that Sphinx that I want," he continued. "If I were a composer I would put the duo itself to music. I know of no prose more admirable. I have the scene on canvas, all of it, that is, except the Sphinx's face, and that, of course, is the most important. I want a face that she alone could possess. I may find it, I may not. At all events, you see that just at present I too am in pursuit of the intangible. But there, tell me of the artist who is not. It is true, you go to the Academy, and in the Cleopatras and Psyches you recognize the same Mary Jane who the day before offered herself as model to you. My Sphinx, however, was not born in Clapham. Nor does she dwell in Pimlico. But, apropos to Pimlico, I have a fancy that that little friend of yours is on her way to St. John's Wood."

"What little friend?"

"Why, the girl that sits opposite. And what's more to the point, she's in love with you. *Tous mes compliments, c'est un vrai morceau de roi.*"

At this Tristrem blushed in spite of himself. She might have been the Helen for whom the war of the world was fought; she might have been Mylitta or Venus Basilea, and still would she have left him unimpressed. He would not have recognized the divinity—he bowed but to one.

"You remind me," said Yorke, who had watched his expression—"you remind me of De Marsay, who did not know what he did to the women to make them all fall in love with him. There is nothing as fetching as that. And there is nothing, at least to my thinking, that compares with that charm which a woman in love exhales to her lover. It is small matter whether the woman is the daughter of an earl or whether she is a cocotte. There are, I know, people who like their claret in decanters, but so long as the wine is good, what does the bottle matter?

"*Aimer est le grand point, qu' importe la maitresse? Qu' importe le flacon, pourvu qu'on ait l'ivresse?*'"

"De Musset was drunk when he wrote that," said Tristrem. "But whether he was drunk or sober, I don't agree with him. I don't agree with him at all. It is the speech of a man who can think himself in love over and over again, and who discovers in the end that through all his affairs he has loved no one but himself."

THE TRUTH ABOUT TRISTREM VARICK.

All of which Mr. Yorke pooh-poohed in the civilest manner, and when Tristrem had finished his little speech, expounded the principles of love as they are formulated in the works of a German metaphysician, supporting them as he did so with such clarity and force of argument that Tristrem, vanquished but unconvinced, left him in disgust.

The next day they were at Liverpool. In the confusion that is incidental to every debarcation Tristrem had had no opportunity of exchanging a word with his *vis-à-vis*. But in the custom-house he caught sight of her, and went forward to bid her good-bye.

"Good-bye," she answered, when he had done so, and putting out her hand, she looked at him with mischievous eyes. "Good-bye," she repeated, lightly, and then, between her teeth, she added, "Imbecile that you are!"

Though what she may have meant by that, Tristrem never understood.

XIII.

It was under cover of a fog of leprous brown striated with ochre and acrid with smoke that Tristrem entered London. In allusion to that most delightful of cities, someone has said somewhere that hell must be just such another place. If the epigrammatist be right, then indeed is it time that the rehabilitation of the lower regions began. London is subtle and cruel, perhaps, and to the meditative traveller it not infrequently appears like an invocation to suicide writ in stone. But whoso has once accustomed himself to its breath may live ever after in flowerful Arcadias and yet dream of its exhalations with regret. In Venice one may coquette with phantoms; Rome has ghosts and memories of her own; in Paris there is a sparkle that is headier than absinthe; Berlin resounds so well to the beat of drums that even the pusillanimous are brave; but London is the great enchantress. It is London alone that holds the secret of inspiring love and hatred as well.

Tristrem sniffed the fog with a sensation of that morbid pleasure which girls in their teens and women in travail experience when they crave and obtain repulsive food. Had he not hungered for it himself? and did she not breathe it too?

The journey from Euston Square to the hotel in Jermyn Street at which he proposed to put up, was to him a confusion of impatience and anticipation. He was sure of finding a cablegram from Mrs. Raritan's attorney, and was it not possible that he might see Viola that very night? In Jermyn Street, however, no message awaited him. Under the diligent supervision of a waiter who had the look and presence of a bishop he managed later to eat some dinner. But the evening was a blank: he passed it twirling his thumbs, dumbly irritated, incapable of action, and perplexed as he had never been before.

The next morning his Odyssey began. He cabled to Mr. Meggs, and saw the clerk put beneath the message the cabalistic letters *A. P.* And then, in an attempt to frighten Time, he had his measure taken in Saville Row and his hair cut in Bond Street. But in vain—the day dragged as though its wheels were clogged. By noon he had exhausted every possible resource. Another, perhaps, might have beguiled the tedium with drink, or cultivated what Balzac has called the gastronomy of the eye, and which consists in idling in the streets. But unfortunately for Tristrem, he was none other than himself. The mere smell of liquor was distasteful to him, and he was too nervous to be actively inactive. Moreover, as in September there are never more than four million people in London, his chance of encountering an acquaintance was slight. Those that he possessed were among the absent ten thousand. They were in the country, among the mountains, at the seaside, on the Continent—anywhere, in fact, except in the neighborhood of Pall Mall. And even had it been otherwise, Tristrem was not in a mood to suffer entertainment. He had not the slightest wish to be amused. Wagner might have come to Covent Garden from the grave to conduct Parsifal in person and Tristrem would not have so much as bought a stall. He wanted Miss Raritan's address, and until he got it a comet that bridged the horizon would have left him incurious as the dead.

On the morrow, with his coffee, there came to him a yellow envelope. The message was brief, though not precisely to the point *"Uninformed of Mrs. Raritan's address,"* it ran, and the signature was *Meggs.*

For the first time it occurred to Tristrem that Fate was conspiring against him. It had been idiocy on his part to leave New York before he had obtained the address; and now that he was in London, it would be irrational to write to any of her friends—the Wainwarings, for instance—and hope to get it. He knew the Wainwarings just well enough to attend a reception if they gave one, and a slighter acquaintance than that it were idle to describe.

Other friends the girl had in plenty, but to Tristrem they were little more than shadows. There seemed to be no one to whom he could turn. Indeed he was sorely perplexed. Since the hour in which he learned that his father and Viola's were not the same he had been possessed of but one thought—to see her and kneel at her feet; and in the haste he had not shown the slightest forethought—he had been too feverishly energetic to so much as wait till he got her address; and now in the helter-skelter he had run into a *cul-de-sac* where he could absolutely do nothing except sit and bite his thumb. The enforced inactivity was torturesome as suspense. In his restlessness he determined to retrace his steps; he would return to New York, he told himself, learn of her whereabouts, and start afresh. Already he began to calculate the number of days which that course of action would necessitate, and then suddenly, as he saw himself once more on Fifth Avenue, he bethought him of Alphabet Jones. What man was there that commanded larger sources of social information than he? He would cable to him at once, and on the morrow he would have the address.

The morrow dawned, and succeeding morrows—a

week went by, and still no word from Jones. A second week passed, and when a third was drawing to a close and Tristrem, outwearied and enervated, had secured a berth on a returning steamer, at last the answer came—an answer in four words—*"Brown Shipley, Founders' Court."* That was all, but to Tristrem, in his over-wrought condition, they were as barbs of flame. "My own bankers!" he cried; "oh, thrice triple fool! why did I not think of them before?" He was so annoyed at his stupidity that on his way to the city his irritation counterbalanced the satisfaction which the message brought. "Three whole weeks have I waited," he kept telling himself—"three whole weeks! H'm! Jones might better have written. No, I might better have shown some common-sense. Three whole weeks!"

He was out of the cab before it had fairly stopped, and breathless when he reached the desk of the clerk whose duty it was to receive and forward the letters of those who banked with the house.

"I want Mrs. Raritan's address," he said—"Mrs. R. F. Raritan, please."

The clerk fumbled a moment over some papers. "Care of Munroe, Rue Scribe," he answered.

"Thank God!" Tristrem exclaimed; "and thank you. Send my letters there also."

That evening he started for Paris, and the next morning he was asking in the Rue Scribe the same question which he had asked the previous afternoon in Founders' Court. There he learned that Mrs. Raritan had sent word, the day before, that all letters should be held for her until further notice. She had been stopping with her daughter at the Hôtel du Rhin, but whether or not she was still there the clerk did not know. The Rue Scribe is not far from the Place Vendôme, in which the Hôtel du Rhin is situated, and it took Tristrem a little less than five minutes to get there. The concierge was lounging in her cubby-hole.

"Madame Raritan?" Tristrem began.

"*Partie, m'sieu, partie d'puis hier—*"

And then from Tristrem new questions came thick and fast. The concierge, encouraged by what is known as a white piece, and of which the value is five francs in current coin, became very communicative. Disentangled from layers of voluble digression, the kernel of her information amounted to this: Mrs. Raritan and her daughter had taken the Orient Express the day before. On the subject of their destination she declared herself ignorant. Suppositions she had in plenty, but actual knowledge none, and she took evident pleasure in losing herself in extravagant conjectures. "*Bien le bonjour,*" she said when Tristrem, passably disheartened, turned to leave—"*Bien le bonjour, m'sieu; si j'ose m'exprimer ainsi.*"

The Orient Express, as Tristrem knew, goes through Southern Germany into Austria, thence down to Buda-Pest and on to Constantinople. That Viola and her mother had any intention of going farther than Vienna was a thing which he declined to consider. On the way to Vienna was Stuttgart and Munich. In Munich there was Wagner every other night. In Stuttgart there was a conservatory of music, and at Vienna was not the Opera world-renowned? "They have gone to one of those three cities," he told himself. "Viola must have determined to relinquish the Italian school for the German. H'm," he mused, "I'll soon put a stop to that. As to finding her, all I have to do is go to the police. They keep an eye on strangers to some purpose. Let me see—I can get to Stuttgart by to-morrow noon. If she is not there

I will go to Munich. I rather like the idea of a stroll on the Maximilien Strasse. It would be odd if I met her in the street. Well, if she isn't in Munich she is sure to be in Vienna." And as he entered the Grand Hôtel he smiled anew in dreams forecast.

Tristrem carried out his programme to the end. But not in Stuttgart, not in Munich, nor in Vienna either, could he obtain the slightest intelligence of her. In the latter city he was overtaken by a low fever, which detained him for a month, and from which he arose enfeebled but with clearer mind. He wrote to Viola two letters, and two also to her mother. One of each he sent to the Rue Scribe, the others to Founders' Court. When ten days went by, and no answer came, he understood for the first time what the fable of Tantalus might mean, and that of Sisyphus too. He wrote at length to his grandfather, describing his Odyssey, his perplexities, and asking advice. He even wrote to Jones—though much more guardedly, of course—thanking him for his cable, and inquiring in a post-scriptum whether he had heard anything further on the subject of the Raritans' whereabouts. These letters were barely despatched when he was visited by a luminous thought. The idea that Viola intended to relinquish Italian music for that of Wagner had never seemed to him other than an incongruity. "Idiot that I am!" he exclaimed; "she came abroad to study at Milan, and there is where she is. She must have left the Orient Express at Munich and gone straight down through the Tyrol." And in the visitation of this comforting thought Tantalus and Sisyphus went back into the night from which they had come; in their place came again the blue-eyed divinity whose name is Hope.

It is not an easy journey, nor a comfortable one, from Vienna to Milan, but Hope aiding, it can be accomplished without loss of life or reason. And Hope aided Tristrem to his destination, and there disappeared. In all Milan no intelligence of Viola could be obtained. He wrote again to her. The result was the same. "I am as one accursed," he thought, and that night he saw himself in dream stopping passers in the street, asking them with lifted hat had they seen a girl wonderfully fair, with amber eyes. He asked the question in French, in German, in Italian, according to the nationality of those he encountered, and once, to a little old woman, he spoke in a jargon of his own invention. But she laughed, and seemed to understand, and gave him the address of a lupanar.

He idled awhile in Milan, and then went to Florence, and to Rome, and to Naples, crossing over, even, to Palermo; and then retracing his steps, he visited the smaller cities and outlying, unfrequented towns. Something there was which kept telling him that she was near at hand, waiting, like the enchanted princess, for his coming. And he hunted and searched, outwearied at times, and refreshed again by resuscitations of hope, and intussusceptions of her presence. But in the search his nights were white. It was rare for him to get any sleep before the dawn had come.

Early in spring he reached Milan again. He had written from Bergamo to the Rue Scribe, asking that his letters should be forwarded to that place, and among the communications that were given him on his arrival was a cablegram from New York. *Come back*, it ran; *she is here*. It was from his grandfather, Dirck Van Norden, and as Tristrem read it he trembled from head to foot. It was on a Tuesday that this occurred, and he reflected that he would just about be able to get to Havre in time for the Saturday steamer. An hour later he was in the train bound for Desenzano, from which place he proposed to go by boat to Riva, and thence up to Munich, where he could catch the Orient Express on its returning trip to France.

XIV.

When the boat entered the harbor it was already night. Tristrem was tired, but his fatigue was pleasant to him. His Odyssey was done. New York, it is true, was many days away, but he was no longer to wander feverishly from town to town. If he was weary, at least his mind was at rest. Riva is on the Austrian frontier, and while the luggage was being examined Tristrem hummed contentedly to himself. He would get some dinner at the hotel, for he was hungry as he had not been in months. At last he would have a good night's rest; there would be no insomnia now. In the magic of a cablegram that succube had been exorcised forever. On the morrow he would start afresh, and neither stop nor stay till the goal was reached. It was no longer vague and intangible—it was full in sight. And so, while the officers were busy with his traps, he hummed the unforgotten air, *O Magali, ma bien aimée.*

The hotel to which he presently had himself conveyed stands in a large garden that leans to the lake. It is a roomy structure, built quadrangularwise. On one side is a little châlet. Above, to the right and left, precipitous cliffs and trellised mountains loom like battlements of Titan homes. The air is very sweet, and at that season of the year almost overweighted with the scent of flowers. In spite of the night, the sky was visibly blue, and high up in the heavens the moon glittered with the glint of sulphur.

As the carriage drew up at the door there was a clang of bells; an individual in a costume that was brilliant as the uniform of a field-officer hastened to greet the guest; at the threshold was the Oberkellner; a few steps behind him the manager stood bowing persuasively; and as Tristrem entered, the waiters, hastily marshalled, ranged themselves on either side of the hall.

"Vorrei," Tristrem began, and then remembering that he was no longer in Italy, continued in German.

The answer came in the promptest English.

"Yes, my lord; will your lordship dine at *table d'hôte*? Du, Konrad, schnell, die Speise-karte."

Tristrem examined the bill of fare which was then brought him, and while he studied the contents he heard himself called by name. He looked up, and recognized Ledyard Yorke, his companion of months before on the outward-bound Cunarder, who welcomed him with much warmth and cordiality.

"And whatever became of Miss Tippity-fitchet? You don't mean to say you did not see her again? Fancy that! It was through no fault of hers, then. But there, in spite of your promise, you didn't so much as look *me* up. I am just in from a tramp to Mori; suppose we brush up a bit and have dinner together?" He turned to the waiter. "Konrad, wir speisen draussen; verschaffen Sie 'was Monkenkloster."

"Zu Befehl, Herr Baron."

Half an hour later, when the brushing up was done and the Monkenkloster was uncorked, Tristrem and Yorke seated themselves in an arbor that overhung the lake.

"It's ever so much better here than at *table d'hôte*," Yorke began. "I hate that sort of business—don't you? I have been here over two months, but after a week or so of it I gave up promiscuous feeding. Since then, whenever I have been able, I have dined out here. I don't care to have every dish I eat seasoned with the twaddle of cheap-trippers. To be sure, few of them get here. Riva is well out of the beaten track. But one *table d'hôte* is just like another, and they are all of them wearying to the spirit and fatiguing to digestion. Look at that water, will you. It's almost Venice, isn't it? I can tell you, I have done some good work in this place. But what have you been doing yourself?"

"Nothing to speak of," Tristrem answered. "I have been roaming from pillar to post. It's the second time I have been over the Continent, and now I am on my way home. I am tired of it; I shall be glad to be back."

"Yes you were the last person I expected to meet. If I remember rightly, you said on the steamer that you were to be on this side but a short time. It's always the unexpected that occurs, isn't it? By the way, I have got my sphinx."

"What sphinx?"

"I thought I told you. I have been looking for years for a certain face. I wanted one that I could give to a sphinx. The accessories were nothing. I put them on canvas long ago, but the face I never could grasp. Not one of all that I tried suited me. I had almost given it up; but I got it—I got it at last. I'll show it to you to-morrow."

"I am afraid——You see, I leave very early."

"I'll show it to you to-night, then; you must see it. If I had had it made to order it could not suit me better. It came about in such an odd way. All winter I have been at work in Munich. I intended to remain until June, but the spring there is bleaker than your own New England. One morning I said to myself, Why not take a run down to Italy? Two days later, I was on my way. But at Mori, instead of pushing straight on to Verona, I drove over here, thinking it would be pleasanter to take the boat. I arrived here at midnight. The next morning I looked out of the window, and there, right in front of me, in that châlet, was my sphinx. Well, the upshot of it was, I have been here ever since. I repainted the entire picture—the old one wasn't good enough."

"I should like to see it very much," said Tristrem, less from interest than civility.

"I wish you had come in time to see the original. She never suspected that she had posed as a model, and though her window was just opposite mine, I believe she did not so much as pay me the compliment of being aware of my existence. There were days when she sat hour after hour looking out at the lake, almost motionless, in the very attitude that I wanted. It was just as though she were repeating the phrase that Flaubert puts in the Sphinx's mouth, 'I am guarding my secret—I calculate and I dream.' Wasn't it odd, after all, that I should have found her in that hap-hazard way?"

"It was odd," Tristrem answered; "who was she?"

"I don't know. French, I fancy. Her name was Dupont, or Duflot—something utterly *bourgeois*. There was an old lady with her, her mother, I suppose. I remember, at *table d'hôte* one evening, a Russian woman, with an 'itch' in her name, said she did not think she was comme il faut. 'She is comme il *m'en* faut,' I answered, and mentally I added, 'which is a deuced sight more than I can say of you, who are comme il n'en faut pas.' The Russian woman was indignant at her, I presume, because she did not come to the public table. You know that feeling, 'If it's good enough for me, it's good enough for you.' But my sphinx not only did not appear at *table d'hôte*, she did not put her foot outside of the châlet. One bright morning she disappeared from the window, and a few days later I heard that she had been confined. Shortly after she went away. It did not matter, though, I had her face. Let me give you another glass of Monkenkloster."

"She was married, then?"

"Yes, her husband was probably some brute that did not know how to appreciate her. I don't mean, though, that she looked unhappy. She looked impassible, she looked exactly the way I wanted to have her look. If you have finished your coffee, come up to my little atelier. I wish you could see the picture by daylight, but you may be able to get an idea of it from the candles." And as Mr. Yorke led the way, he added, confidentially, "I should really like to have your opinion."

The atelier to which Yorke had alluded as "little" was, so well as Tristrem could discern in the darkness, rather spacious than otherwise. He loitered in the door-way until his companion had lighted and arranged the candles, and then, under his guidance, went forward to admire. The picture, which stood on an easel, was really excellent; so good, in fact, that Tristrem no sooner saw the face of the sphinx than to his ears came the hum of insects, the murmur of distant waters. It was Viola Raritan to the life.

"She guarded her secret, indeed," he muttered, huskily. And when Yorke, surprised at such a criticism, turned to him for an explanation, he had just time to break his fall. Tristrem had fallen like a log.

As he groped back through a roar and turmoil to consciousness again, he thought that he was dead and that this was the tomb. "That Monkenkloster must have been too much for him," he heard Yorke say, in German, and then some answer came to him in sympathetic gutturals. He opened his eyes ever so little, and then let the lids close down. Had he been in a nightmare, he wondered, or was it Viola? "He's coming too," he heard Yorke say. "Yes, I am quite right now," he answered, and he raised himself on his elbow. "I think," he continued, "that I had better get to my room."

"Nonsense. You must lie still awhile."

For the moment Tristrem was too weak to rebel, and he fell back again on the lounge on which he had been placed, and from which he had half arisen. Was it a dream, or was it the real? "There, I am better now," he said at last; "I wonder, I——Would you mind ordering me a glass of brandy?"

"Why, there's a carafon of it here. I thought you had had too much of that wine."

Some drink was then brought him, which he swallowed at a gulp. Under its influence his strength returned.

"I am sorry to have put you to so much trouble," he said collectedly to Yorke and to a waiter who had been summoned to his assistance; "I am quite myself now." He stood up again and the waiter, seeing that he was fully restored, withdrew. When the door closed behind him, Tristrem went boldly back to the picture.

It was as Yorke had described it. In the background was a sunset made of cymbal strokes of vermilion, splattered with gold, and seamed with fantasies of red. In the foreground fluttered a chimera, so artfully done that one almost heard the whir of its wings. And beneath it crouched the Sphinx. From the eyrie of the years the ages had passed unmarked, unnoticed. The sphinx brooded, motionless and dumb.

With patient, scrutinizing attention Tristrem looked in her eyes and at her face. There was no mistake, it was Viola. Was there ever another girl in the world such as she? And this was her secret! Or was there a secret, after all, and might he not have misunderstood?

"Tell me," he said—"I will not praise your picture; in many respects it is above praise—but tell me, is what you said true?"

"Is what true?"

"What you said of the model."

"About her being in the châlet? Of course it is. Why do you ask?"

"No, not that, tell me—Mr. Yorke, I do not mean to be tragic; if I seem so, forgive me and overlook it. But as you love honor, tell me, is it true that she had a child in this place?"

"Yes, so I heard."

"And you say her name was——"

"Madame Dubois—Dupont—I have forgotten; they can tell you at the bureau. But it seems to me——"

"Thank you," Tristrem answered. "Thank you," he repeated. He hesitated a second and then, with an abrupt good-night, he hurried from the atelier and down the corridor till he reached his room.

Through the open window, the sulphur moon poured in. He looked out in the garden. Beyond, half concealed in the shadows, he could see the outline of the châlet. And it was there she had hid! He pressed his hands to his forehead; he could not understand. For the moment he felt that if he could lose his reason it would be a grateful release. If only some light would come! He drew a handkerchief from his pocket and mopped his face. And then suddenly, as he did so, he caught a spark of that for which he groped. The room turned round, and he sank into a chair.

Yes, he remembered, it was at Bergamo, no, at Bologna. Yes, it was at Bergamo, he remembered perfectly well. He had taken from one of his trunks a coat that he had not

THE TRUTH ABOUT TRISTREM VARICK.

worn since he went into mourning. It had been warm that day, and he wanted some thinner clothing. He remembered at the time congratulating himself that he had had the forethought to bring it. And later in the day he had taken from the pocket a handkerchief of a smaller size than that which he habitually used. He had looked at it, and in the corner he had found the Weldon crest. As to how it had come in his possession, he had at the time given no thought. Weldon, in one of his visits, might have left it at Waverley Place, or he himself might have borrowed it when dining at Weldon's house. He was absent-minded, he knew, and apt to be forgetful, and so at the time he had given the matter no further thought. After all, what incident could be more trivial? But now the handkerchief, like a magician's rug, carried him back to Narragansett. As well as he could remember, the last occasion on which he wore that coat was the day on which the butler's telegram had summoned him to town. Then, on learning of his father's death, he had put on other things, of sombrer hue. Harris, without rummaging in the pockets, had folded the coat and put it away. And it had remained folded ever since till the other day at Bologna—no, at Bergamo.

That morning at Narragansett, when he was hurrying into the cottage, the man who had aided Viola home the preceding evening drove up with her hat, with this very handkerchief, and the story of a dream. Aye, and his own dream. So this was Truth. She had pursued him, indeed. He could feel her knees on his arms, her fetid breath in his face. But this time it was not a nightmare. It was the real.

Yes, it was that. One by one he recalled the incidents of the past—incidents on which his mind loathed to dwell, rebelling against its own testimony until he coerced the shuddering memories to his will. There were the number-less times in which he had encountered Weldon coming in or leaving her house, almost haunting it with his presence. There was that wanton lie, and the unexplained and inter-rupted scene between them. It was then, perhaps, that he had first shown the demon that was in him. And then, after-ward, was that meeting on the cars—he with a bruise on his cheek and a gash on his neck. Why was Viola's whip broken, if it were not that she had broken it on his face? Why did the nails of her ungloved hand look as though they had been stained with the juice of berries? Why, indeed, if it were not that she had sunk them in his flesh. Why had he heard her calling "Coward" to the night? It was for this, then, that the engagement had been broken; it was for this that she had hidden herself abroad.

For the first time since his boyhood, he threw himself on the bed and sobbed aloud. To stifle his grief he buried his face in the pillow, and bit it with his teeth. It was more than grief, it was anguish, and it refused to be choked. But presently it did leave him. It left him quivering from head to foot, and in its place came another visitor. An obsession, from which he shrank, surged suddenly, and claimed him for its own. In a combat, of which his heart was the one dumb witness, he battled with it. He struggled with it in a conflict that out-lasted hours; but presumably he coped in vain. The next morning his face was set as a captive's. In a fortnight he was in New York.

XV.

The return journey was unmarked by incident or adventure. Nothing less than a smash-up on the railway or the wrecking of the ship would have had the power to distract his thoughts. It may even be that his mind was unoccupied, empty as is a vacant bier, and yet haunted by an overmastering obsession. The ordinary functions of the traveller he performed mechanically, with the air and manner of a subject acting under hypnotic suggestion. One who crossed the ocean with him has since said that the better part of the time the expression of his face was that of utter vacuity. He would remain crouched for hours, in the same position, a finger just separating the lips, and then he would start with the tremor of one awakening from a debauch.

Mrs. Manhattan, who was returning with spoils from the Rue de la Paix, asked him one afternoon, as he happened to descend the cabin-stair in her company, where he had passed the winter.

"Yes, indeed," Tristrem answered, and went his way unconcernedly.

Mrs. Manhattan complained of this conduct to Nicholas, her husband, alleging that the young man was fatuous in his impertinence.

"My dear," returned that wise habitué of the Athenæum, "when a man gives away seven million, it is because he has forgotten how to be conventional."

It was on a Sunday that the ship reached New York, and it was late in the afternoon before the passengers were able to disembark. Tristrem had his luggage passed, and expressed to his grandfather's house, and then, despite the aggressive solicitations of a crew of bandits, started up-town on foot. In the breast-pocket of his coat he carried a purchase which he had made in Naples, a fantastic article which he had bought, not because he wanted it, but because the peddler who pestered him with wares and offers happened to be the best-looking and most unrebuffably good-natured scoundrel that he had ever encountered. And now, at intervals, as he walked along, he put his hand to the pocket to assure himself that it was still in place. Presently he reached Broadway. That thoroughfare, which on earlier Sundays was wont to be one of the sedatest avenues of the city, was starred with globes of azure light, and its quiet was broken by the passing of orange-colored cars. On the corner he stopped and looked at his watch. It was after seven. Then, instead of continuing his way up-town, he turned down in the direction of the Battery. His head was slightly bent, and as he walked he had the appearance of one perplexed. It was a delightful evening. The sky was as blue as the eyes of a girl beloved. The air was warm, and had the street been less noisy, less garish, and a trifle cleaner it might have been an agreeable promenade. But to Tristrem the noise, the dirt, the glare, the sky itself were part and parcel of the non-existent. He neither saw nor heeded, and, though the air was warm, now and then he shivered.

It seemed to him impossible that he should do this thing. And yet, since that night at Riva, his mind had been as a stage in which it was in uninterrupted rehearsal. If it were unsuccessful, then come what sorrow could. But even

THE TRUTH ABOUT TRISTREM VARICK.

though its success were assured, might not the success be worse than failure, and viler to him than the most ignoble defeat? Meditatively he looked at his hand; it was slight as a girl's.

"I cannot," he said, and even as he said it he knew that he would. Had he not said it ten thousand times of times before? It was not what he willed, it was what he must. He was in the lap of a necessity from which, struggle as he might, he could not set himself free. He might make what resolutions he chose, but the force which acted on him and in him snuffed them out like candles. And yet, what had he done to fate that it should impel him to this? Why had he been used as he had? What wrong had he committed? For the past twelvemonth his life had been a continuous torture. Truly, he could have said, "no one save myself, in all the world, has learned the acuity of pain. I alone am its depository."

"And yet," he mused, "perhaps it is right. Long ago, when I was comparing my nothingness to her beauty, did I not know that to win her I must show myself worthy of the prize? She will think that I am when I tell her. Yes, she must think so when it is done. But will it be done? O God, I cannot."

For the instant he felt as though he must turn to the passers and claim their protection from himself. He had stopped again, and was standing under a great pole that supported an electric light. In the globe was a dim, round ball of red, and suddenly it flared up into a flame of the palest lemon, edged with blue. "It is my courage," he said, "I have done with hesitation now." He hailed and boarded a passing car. "Hesitation, indeed!" he repeated. "As if I had not known all through that when the time came there would be none!" He put his hand again to his breast-pocket; it was there.

He had taken the seat nearest to the door, absently, as he would have taken any other, and the conductor found it necessary to touch him on the shoulder before he could extract the fare. He had no American money, he discovered, and would have left the car had not the conductor finally agreed to take his chances with a small piece of foreign gold, though not, however, until he had bit it tentatively with his teeth. It was evident that he viewed Tristrem with suspicion.

At Twentieth Street Tristrem swung himself from the moving vehicle, and turned into Gramercy Park. He declined to think; the rehearsals were over, he did not even try to recall the rôle. He had had a set speech, but it was gone from him as the indecision had gone before. Now he was to act.

He hurried up the stoop of Weldon's house and rang the bell, and as there seemed to him some unnecessary delay, he rang again, not violently, but with the assurance of a creditor who has come to be paid. But when at last the door was opened, he learned that Weldon was not at home.

As he went down the steps again there came to him a great gust and rush of joy. He would go now, he had been fully prepared, he had tried his best. If Weldon had been visible, he would not have hesitated. But he had not been; that one chance had been left them both, and now, with a certitude that had never visited his former indecisions, he felt it was written that that deed should never be done. He gasped as one gasps who has been nearly stifled. The obsession was gone. He was free.

In the street he raised his arms to testify to his liberty reconquered. Yet, even as they fell again, he knew that he was tricking himself. A tremor beset him, and to steady himself he clutched at an area-rail. Whether he stood there

THE TRUTH ABOUT TRISTREM VARICK.

one minute or one hour he could not afterward recall. He remembered only that while he loitered Weldon had rounded the corner, and that as he saw him approach, jauntily, in evening dress, a light coat on his arm, his strength returned.

"Royal," he exclaimed, for the man was passing him without recognition. "Royal," he repeated, and Weldon stopped. "I have come to have a word with you."

The voice in which he spoke was so unlike his own, so rasping and defiant, that Weldon, with the dread which every respectable householder has of a scene at his own front door, motioned him up the steps. "Come in," he said, mellifluously, "I am glad to see you."

"I will," Tristrem answered, in a tone as arrogant as before.

"I am sorry," Weldon continued, "Nanny——"

"I did not come to see your wife; you know it."

Weldon had unlatched the door, and the two men passed into the sitting-room. There Weldon, with his hat unremoved, dropped in a chair, and eyed his visitor with affected curiosity.

"I say, Trissy, you're drunk."

"I am come," Tristrem continued, and this time as he spoke his voice seemed to recover something of its former gentleness, "I am come to ask whether, in the purlieus of your heart, there is nothing to tell you how base you are."

Weldon stretched himself languidly, took off his hat, stood up, and lit a cigarette. "Have an Egyptian?" he asked.

"Do you remember," Tristrem went on, "the last time I saw you?"

Weldon tossed the match into an ash-receiver, and, with the cigarette between his teeth, sprawled himself out on a sofa. "Well, what of it?"

"When I saw you, you had just contracted a debt. And now you can liquidate that debt either by throwing yourself in the river or——"

"Charming, Triss, charming! You have made a *bon mot*. I will get that off. Liquidate a debt with water is really good. There's the advantage of foreign travel for you."

"Do you know what became of your victim? Do you know? She went abroad and hid herself. Shall I give you details?"

For the first time Weldon scowled.

"Would you like the details?" Tristrem repeated.

Weldon mastered his scowl. "No," he answered, negligently. "I am not a midwife. Obstetrics do not interest me. On the contra——"

That word he never finished. Something exploded in his brain, he saw one fleeting flash, and he was dead. Even as he spoke, Tristrem had whipped an instrument from his pocket, and before Weldon was aware of his purpose, a knife, thin as a darning-needle and long as a pencil—a knife which it had taken the splendid wickedness of mediæval Rome to devise—had sunk into his heart, and was out again, leaving behind it a pin's puncture through the linen, one infinitesimal bluish-gray spot on the skin, and death.

Tristrem looked at him. The shirt was not even rumpled. If he had so much as quivered, the quiver had been imperceptible, and on the knife there was no trace of blood. It fell from his fingers; he stooped to pick it up, but his hand trembled so that, on recovering it, he could not insert the point into the narrow sheath that belonged to it, and, throwing the bit of embroidered leather in a corner, he put the weapon in his pocket.

"It was easier than I thought," he mused. "I suppose—h'm—I seem to be nervous. It's odd. I feared that afterward I should collapse like an omelette soufflée. And to think that it is done!"

He turned suspiciously, and looked at the body again. No, he could see it was really done. "And so, this is afterward," he continued. "And to think that it was here I first saw her. She came in that door there. I remember I thought of a garden of lilies."

From the dining-room beyond he caught the glimmer of a lamp. He crossed the intervening space, and on the sideboard he found some decanters. He selected one, and pouring a little of its contents into a tumbler he drank it off. Then he poured another portion, and when he had drunk that too, he went out, not through the sitting-room, but through the hall, and, picking up the hat which on entering he had thrown on the table, he left the house.

XVI.

Several thousand years ago a thinker defined virtue as the agreement of the will and the conscience. If the will were coercible the definition would be matchless. Unfortunately it is not. Will declines to be reasoned with; it insists, and in its insistence conscience, horrified or charmed, stands a witness to its acts.

For a fortnight Tristrem had been married to an impulse against which his finer nature rebelled. It was not that the killing of such a one as Weldon was unjustifiable; on the contrary, it was rather praiseworthy than otherwise. His crime was one for which the noose is too good. But to Weldon, in earlier days, he had felt as to a brother; and though affection may die, does it not leave behind it a memory which should thereafter serve as a protecting shield? It had been the bonds of former attachment, bonds long loosened, it is true, but of which the old impress still lingered, that seemed to Tristrem to tie his hands. Then, too, was the horror of such a thing. There is nothing, a Scandinavian poet has said, more beautiful than a beautiful revenge; yet when a man is so tender of heart that if it be raining he will hesitate to shoo a persistent fly out of the window, it is difficult for that man, however great the aggravation, to take another's life. Besides, the impulse which had acted in Tristrem was not one of revenge. He had not the slightest wish to take the law into his own hands. The glaive of atonement was not one which he felt himself called upon to wield. That which possessed him was the idea that until the world was rid of Weldon there was a girl somewhere who could not look her own mother in the face. And that girl was the girl whom he loved, a girl who apparently had no other protector than himself.

In the rehearsals, it was this that had strung his nerves to acting pitch. When it was done he proposed to go to her with a reverence even greater than before, with a sympathy unspoken yet sentiable, and leave her with the knowledge that the injury had been obliterated and the shame effaced. For himself, whatever he may have hoped, he determined to ask for nothing. It was for her he defied the law; he was her agent, one whom she might recompense or not with her lithe white arms, but one to whom she would at least be grateful. And how beautiful her gratitude might be! Though she gave him nothing else, would not the thanks of her eyes be reward enough? And then, as he worked himself up with the thought of these things to acting pitch, then would come the horror of it all, the necessity of taking the life of one who had been his nearest friend, the dread of the remorse which attaches to death, the soiling of his own hands. It was in this fashion that he had wavered between indecision and determination, until, at last, stung by the cynicism of Weldon's speech, there had come to him a force such as he had never possessed before, and suddenly the deed had been done.

The possible arraignment that might follow the inquest, he had never considered. It is said that the art of killing has been lost. The tribunals, assizes, and general sessions have doubtless led somewhat to its discouragement, and yet it must be admitted that the office of police justice in one way resembles that of lover in the tropics—it is not exactly a sinecure. Perhaps, nowadays, it is only the blunderers that are detected; yet, however numerous they may or may not be, Tristrem, without giving a single thought as to how such a thing should be done and remain undetected, had had such chances in his favor that Vidocq himself might have tried in vain to fasten the death of Weldon on him. No one had seen him enter the house, no one had seen him leave it. Even the instrument which he had used, and which he had bought hap-hazard, as one buys a knick-knack, had served his end as cleanly as a paralysis of the heart. It had not spilled a drop of blood.

As Tristrem walked on, he did not think of these things; the possibility of detection had not troubled him, and now the probability that Weldon's death would be attributed to natural causes brought him no satisfaction. Of himself he gave no thought. He had wondered, indeed, that his presence of mind had not deserted him; he had marvelled at his own calm. But now his thoughts were wholly with Viola, and when he reached Fifth Avenue he determined to go to her at once.

A vagabond hansom was loitering near, and with its assistance he presently reached her door. Even as he entered, it was evident that she was not alone. On putting his hat down in the hall he noticed two others, and through the portière came the sound of voices. But he pushed the curtain aside, and entered the room with the air of one to whom the conventional has lost its significance. Yet, as he did so, he felt that he was wrong. If he wished to see Viola, would it not have been more courteous to her to get into evening dress than to appear among her guests in a costume suitable only for the afternoon? Society he knew to be a despot. Though it has no dungeons, at least it can banish, and to those that have been brought up in its court there are no laws rigider than its customs. Besides, was he in a mood to thrust himself among those whose chiefest ambition was to be ornate? He was aware of his mistake at once, but not until it was too late to recede.

Among those present he recognized a man who, though well on in life, devoted his entire time to matters appertaining to the amusements of the selectest circles. He was talking to a girl who, moist as to the lips and eyes, looked as had she just issued from a vapor-bath. Near to her was Mrs. Raritan. Tristrem noticed that her hair had turned almost white. And a little beyond, a young man with a retreating forehead and a Pall Mall accent sat, splendidly attired, talking to Viola.

Mrs. Raritan was the first to greet him, and she did so in the motherly fashion that was her own. And as she spoke Viola came forward, said some simple word, and went back to her former place.

"Come with me," said Mrs. Raritan, and she led him to an S in upholstery, in which they both found seats. "And now tell me about yourself," she added. "And where have you been?"

Truly it was pitiful. She looked ten years older. From a handsome, well-preserved woman she had in a twelvemonth been overtaken by age.

"I have been in Europe, you know," Tristrem answered; "I wrote to you from Vienna, and again from Rome."

"I am sorry," Mrs. Raritan replied; "the bankers are so negligent. There were many letters that must have gone astray. Were you—you had a pleasant winter, of course. And how is your grandfather?"

"I have not seen him. I am just off the ship."

At this announcement Mrs. Weldon looked perplexed.

"Is it possible that you only arrived this evening?" she asked.

"Yes, I wanted to see Viola. You know it is almost a year since—since—I tried to find you both in Europe, but——"

"Mr. Varick, did I hear you say that you arrived from Europe to-day?" It was the gentleman who devoted himself to the interests of society that was speaking.

"Yes, I came on the Bourgogne."

"Was Mrs. Manhattan on board?"

Tristrem answered that she was, and then the gentleman in question entered into an elaborate discourse on the subject of Mrs. Manhattan's summer plans. While he was still speaking a servant informed the vaporous maiden that her maid and carriage had arrived, and presently that young lady left the room. Soon after the society agent disappeared, and a little later the youth that had been conversing with Miss Raritan took his splendor away.

As yet Tristrem had had no opportunity of exchanging a word with Viola. To his hostess he had talked with feverish animation on the subject of nothing at all; but as the adolescent who had been engaging Viola's attention came to Mrs. Raritan to bid that lady good-night, Tristrem left the upholstered S and crossed the room to where the girl was seated.

"Viola," he began, but she stayed his speech with a gesture.

The young man was leaving the room, and it was evident from Mrs. Raritan's attitude that it was her intention to leave it also.

"I am tired," that lady said, as the front door closed; "you won't mind?" And Tristrem, who had arisen when he saw her standing, went forward and bowed over her hand, and then preceded her to the portière, which he drew aside that she might pass.

"Good-night, Mrs. Raritan," he said; "good-night, and pleasant dreams."

Then he turned to the girl. She, too, looked older, or, perhaps, it would be more exact to say she looked more mature. Something of the early fragrance had left her face, but she was as beautiful as before.

Her gold eyes were brilliant as high noon, and her cheeks bore an unwonted color. She was dressed in white, her girdle was red with roses, and her arms and neck were bare.

As Mrs. Raritan passed from the room, Tristrem let the portière fall again, and stood a moment feasting his famished eyes in hers. At last he spoke.

"*He* is dead, Viola."

The words came from him very gravely, and when he had uttered them he looked down at the rug.

"Dead! Who is dead? What do you mean?"

"He is dead," he repeated, but still he kept his eyes lowered.

"He! What he? What are you talking about?" She had left her seat and fronted him.

"Royal Weldon," he made answer, and as he did so he looked up at her.

Her hands fluttered like falling leaves. An increased color mounted to her cheeks, and disappearing, left them white. Her lips trembled.

"I do not understand," she gasped. And then, as her dilated eyes stared into his own, he saw that she understood at last. Her fluttering hands had gone to her throat, as though to tear away some invisible clutch. Her lips had grown gray. She was livid.

"It is better so, is it not?" he asked, and searched her face for some trace of the symptoms of joy. As he gazed at her, she retreated. Her hands had left her throat, her forehead was pinioned in their grasp, and in her eyes the expression of terrified wonder was seamed and obscured by another that resembled hate.

"And it was you," she stammered, "it was you?"

"Yes," he answered, with an air of wonder that equalled her own; "yes——"

"You tell me that Royal Weldon is dead, and that you—that you——"

"It was this way," he began, impelled, in his own surprise, to some form of explanation. "It was this way—you see—well, I went to Riva. That man that brought back your hat——Good God, Viola, are you not glad?"

She had fallen into a chair, and he was at her feet.

"Are you not glad?" he insisted. "Now, it will be——" But whatever he intended to say, the speech remained uncompleted. The girl had drawn from him as from an adder unfanged.

"Assassin!" she hissed. "Assassin!" she hissed again. "What curse——"

"Viola, it was for your sake."

She clinched her hand as though she sought the strength wherewith to strike. And then the fingers loosened again. She moved still farther away. The hatred left her eyes, as the wonder had done before. With the majesty which Mary Stuart must have shown when she bade farewell to England, to the sceptre, and to life, Viola Raritan turned to him again:

"I loved him," she muttered, yet so faintly that she had left the room before Tristrem, who still crouched by the chair which she had vacated, fully caught the import of her words.

"Viola!" he called. But she had gone. "Viola! No, no; it is impossible. It is impossible," he repeated, as he rose up again; "it is impossible."

He staggered to the door and let himself out. And then, as the night-air affects one who has loitered over the wine, he reeled.

In a vision such as is said to visit the ultimate consciousness of they that drown, a riot of long-forgotten incidents surged to his mind. He battled with them in vain; they were trivial, indeed, but in their onslaught he saw that the impossible was truth.

With the aimlessness of a somnambulist, and reasoning with himself the while, he walked down through Madison Avenue until he reached the square. There, turning into Lexington, he entered Gramercy Park. Presently he found himself standing at Weldon's door. "But what am I doing here?" he mused. For a little time, he leaned against the rail, endeavoring to collect his thoughts. Then, as an individual, coated in blue and glistening as to his buttons, sauntered by, he seemed to understand. He left the railing at which he had stood, and, circling the park, set out in the direction of the river. As he reached Second Avenue, a train of the elevated railway flamed about an adjacent corner, and swept like a dragon in mid-air, on, beyond, and out of sight. To the right was a great factory, and as Tristrem continued his way through the unfamiliar street he wondered what the people in the train, what the factory-hands, and the dwellers in the neighborhood would say if they could surmise his errand. The river was yet some distance away. It was such a pity, he told himself, such a pity, that he had not accepted the invitation of the sea. That would have been so much better, so much surer, and so much more discreet. And then he fell to wondering about his grandfather, and his heart was filled with anguish. He would have done anything to save that old man from pain. But it was too late now. A gas-jet that lighted a wide and open door attracted his attention; he looked in, the building seemed empty as a lecture-hall. After all, he decided, perhaps that would be best.

Half an hour later, Tristrem Varick was the occupant of a room that was not as large as one of the closets in his grandfather's house. The furniture consisted of a wooden bench. The sole fixture was an apparatus for drawing water. The floor was tiled and the upper part of the walls was white; the lower, red. The room itself was very clean. There was no window, and the door, which was of grated iron, had been locked from without. From an adjoining cell, a drunken harlot rent the night with the strain of a maudlin ditty.

XVII.

It was some little time before the powers that are could be convinced that Tristrem Varick was guilty of the self-accused murder. It was not that murders are rare, but a murder such as that was tolerably uncommon. The sergeant who presided over the police-station in which Tristrem had delivered himself up was a mild-mannered man, gentle of voice, and sceptical as a rag-picker. He received Tristrem's statement without turning a hair.

"What did you do it for?" he asked, and when Tristrem declined to enter into any explanation, he smiled with affable incredulity. "I can, if you insist," he said, "accommodate you with a night's lodging." And he was as good as his word; but the cell which Tristrem subsequently occupied was not opened for him until the sergeant was convinced that death had really visited the precinct.

Concerning the form in which that death had come, there was at first no doubt. Weldon had been found stretched lifeless on a sofa. The physician who was then summoned made a cursory examination, and declared that death was due to disease of the heart. Had Tristrem held his tongue, that verdict, in all probability, would never have been questioned; indeed, it was not until the minuter autopsy which Tristrem's statement instigated that the real cause was discovered.

It was then that it began to be admitted that violence

had been used, but as to whether that violence was accidental or intentional, and if intentional, whether or not it was premeditated, was a matter which, according to our archaic law, twelve men in a pen could alone decide. The case was further complicated by a question of sanity. Granting that some form of manslaughter had been committed, was it the act of one in full possession of his faculties, or was it the act of one bereft of his senses?

Generally speaking, public opinion inclined to the latter solution. Indeed, there seemed to be but one other in any way tenable, and that was, that the blow was self-inflicted. This theory had many partisans. The records, if not choked, are well filled with the trials of individuals who have confessed to crimes of which they were utterly guiltless. It was discovered that a recent slump in Wall Street had seriously affected Weldon's credit. It was known that his manner of living had compelled his wife to return to her father's house, and it was shown that she had begun an action for divorce. It seemed, therefore, possible that he had taken his own life in Tristrem's presence, and that Tristrem, in the horror of the spectacle, had become mentally unhinged.

In addition to this, there was against Tristrem—aside, of course, from the confession—barely a scintilla of evidence. The very instrument which was found on his person, and with which he declared the murder had been committed, was said not to belong to him. A servant of Weldon's thought she had once seen it in the possession of her late master. And it was argued that Tristrem had caught it up when it fell from the hand of the dead, and, in the consternation of the moment, had thrust it in his own pocket. Moreover, as suicides go, there was in Weldon's case a tangible excuse. He was on the edge of bankruptcy, and his matrimonial venture was evidently infelicitous. His life was an apparent failure. Many other men have taken their own lives for causes much minor.

The theory of suicide was therefore not untenable, and those who preferred to believe that a murder had been really committed were at a loss for a motive. Tristrem and Weldon were known to have been on terms of intimacy. Tristrem had been absent from the country a number of months, while Weldon had steadfastly remained in New York. During the intervening period it was impossible to conjecture the slightest cause of disagreement. And yet, no sooner did the two men have the opportunity of meeting, than one fell dead, and the other gave himself up as his murderer. And if that murder had been really committed, then what was the motive?

This was the point that particularly perplexed the District Attorney. It could not have been money. Tristrem had never speculated, and his financial relations with Weldon were confined to certain loans made to the latter, and long since repaid. Nor, through the whole affair, could the sharpest ear detect so much as the rustle of a petticoat. Inasmuch, then, as neither of the two great motor forces, woman and gold, was discernible, it is small wonder that the District Attorney was perplexed. To that gentleman the case was one of peculiar importance. His term of office had nearly expired, and he ardently desired re-election. Two wealthy misdemeanants had recently slipped through his fingers—not through any fault of his own, but they had slipped, none the less—and some rhetoric had been employed to show that there was a law for the poor and a more elastic one for the rich. Now Tristrem's conviction would be the finest plume he could stick in his hat. The possessor of an historic name, a member of what is known as the best society, an habitué of exclusive clubs—a representative, in fact, of everything that is most hateful to the mob—and yet a murderer. No, such a prize as that must not be allowed to escape. The District Attorney felt that, did such a thing occur, he might bid an eternal farewell to greatness and the bench.

But what was the motive of the crime? Long before that question, which eventually assumed the proportions of a pyramid, was seriously examined, it had been demonstrated that the wound from which Weldon had died was not one that could have been self-inflicted. The theory of suicide was thereupon and at once abandoned. And those who had been most vehement in its favor now asserted that Tristrem was insane. What better evidence of insanity could there be than the giving away of seven millions? But apart from that, there were a number of people willing to testify that on shipboard Tristrem's demeanor was that of a lunatic—moreover, did he not insist that he was perfectly sane, and where was the lunatic that ever admitted himself to be demented? Of course he was insane.

A committee, however, composed of a lawyer, a layman, and a physician, visited Tristrem, and announced exactly the contrary. According to their report, he was as sane as the law allows, and, although that honorable committee did not seem to suspect it, it may be that he was even a trifle saner. One of the committee—the layman—started out on his visit with no inconsiderable trepidation. In after-conversation, he said that it had never been his privilege to exchange speech with one gentler and more courteous than that self-accused murderer.

Yet still the motive was elusive. In this particular, Tristrem hindered everybody to the best of his ability. He was resolutely mute.

The attorney who was retained for the defence—not, however, through any wish of Tristrem's—could make nothing of his client. "It is pathetic," he said; "he keeps telling me that he is guilty, that he is sane, that he is infinitely indebted for my kindness and sympathy, but that *he does not wish to be defended.* Sane? He is no more sane than the King of Bavaria. Who ever heard of an inmate of the Tombs that did not want to be defended? Isn't that evidence enough?"

It was possible, of course, to impugn the testimony of the committee, but the attorney in this instance deemed it wiser to let it go for what it was worth, while showing that Tristrem, if sane at the time of the committee's examination, was insane at the time the crime, if crime there were, was committed. It was his settled conviction that if Tristrem would only explain the motive, it would be of such a nature that the chances of acquittal would be in his favor. In this, presumably, he was correct. But, in default of any explanation, he determined that the only adoptable line of defence was the one already formulated; to wit, that in slaying Weldon his client was temporarily deranged.

Meanwhile he expressed his conviction to the grief-stricken old man by whom he had been retained, and who himself had tried, unavailingly, to learn the cause. Whether he divined, or not, what it really was, is a matter of relative unimportance. In any event, he had discovered that on leaving Weldon's house Tristrem, instead of giving himself up at once, which he would have done had he at the time intended to do so at all, had gone directly to Miss Raritan.

And one day he, too, went to her. "You can save him," he said.

He might as well have asked alms of a statue. He went again, but the result was the same. And then a third time he went to her, and on his knees, with clasped and trembling hands, in a voice broken and quavering, he besought her to save his grandson from the gallows. "Come to court," he pleaded; "if you will only come to court!"

"I will come," the girl at last made answer, "I will come to see him sentenced."

Such is the truth about Tristrem Varick. In metropolitan drawing-rooms it was noticed that since Miss Raritan's return from Europe the quality of her voice had deteriorated. Mrs. Manhattan said that for her part she did not approve of the French method.

THE END.

MR. INCOUL'S MISADVENTURE.

To
E.A.S.

I.
MR. INCOUL.

When Harmon Incoul's wife died, the world in which he lived said that he would not marry again. The bereavement which he had suffered was known to be bitter, and it was reported that he might betake himself to some foreign land. There was, for that matter, nothing to keep him at home. He was childless, his tastes were too simple to make it necessary for him to reside as he had, hitherto, in New York, and, moreover, he was a man whose wealth was proverbial. Had he so chosen, he had little else to do than to purchase a ticket and journey wheresoever he listed, and the knowledge of this ability may have been to him not without its consolations. Yet, if he attempted to map some plan, and think which spot he would prefer, he probably reflected that whatever place he might choose, he would, in the end, be not unlike the invalid who turns over in his bed, and then turns back again on finding the second position no better than the first. However fair another sky might be, it would not make his sorrow less acute.

He was then one of those men whose age is difficult to determine. He had married when quite young, and at the time of his widowerhood he must have been nearly forty, but years had treated him kindly. His hair, it is true, was inclined to scantiness, and his skin was etiolated, but he was not stout, his teeth were sound, he held himself well, and his eyes had not lost their lustre. At a distance, one might have thought him in the thirties, but in conversation his speech was so measured, and about his lips there was a compression such that the ordinary observer fancied him older than he really was.

His position was unexceptionable. He had inherited a mile of real estate in a populous part of New York, together with an accumulation of securities sufficient for the pay and maintenance of a small army. The foundations of this wealth had been laid by an ancestor, materially increased by his grandfather, and consolidated by his father, who had married a Miss Van Tromp, the ultimate descendant of the Dutch admiral.

His boyhood had not been happy. His father had been a lean, taciturn, unlovable man, rigid in principles, stern in manner, and unyielding in his adherence to the narrowest tenets of Presbyterianism. His mother had died while he was yet in the nursery, and, in the absence of any softening influence, the angles of his earliest nature were left in the rough.

At school, he manifested a vindictiveness of disposition which made him feared and disliked. One day, a comrade raised the lid of a desk adjoining his own. The raising of the lid was abrupt and possibly intentional. It jarred him in a task. The boy was dragged from him senseless and bleeding. In college, he became aggrieved at a tutor. For three weeks he had him shadowed, then, having discovered an irregularity in his private life, he caused to be laid before the faculty sufficient evidence to insure his removal. Meanwhile, acting presumably on the principle that an avowed hatred is powerless, he treated the tutor as though the grievance had been forgotten. A little later, owing to some act of riotous insubordination, he was himself expelled, and the expulsion seemed to have done him good. He went to Paris and listened decorously to lectures at the Sorbonne, after which he strayed to Heidelberg, where he sat out five semesters without fighting a duel or making himself ill with beer. In his fourth summer abroad, he met the young lady who became his wife. His father died, he returned to New York, and thereafter led a model existence.

He was proud of his wife and indulgent to her every wish. During the years that they lived together, there was no sign or rumor of the slightest disagreement. She was of a sweet and benevolent disposition, and though beyond a furtive coin he gave little to the poor, he encouraged her to donate liberally to the charities which she was solicited to assist. She was a woman with a quick sense of the beautiful, and in spite of the simplicity of his own tastes, he had a house on Madison avenue rebuilt and furnished in such a fashion that it was pointed out to strangers as one of the chief palaces of the city. She liked, moreover, to have her friends about her, and while he cared as much for society as he did for the negro minstrels, he insisted that she should give entertainments and fill the house with guests. In the winter succeeding the fifteenth anniversary of their marriage, Mrs. Incoul caught a chill, took to her bed and died, forty-eight hours later, of pneumonia.

It was then that the world said that he would not marry again. For two years he gave the world no reason to say otherwise, and for two years time hung heavy on his hands. He was an excellent chess-player, and interested in archaeological pursuits, but beyond that his resources were limited. He was too energetic to be a dilettante, he had no taste for horseflesh, the game of speculation did not interest him, and his artistic tendencies were few. Now and then, a Mr. Blydenburg, a florid, talkative man, a widower like himself, came to him of an evening, and the chessboard was prepared. But practically his life was one of solitude, and the solitude grew irksome to him.

Meanwhile his wound healed as wounds do. The cicatrix perhaps was ineffaceable, but at least the smart had subsided, and in its subsidence he found that the great house in which he lived had taken on the silence of a tomb. Soon he began to go out a little. He was seen at meetings of the Archaeological Society and of an afternoon he was visible in the Park. He even attended a reception given to an English thinker, and one night applauded Salvini.

At first he went about with something of that uncertainty which visits one who passes from a dark room to a bright one, but in a little while his early constraint fell from him, and he found that he could mingle again with his fellows.

At some entertainment he met a delicious young girl, Miss Maida Barhyte by name, whom for the moment he admired impersonally, as he might have admired a flower, and until he saw her again, forgot her very existence. It so happened, however, that he saw her frequently. One evening he sat next to her at a dinner and learning from her that she was to be present at a certain reception, made a point of being present himself.

This reception was given by Mrs. Bachelor, a lady, well known in society, who kept an unrevised list, and at stated intervals issued invitations to the dead, divorced and defaulted. When she threw her house open, she liked to have it filled, and to her discredit it must be said that in that she invariably succeeded. On the evening that Mr. Incoul crossed her vestibule, he was met by a hum of voices, broken by the rhythm of a waltz. The air was heavy, and in the hall was a smell of flowers and of food. The rooms were crowded. His friend Blydenburg was present and with him his daughter. The Wainwarings, whom he had always known, were also there, and there were other people by whom he had not been forgotten, and with whom he exchanged a word, but for Miss Barhyte he looked at first in vain.

He would have gone, a crowd was as irksome to him as solitude, but in passing an outer room elaborately supplied with paintings and bric-à-brac, he caught a glimpse of the girl talking with a young man whom he vaguely remembered to have seen in earlier days at his own home.

He walked in: Miss Barhyte greeted him as an old friend: there were other people near her, and the young man with whom she had been talking turned and joined them, and presently passed with them into another room.

Mr. Incoul found a seat beside the girl, and, after a little unimportant conversation asked her a question at which she started. But Mr. Incoul was not in haste for an answer, he told her that with her permission, he would do himself the honor of calling on her later, and, as the room was then invaded by some of her friends, he left her to them, and went his way.

II.

MISS BARHYTE AGREES TO CHANGE HER NAME

A day or two after Mrs. Bachelor's reception, Mr. Incoul walked down Madison avenue, turned into one of the adjacent streets and rang the bell of a private boarding-house.

As he stood on the steps waiting for the door to be opened, a butcher-boy passed, whistling shrilly. Across the way a nurse-maid was idling with a perambulator, a slim-figured girl hurried by, a well-dressed woman descended from a carriage and a young man with a flower in his button-hole issued from a neighboring house. The nurse-maid stayed the perambulator and scrutinized the folds of the woman's gown; the young man eyed the hurrying girl; from the end of the street came the whistle of the retreating butcher, and as it fused into the rumble of Fifth avenue, Mr. Incoul heard the door opening behind him.

"Is Miss Barhyte at home?" he asked. The servant, a negro, answered that she was. "Then be good enough," said Mr. Incoul, "to take her this card."

The drawing-room, long and narrow, as is usual in many New York houses, was furnished in that fashion which is suggestive of a sheriff's sale, and best calculated to jar the nerves. Mr. Incoul did not wince. He gave the appointments one cursory, reluctant glance, and then went to the window. Across the way the nurse-maid still idled, the young man with a flower was drawing on a red glove, stitched with black, and as he looked out at them he heard a rustle, and turning, saw Miss Barhyte.

"I have come for an answer," he said simply.

"I am glad to see you," she answered, "very glad; I have thought much about what you said."

"Favorably, I hope."

"That must depend on you." She went to a bell and touched it. "Archibald," she said, when the negro appeared, "I am out. If any visitors come take them into the other room. Should any one want to come in here before I ring, say the parlor is being swept."

The man bowed and withdrew. He would have stood on his head for her. There were few servants that she did not affect in much the same manner. She seemed to win willingness naturally.

She seated herself on a sofa, and opposite to her Mr. Incoul found a chair. Her dress he noticed was of some dark material, tailor-made, and unrelieved save by a high white collar and the momentary glisten of a button. The cut and sobriety of her costume made her look like a handsome boy, a young Olympian as it were, one who had strayed from the games and been arrayed in modern guise. Indeed, her features suggested that combination of beauty and sensitiveness which was peculiar to the Greek lad, but her eyes were not dark—they were the blue victorious eyes of the Norseman—and her hair was red, the red of old gold, that red which partakes both of orange and of flame.

"I hope—" Mr. Incoul began, but she interrupted him.

"Wait," she said, "I have much to tell you of which the telling is difficult. Will you bear with me a moment?"

"Surely," he answered.

"It is this: It is needless for me to say I esteem you; it is unnecessary for me to say that I respect you, but it is because I do both that I feel I may speak frankly. My mother wishes me to marry you, but I do not. Let me tell you, first, that when my father died he left very little, but the little that he left seems to have disappeared, I do not know how or where. I know merely that we have next to nothing, and that we are in debt beside. Something, of course, has had to be done. I have found a position. Where do you suppose? " she asked, with a sudden smile and a complete change of key.

But Mr. Incoul had no surmises.

"In San Francisco! The MacDermotts, you know, the Bonanza people, want me to return with them and teach their daughter how to hold herself, and what not to say. It has been arranged that I am to go next week. Since the other night, however, my mother has told me to give up the MacDermotts and accept your offer. But that, of course, I cannot do."

"And why not?"

To this Miss Barhyte made no answer.

"You do not care for me, I know; there is slight reason why you should. Yet, might you not, perhaps, in time?"

The girl raised her eyebrows ever so slightly. "So you see," she continued, "I shall have to go to San Francisco."

Mr. Incoul remained silent a moment. "If," he said, at last, " if you will do me the honor to become my wife, in time you will care. It is painful for me to think of you accepting a position which at best is but a shade better than that of a servant, particularly so when I am able—nay, anxious," he added, pensively—" to surround you with everything which can make life pleasant. I am not old," he went on to say, "at least not so old that a marriage between us should seem incongruous. I find that I am sincerely attached to you—unselfishly, perhaps, would be the better word—and, if the privilege could be mine, the endeavor to make you happy would be to me more grateful than a second youth. Can you not accept me?"

He had been speaking less to her than to the hat which he held in his hand. The phrases had come from him haltingly, one by one, as though he had sought to weigh each mentally before dowering it with the wings of utterance, but, as he addressed this question he looked up at her. "Can you not?" he repeated.

Miss Barhyte raised a handkerchief to her lips and bit the shred of cambric with the *disinvoltura* of an heiress.

"Why is it," she queried, "why is it that marriage ever was invented? Why cannot a girl accept help from a man without becoming his wife?"

Mr. Incoul was about to reply that many do, but he felt that such a reply would be misplaced, and he called a platitude to his rescue. "There are wives and wives," he said.

"That is it," the girl returned, the color mounting to her cheeks; "if I could but be to you one of the latter."

He stared at her wonderingly, almost hopefully. "What do you mean?" he asked.

"Did you ever read *Eugénie Grandet*?"

"No," he answered, "I never have."

"Well, I read it years ago. It is, I believe, the only one of Balzac's novels that young girls are supposed to read. It is tiresome indeed; I had almost forgotten it, but yesterday I remembered enough of the story to help me to come to some decision. In thinking the matter over and over again as I have done ever since I last saw you it has seemed that I could not become your wife unless you were willing to make the same agreement with me that Eugenie Grandet's husband made with her."

"What was the nature of that agreement?"

"It was that, though married, they were to live as though they were not married—as might brother and sister."

"Always?"

"Yes."

"No," Mr. Incoul answered, "to such an agreement I could not consent. Did I do so, I would be untrue to myself, unmanly to you. But if you will give me the right to aid you and yours, I will—according to my lights—leave nothing undone to make you contented; and if I succeed in so doing, if you are happy, then the agreement which you have suggested would fall of itself. Would it not?" he continued. "Would it not be baseless? See—" he added, and he made a vague gesture, but before he could finish the phrase, the girl's hands were before her face and he knew that she was weeping.

Mr. Incoul was not tender-hearted. He felt toward Miss Barhyte as were she some poem in flesh that it would be pleasant to make his own. In her carriage as in her looks, he had seen that stamp of breeding which is coercive even to the dissolute. In her eyes he had discerned that promise of delight which it is said the lost goddesses could convey; and at whose conveyance, the legend says, the minds of men were enraptured. It was in this wise that he felt to her. Such exhilaration as she may have brought him was of the spirit, and being cold by nature and undemonstrative, her tears annoyed him. He would have had her impassive, as befitted her beauty. Beside, he was annoyed at his own attitude. Why should there be sorrow where he had sought to bring smiles? But he had barely time to formulate his annoyance into a thing even as volatile as thought—the girl had risen and was leaving the room.

As she moved to the door Mr. Incoul hastened to open it for her, but she reached it before him and passed out unassisted.

When she had gone he noticed that the sun was setting and that the room was even more hideous than before. He went again to the window wondering how to act. The entire scene was a surprise to him. He had come knowing nothing of the girl's circumstances, and suddenly he learned that she was in indigence, unable perhaps to pay her board bills and worried by small tradesmen. He had come prepared to be refused and she had almost accepted him. But what an acceptance! In the nature of it his thoughts roamed curiously: he was to be a little more than kin, a little less than kind. She would accept him as a husband for out-of-door purposes, for the world's sake she would bear his name—at arm's length. According to the terms of her proposition were she ever really his wife it would be tantamount to a seduction. He was to be with her, and yet, until she so willed it, unable to call her his own. And did he refuse these terms, she was off, no one knew whither. But he had not refused, he told himself, he had indeed not refused, he had merely suggested an amendment which turned an impossibility into an allurement. What pleasanter thing could there be than the winning of one's own wife? The idea was so novel it delighted him. For the moment he preferred it to any other; beside it his former experience seemed humdrum indeed. But why had she wept? Her reasons, however, he had then no chance to elucidate. Miss Barhyte returned as abruptly as she had departed.

"Forgive me," she said, advancing to where he stood, "it was stupid of me to act as I did. I am sorry—are we still friends?" Her eyes were clear as had she never wept, but there were circles about them, and her face was colorless.

"Friends," he answered, "yes, and more —" He hesitated a moment, and then hastily added, "It is agreed, then, is it not, you will be my wife?"

"I will be your wife?"

"As Balzac's heroine was to her husband?"

"You have said it."

"But not always. If there come a time when you care for me, then I may ask you to give me your heart as to-day I have asked for your hand?"

"When that day comes, believe me," she said, and her delicious face took on a richer hue, "when that day comes there will be neither asking nor giving, we shall have come into our own."

With this assurance Mr. Incoul was fain to be content, and, after another word or two, he took his leave.

For some time after his departure, Miss Barhyte stood thinking. It had grown quite dark. Before the window a street lamp burned with a small, steady flame, but beyond, the azure of the electric light pervaded the adjacent square with a suggestion of absinthe and vice. One by one the op-posite houses took on some form of interior illumination. A newsboy passed, hawking an extra with a noisy, aggressive ferocity as though he were angry with the neighborhood, and dared it come out and wrestle with him for his wares. There was a thin broken stream of shopgirls passing east-ward; at intervals, men in evening dress sauntered leisurely to their dinners, to restaurants, or to clubland, and over the rough pavement there was a ceaseless rattle of traps and of wagons; the air was alive with the indefinable murmurs of a great city.

Miss Barhyte noticed none of these things. She had taken her former seat on the sofa and sat, her elbow on her crossed knee, her chin resting in her hand, while the fingers touched and barely separated her lips. The light from without was just strong enough to reach her feet and make visible the gold clock on her silk stocking, but her face was in the shadow as were her thoughts.

Presently she rose and rang the bell. "Archibald," she said, when the man came, and who at once busied himself with lighting the gas, " I want to send a note; can't you take it? It's only across the square."

"I'll have to be mighty spry about it, miss. The old lady do carry on most unreasonable if I go for anybody but herself. She has laws that strict they'd knock the Swedes and Prussians silly. Why, you wouldn't believe if I told you how—"

And Archibald ran on with an unbelievable tale of recent adventure with the landlady. But the girl feigned no interest. She had taken a card from her case. On it she wrote, *Veins ce soir,* and after running the pencil through her name, she wrote on the other side, Lenox Leigh, esq., Athenæum Club.

"There," she said, interrupting the negro in the very climax of his story, "it's for Mr. Leigh; you are sure to find him, so wait for an answer."

A fraction of an hour later, when Miss Barhyte took her seat at the dinner table, she found beside her plate a note that contained a single line: "Will be with you at nine. I kiss your lips. L. L."

III.
AFTER DARKNESS

When Miss Barhyte was one year younger she had gone with her mother to pass the summer at Mt. Desert; and there, the morning of her arrival, on the monster angle of Rodick's porch, Lenox Leigh had caused himself to be presented.

A week later Miss Barhyte and her new acquaintance were as much gossiped about as was possible in that once unconventional resort.

Lenox Leigh was by birth a Baltimorean, and by profession a gentleman of leisure, yet as the exercise of that profession is considered less profitable in Baltimore than in New York, he had, for some time past, been domiciled in the latter city. From the onset he was well received; one of the Amsterdams had married a Leigh, his only sister had charmed the heart of Nicholas Manhattan, and being in this wise connected with two of the reigning families, he found the doors open as a matter of course. But even in the absence of potent relatives, there was no reason why he should not have been cordially welcomed. He was, it is true, better read than nineteen men out of twenty; when he went to the opera he preferred listening to the music to wandering from box to box; he declined to figure in cotillons and at no dinner, at no supper had he been known to drink anything stronger than claret and water.

But as an offset to these defects he was one of the most admirably disorganized young men that ever trod Fifth avenue. He was without beliefs and without prejudices; added to this he was indulgent to the failings of others, or perhaps it would be better to say that he was indifferent. It may be that the worst thing about him was that he was not bad enough; his wickedness, such as there was of it, was purely negative. A poet of the decadence of that period in fact when Rome had begun to weary of debauchery without yet acquiring a taste for virtue, a pre-mediæval Epicurean, let us say, could not have pushed a creedless refinement to a greater height than he. There were men who thought him a prig, and who said so when his back was turned.

It was in the company of this patrician of a later day that Miss Barhyte participated in the enjoyments of Mt. Desert. Leigh was then in his twenty-fifth year, and Miss Barhyte was just grazing the twenties. He was attractive in appearance, possessed of those features which now and then permit a man to do without beard or moustache, and his hair, which was black, clung so closely to his head that at a distance it might have been taken for the casque of a Saracen. To Miss Barhyte, as already noted, a full share of beauty had been allotted. Together they formed one of the most charming couples that it has ever been the historian's privilege to admire. And being a charming couple, and constantly together, they excited much interest in the minds of certain ladies who hailed from recondite Massachusettsian regions.

To this interest they were indifferent. At first, during the early evenings when the stars were put out by the Northern Lights, they rowed to the outermost shore of a neighboring island and lingered there for hours in an enchanted silence. Later, in the midsummer nights, when the harvest-moon was round and mellow, they wandered through the open fields back into the Dantesque forests and strayed in the clinging shadows and inviting solitudes of the pines.

From one such excursion they returned to the hotel at an hour which startled the night porter, who, in that capricious resort, should have lost his ability to be startled at anything.

That afternoon Mrs. Bunker Hill—one of the ladies to whom allusion has been made—approached Miss Barhyte on the porch. "And are you to be here much longer?" she asked, after a moment or two of desultory conversation.

"The holidays are almost over," the girl answered, with her radiant smile.

"*Holidays* do you call them? *Holidays* did I understand you to say? *I* should have called them *fast* days." And, with that elaborate witticism, Mrs. Bunker Hill shook out her skirts and sailed away.

Meanwhile an enveloping intimacy had sprung up between the two young people. Their conversation need not be chronicled. There was in it nothing unusual and nothing particularly brilliant; it was but a strain from that archaic duo in which we have all taken part and which at each repetition seems an original theme.

For the first time Miss Barhyte learned the intoxication of love. She gave her heart ungrudgingly, without calculation, without forethought, wholly, as a heart should be given and freely as had the gift been consecrated in the nave of a cathedral. If she were generous why should she be blamed? In the giving she found that mite of happiness, that one unclouded day that is fair as June roses and dawns but once.

In September Miss Barhyte went with her mother on a visit in the Berkshire Hills. Leigh journeyed South. A matter of business claimed his attention in Baltimore, and when, early in November, he reached New York the girl had already returned.

Since the death of Barhyte *père* she had lived with her mother in a small house in Irving Place, which they rented, furnished, by the year. But on this particular autumn affairs had gone so badly, some stock had depreciated, some railroad had been mismanaged, or some trustee had speculated—something, in fact, had happened of which no one save those personally interested ever know or ever care, and, as a result, the house in Irving Place was given up, and the mother and daughter moved into a boarding-house.

Of all this Lenox Leigh was made duly aware. Had he been able, and could such a thing have been proper and conventional, he would have been glad indeed to offer assistance; he was not selfish, but then he was not rich, a condition which always makes unselfishness easy. Matrimony was out of the question; his income was large enough to permit him to live without running into debt, but beyond that its flexibility did not extend, and in money matters, and in money matters alone, Lenox Leigh was the most scrupulous of men. Beside, as the phrase goes, he was not a marrying man—marriage, he was accustomed to assert, means one woman more and one man less, and beyond that definition he steadfastly declined to look, except to announce that, like some other institutions, matrimony was going out of fashion.

That winter Miss Barhyte was more circumspect. It was not that her affection had faltered, but in the monochromes of a great city the primal glamour that was born of the fields and of the sea lost its lustre. Then, too, Lenox in the correctness of evening dress was not the same adorer who had lounged in flannels at her side, and the change from the open country to the boarding-house parlor affected their spirits unconsciously.

And so the months wore away. There were dinners and routs which the young people attended in common, there were long walks on avenues unfrequented by fashion, and there were evenings prearranged which they passed together and during which the girl's mother sat upstairs and thought her own thoughts.

Mrs. Barhyte had been a pretty woman and inconsequential, as pretty women are apt to be. Her girlhood had been of the happiest, without a noteworthy grief. She married one whose perfection had seemed to her impeccable, and then suddenly without a monition the tide of disaster set in. After the birth of a second child, Maida, her husband began to drink, and drank, after each debauch with a face paler than before, until disgrace came and with it a plunge into the North River. Her elder child, a son, on whom she placed her remaining hopes, had barely skirted manhood before he was taken from her to die of small-pox in a hospital. Then came a depreciation in the securities which she held and in its train the small miseries of the shabby genteel. Finally, the few annual thousands that were left to her seemed to evaporate, and as she sat in her room alone her thoughts were bitter. The pretty inconsequential girl had developed into a woman, hardened yet unresigned. At forty-five her hair was white, her face was colorless as her widow's cap, her heart was dead.

On the night when her daughter, under the chaperonage of Mrs. Hildred, one of her few surviving relatives—returned from the reception, she was still sitting up. At Mrs. Hildred's suggestion a position, to which allusion has been made, had been offered to her daughter, and that position—the bringing up or rather the bringing out of a child of the West—she determined that her daughter should accept. Afterwards—well, perhaps for Maida there were other things in store, as for herself she expected little. She would betake herself to some Connecticut village and there wait for death.

When her daughter entered the room she was sitting in the erect impassibility of a statue. Her eyes indeed were restless, but her face was dumb, and in the presence of that silent desolation, the girl's tender heart was touched.

"Mother!" she exclaimed, "why did you wait up for me?" And she found a seat on the sofa near her mother and took her hand caressingly in her own. "Why are you up so late," she continued, "are you not tired? Oh, mother," the girl cried, impetuously, "if you only knew what happened to-night—what do you suppose?"

But Mrs. Barhyte shook her head, she had no thoughts left for suppositions. And quickly, for the mere sake of telling something that would arouse her mother if ever so little from her apathy, Maida related Mr. Incoul's offer. Her success was greater, if other, than she anticipated. It was as though she had poured into a parching throat the very waters of life. It was the *post tenebras, lux*. And what a light! The incandescence of unexpected hope. A cataract of gold pieces could not have been more dazzling; it was blinding after the shadows in which she had groped. The color came to her cheeks, her hand grew moist. "Yes, yes," she cried, urging the girl's narrative with a motion of the head like to that of a jockey speeding to the post; "yes, yes," she repeated, and her restless eyes flamed with the heat of fever.

"Wasn't it odd?" Maida concluded abruptly.

"But you accepted him?" the mother asked hoarsely, almost fiercely.

"Accepted him? No, of course not—he—why, mother, what is the matter?"

Engrossed in the telling of her story, the girl had not noticed her mother's agitation, but at her last words, at the answer to the question, her wrist had been caught as in a vise, and eyes that she no longer recognized—eyes dilated with anger, desperation and revulsion of feeling—were staring into her own. Instinctively she drew back—" Oh, mother, what is it?" And the mother bending forward, even as the daughter retreated, hissed, "You shall accept him—I say you shall!"

"Mother, mother," the girl moaned, helplessly.

"You shall accept him, do you hear me?"

"But, mother, how can I?" The tears were rolling down her cheeks, she was frightened—the acute, agonizing fright of a child pursued. She tried to free herself, but the hands on her wrist only tight ened, and her mother's face, livid now, was close to her own.

"You shall accept him," she repeated with the insistence of a monomaniac. And the girl, with bended head, through the paroxisms of her sobs, could only murmur in piteous, beseeching tones, "Mother! mother!"

But to the plaint the woman was as deaf as her heart was dumb. She indeed loosened her hold and the girl fell back on the lounge from which they had both arisen, but it was only to summon from the reservoirs of her being some new strength wherewith to vanquish. For a moment she stood motionless, watching the girl quiver in her emotion, and as the sobbing subsided, she stretched forth her hand again, and caught her by the shoulder.

"Look up at me," she said, and the girl, obedient, rose

from her seat and gazed imploringly in her mother's face. No Neapolitan fish-wife was ever more eager to barter her daughter than was this lady of acknowledged piety and refinement, and the face into which her daughter looked and shrank from bore no trace of pity or compassion. "Tell me if you dare," she continued, "tell me why it is that you refuse? What more do you want? Are you a princess of the blood? Perhaps you will say you don't love him! And what if you don't? I loved your father and look at me now! Beside, you have had enough of that—there, don't stare at me in that way. I know, and so do you. Now take your choice—accept this offer or get to your lover—and this very night. As for me, I disown you, I—"

But the flood of words was interrupted—the girl had fainted. The simulachre of death had extended its kindly arms, and into them she had fallen as into a grateful release.

By the morrow her spirit was broken. Two days later Mr. Incoul called with what success the reader has been already informed, and on that same evening in obedience to the note, came Lenox Leigh.

IV.
AN EVENING CALL

When Leigh entered the drawing-room he found Miss Barhyte already there.

"It is good of you to come," she said, by way of greeting.

The young man advanced to where she stood, and in a tender, proprietary manner, took her hand in his; he would have kissed her, but she turned her face aside.

"What is it?" he asked; "you are pale as Ophelia."

"And you, my prince, as inquisitive as Hamlet."

She led him to a seat and found one for herself. Her eyes rested in his own, and for a moment both were silent.

"Lenox," she asked at last, "do you know Mr. Incoul?"

"Yes, of course; everyone does."

"I mean do you know him well?"

"I never said ten words to him, nor he to me."

"So much the better. What do you suppose he did the other evening after you went away?"

"Really, I have no idea, but if you wish me to draw on my imagination, I suppose he went away too."

"He offered himself."

"For what?"

"To me."

"Maida, that mummy! You are joking."

"No, I am not joking, nor was he."

"Well, what then?"

"Then, as you say, he went away."

"And what did you do?"

"I went away too."

"Be serious; tell me about it."

"He came here this afternoon, and I—well—I am to be Mrs. Incoul."

Lenox bit his lip. Into his face there came an expression of angered resentment. He stood up from his seat; the girl put out her hand as though to stay him: "Lenox, I had to," she cried. But he paid no attention to her words and crossed the room.

On the mantel before him was a clock that ticked with a low, dolent moan, and for some time he stood looking at it as were it an object of peculiar interest which he had never before enjoyed the leisure to examine. But the clock might have swooned from internal pain, he neither saw nor heard it; his thoughts circled through episodes of the winter back to the forest and the fringes of the summer sea. And slowly the anger gave way to wonder, and presently the wonder faded and in its place there came a sentiment like that of sorrow, a doubled sorrow in whose component parts there was both pity and distress.

It is said that the rich are without appreciation of their wealth until it is lost or endangered, and it was not until that evening that Lenox Leigh appreciated at its worth the loveliness that was slipping from him. He knew then that he might tread the highroads and faubourgs of two worlds with the insistence of the Wandering Jew, and yet find no one so delicious as she. And in the first flood of his anger he felt as were he being robbed, as though the one thing that had lifted him out of the brutal commonplaces of the every day was being caught up and carried beyond the limits of vision. And into this resentment there came the suspicion that he was not alone being robbed, that he was being cheated to boot, that the love which he had thought to receive as he had seemed to give love before, was an illusory representation, a phantom constructed of phrases.

But this suspicion faded; he knew untold that the girl's whole heart was his, had been his, was yet his and probably would be his for all of time, till the grave opened and closed again. And then the wonder came. He knew, none better, the purity of her heart, and knowing, too, her gentleness, the sweetness of her nature, her abnegation of self, he began to understand that some tragedy had been enacted which he had not been called upon to witness. Of her circumstances he had been necessarily informed. But in the sensitiveness of her refinement the girl had shrunk from unveiling to a lover's eyes the increasing miseries of her position, and of the poignancy of those miseries he had now, uninformed, an inkling. If she sold herself, surely it was because the sale was imperative. The white impassible face of the girl's mother rose before him and then, at once, he understood her cry, "Lenox, I had to."

As he moved from her, Maida had seen the anger, and knowing the anger to be as just as justice ever is, she shook her head in helpless grief, yet her eyes were tearless as had she no tears left to shed. She had seen the anger, but ignorant of the phases of thought by which it had been transfigured she stole up to where he stood and touched his arm with a shrinking caress.

He turned and would have caught her to him, but she drew back, elusively, as might a swan. "No, not that, Lenox. Only say that you do not hate me. Lenox, if you only knew.

To me it is bitterer than death. You are the whole world to me, yet never must I see you again. If I could but tell you all. If I could but tell him all, if there were anything that I could do or say, but there is nothing, nothing," she added pensively, "except submission."

Her voice had sunk into a whisper: she was pleading as much with herself as with him. Her arms were pendant and her eyes downcast. On the mantel the clock kept up its low, dolorous moan, as though in sympathy with her woe. "Nothing," she repeated.

"But surely it need not be. Things cannot be so bad as that—Maida, I cannot lose you. If nothing else can be done, let us go away; at its best New York is tiresome; we could both leave it without a regret or a wish to return. And then, there is Italy; we have but to choose. Why, I could take a palace on the Grand Canal for less than I pay for my rooms at the Cumberland. And you would love Venice; and in winter there is Capri and Sorrento and Palermo. I have known days in Palermo when I seemed to be living in a haze of turquoise and gold. And the nights! You should see the nights! The stars are large as lilies! See, it would be so easy; in a fortnight we could be in Genoa, and before we got there we would have been forgotten."

He was bending forward speaking rapidly, persuasively, half hoping, half fearing, she would accept. She did not interrupt him, and he continued impetuously, as though intoxicated on his own words.

"When we are tired of the South, there are the lakes and that lovely Tyrol; there will be so much to do, so much to see. After New York, we shall really seem to live; and then, beyond, is Munich—you are sure to love that city." He hated Munich; he hated Germany. The entire land, and everything that was in it, was odious to him; but for the moment he forgot. He would have said more, even to praises of Berlin, but the girl raised her ringless hand and shook her head wearily.

"No, Lenox, it may not be. Did I go with you, in a year—six months, perhaps—we would both regret. It would be not only expatriation; it would, for me at least, be isolation as well, and, though I would bear willingly with both, you would not. You think so now, perhaps, I do not doubt"—and a phantom of a smile crossed her face—" and I thank you for so thinking, but it may not be."

Her hand fell to her side, and she turned listlessly away. "You must forget me, Lenox—but not too soon, will you?"

"Never, sweetheart—never!"

"Ah, but you must. And I must learn to forget you. It will be difficult. No one can be to me what you have been. You have been my youth, Lenox; my girlhood has been yours. I have nothing left. Nothing except regrets—regrets that youth should pass so quickly and that girlhood comes but once."

Her lips were tremulous, but she was trying to be brave.

"But surely, Maida, it cannot be that we are to part forever. Afterwards—" the word was vague, but they both understood—"afterwards I may see you. Such things often are. Because you feel yourself compelled to this step, there is no reason why I, of all others, should be shut out of your life."

"It is the fact of your being the one of all others that makes the shutting needful."

"It shall not be."

"Lenox," she pleaded, "it is harder for me than for you."

"But how can you ask me, how can you think that I will give you up? The affair is wretched enough as it is, and now, by insisting that I am not to see you again, you would make it even worse. People think it easy to love, but it is not; I know nothing more difficult. You are the only one for whom I have ever cared. It was not difficult to do so, I admit, but the fact remains. I have loved you, I have loved you more and more every day, and now, when I love you most, when I love you as I can never love again, you find it the easiest matter in the world to come to me and say, 'It's ended; *bon jour.*'"

"You are cruel, Lenox, you are cruel."

"It is you that are cruel, and there the wonder is, for your cruelty is unconscious, of your own free will you would not know how."

"It is not that I am cruel, it is that I am trying to do right. And it is for you to aid me. I have been true to you, do not ask me now to be false to myself."

If at that moment Mrs. Bunker Hill could have looked into the girl's face, her suspicions would have vanished into air. Maida needed only a less fashionable gown to look like a mediæval saint; and before the honesty that was in her eyes Lenox bowed his head.

"Will you help me?"

"I will," he answered.

"I knew you would; you are too good to try to make me more miserable than I am. And now, you must go; kiss me, it is the last time."

He caught her in his arms and kissed her full upon the mouth. He kissed her wet eyes, her cheeks, the splendor of her hair. And after a moment of the acutest pain of all her life, the girl freed herself from his embrace, and let him go without another word.

V.
A YELLOW ENVELOPE

There is a peculiarity about Baden-Baden which no other watering-place seems to share—it has the aroma of a pretty woman. In August it is warm, crowded, enervating, tiresome as are all warm and crowded places, but the air is delicately freighted and a pervasive fragrance is discerned even by the indifferent.

In the summer that succeeded Maida's marriage Baden was the same tame, perfumed *zwei und funfzig* that it has ever been since the war. The ladies and gentlemen who were to regard it as a sort of continuation of the Bois de Boulogne had departed never to return. Gone was Benazet, gone, too, the click of the roulette ball. The echoes and uproars of the Second Empire had died away, as echoes and uproars ever must, and in place of the paint and cleverness of the *dames dulac* had come the stupid loveliness of the *schwärmerisch Mädchen.*

But though Paris had turned her wicked back, the attitude of that decadent capital in no wise affected other cities. On the particular August to which allusion is made, interminable dinners were consumed by contingents from the politest lands, and also from some that were semi-barbaric.

In the Lichenthal Allee and on the promenade in front of the Kursaal one could hear six languages in as many minutes, and given a polyglottic ear the number could have been increased to ten. Among those who added their little quota to this summer Babel were Mr. and Mrs. Incoul.

The wedding had been very simple. Mrs. Barhyte had wished the ceremony performed in Grace Church, and to the ceremony she had also wished that all New York should be bidden. To her it represented a glory which in the absence of envious witnesses would be lustreless indeed. But in this respect her wishes were disregarded. On a melting morning in early June, a handful of people, thirty at most, assembled in Mrs. Hildred's drawing-room. The grave service that is in usage among Episcopalians was mumbled by a diligent bishop, there was a hurried and heavy breakfast, and two hours later the bride and groom were on the deck of the "Umbria."

The entire affair had been conducted with the utmost dispatch. The *Sunday Sun* chronicled the engagement in one issue, and gave the date of the wedding in the next. It was not so much that Harmon Incoul was ardent in his wooing or that Miss Barhyte was anxious to assume the rank and privileges that belong to the wedded state. The incentives were other if equally prosaic. The ceremony if undergone needed to be undergone at once. Summer was almost upon them, and in the code which society has made for itself, summer weddings are reproved. There was indeed some question of postponing the rites until autumn. But on that Mrs. Barhyte put her foot. She was far from sure of her daughter, and as for the other contracting party, who could tell but that he might change his mind. Such changes had been, and instances of such misconduct presented themselves unsummoned to the woman's mind. The fish had been landed almost without effort, a fish more desirable than any other, a very prize among fishes, and the possibility that he might slip away and without so much as a gill awry float off into clearer and less troubled seas, nerved her to her task anew.

In the interview which she enjoyed with her prospective son-in-law she was careful, however, to display no eagerness. She was sedate when sedateness seemed necessary, but her usual attitude was one of conciliatory disinterestedness. Her daughter's choice she told him had met with her fullest approval, and it was to her a matter of deep regret that neither her husband nor her father—the late Chief Justice Hildred, with whose name Mr. Incoul was of course familiar—that neither of them had been spared to join in the expression of her satisfaction. Of Maida it was unnecessary to speak, yet this at least should be said, she was young and she was impressionable, as young people are apt to be, but she had never given her mother cause for the slightest vexation, not the slightest. "She is a sweet girl," Mrs. Barhyte went on to say, "and one with an admirable disposition; she takes after her father in that, but she has her grandfather's intellect."

"Her beauty, madam, comes from you."

To this Mrs. Barhyte assented. "She is pretty," she said, and then in the voice of an actress who feels her rôle, "Do be good to her," she pleaded, "she is all I have."

Mr. Incoul assured her that on that score she need give herself no uneasiness, and a few days before the wedding, begged as a particular favor to himself that after the ceremony she would take up her residence in his house. The servants, he explained, had been instructed in that respect, and a checkbook of the Chemical Bank would be handed her in defrayment of all expenses. "And to think," Mrs. Barhyte muttered to herself, "to think that I might have died

MR. INCOUL'S MISADVENTURE

in Connecticut!"

The voyage over was precisely like any other. There were six days of discomfort in the open, and between Queenstown and Liverpool unnumbered hours of gloomy and irritating delay. Mrs. Incoul grew weary of the captain's cabin and her husband was not enthusiastic on the subject of the quarters which the first officer had relinquished to him. But in dear old London, as all good Americans are wont to call that delightful city, Mrs. Incoul's spirits revived. The difference between Claridge's and Rodick's would have interested one far more apathetic than she, and as she had never before set her foot on Piccadilly, and as Rotten Row and Regent Circus were as unfamiliar to her as the banks of the Yangtse-Kiang, she had none of that satiated feeling of the *deja-vu* which besets the majority of us on our travels.

The notice of their arrival in the *Morning Post* had been followed by cards without limit and invitations without stint. An evening gazette published an editorial a column in length, in which after an historical review of wealth from Plutus to the Duke of Westminster, the reader learned that the world had probably never seen a man so rich and yet seemingly so unconscious of the power which riches give as was Harmon Incoul, esq., of New York, U. S. A.

During the few weeks that were passed in London the bride and groom were bidden to more crushes, dinners and garden parties than Maida had attended during the entire course of her bud-hood. There was the inevitable presentation and as the girl's face was noticeably fair she and her husband were made welcome at Marlborough House. Afterwards, yet before the season drooped, there was a trip to Paris, a city, which, after the splendors of London, seemed cheap and tawdry indeed, and then as already noted came the villegiatura at Babel-Baden.

Meanwhile Maida had come and gone, eaten and fasted, danced and driven in a constant chase after excitement. To her husband she had acted as she might have done to some middle-aged cousin with whom she was not precisely on that which is termed a familiar footing, one on whom chance not choice had made her dependent, and to whom in consequence much consideration was due. But her relations will be perhaps better understood when it is related that she had not found herself physically capable of calling him by his given name, or in fact anything else than You. It was not that she disliked him, on the contrary, in many ways he was highly sympathetic, but the well-springs of her affection had been dried, and the season of their refreshment was yet obscure.

In the face of this half-hearted platonism Mr. Incoul had displayed a wisdom which was peculiar to himself; he exacted none of those little tributes which are conceded to be a husband's due, and he allowed himself none of the familiarities which are reported to be an appanage of the married state. From the beginning he had determined to win his wife by the exercise of that force which, given time and opportunity, a strong nature invariably exerts over a weaker one. He was indulgent but he was also austere. The ordering of one gown or of five hundred was a matter of which he left her sole mistress. Had she so desired she might have bought a jewelry shop one day and given it back as a free gift on the morrow. But on a question of ethics he allowed no appeal. The Countess of Ex, a lady of dishonor at a popular court, had, during the London season, issued cards for a ball. On the evening on which it was to take place the bride and groom had dined at one house, and gone to a musicale at another. When leaving the latter entertainment Maida told her husband to tell the man "Park Lane." Mr. Incoul, however, ordered the carriage to be driven to the hotel.

"Did you not understand me?" she asked. "I am going to the Countess of Ex's."

"She is not a woman whom I care to have you know," he replied.

"But the Prince is to be there!"

To this he assented. "Perhaps." And then he added in a voice that admitted of no further argument, "But not my wife."

Maida sank back in the carriage startled by an unexperienced emotion. For the first time since the wedding she could have kissed the man whose name she bore. It was in this way that matters shaped themselves.

Soon after reaching Paris, Mr. Blydenburg called. He had brought his daughter abroad because he did not know what else to do with her, and now that he was on the Continent he did not know what to do with himself. He explained these pre-occupations and Mr. Incoul suggested that in the general exodus they should all go to Germany. To this suggestion Blydenburg gave a ready assent and that very day purchased a translation of Tacitus, a copy of Mr. Baring-Gould's Germany, a Baedeker, and a remote edition of Murray.

At the appointed date the little party started for Cologne, where, after viewing a bone of the fabulous virgin Undecemilla, they drifted to Frankfort and from there reached the Oos. In Baden, Blydenburg and his daughter elected domicile at the Englischerhof, while through the foresight of a courier, good-looking, polyglottic, idle and useful, the Incouls found a spacious apartment in the Villa Wilhelmina, a belonging of the Mesmer House.

In the drawer of the table which Maida selected as a suitable place for superfluous rings was a yellow envelope addressed to the Gräfin von Adelsburg. On the back was an attempt at addition, a double column of figures which evidently represented the hotel expenses of the lady to whom the envelope was addressed. The figures were marked carefully that no mistake should be possible, but the sum total had been jotted down in hurried numerals, as though the mathematician had been irritated at the amount, while under all, in an indignant scrawl, was the legend "S. T."

Maida was the least inquisitive of mortals, but one evening, a week or ten days after her arrival, when she happened to be sitting in company with the Blydenburgs and her husband on the broad terrace that fronts the Kursaal, she alluded, for the mere sake of conversation, to the envelope which she had found. The Grafin von Adelsburg it then appeared was the name with which the Empress of a neighboring realm was accustomed to veil her rank, and the legend it was suggested could only stand for *schrechlich theuer*, frightfully dear. The Empress had vacated the Villa Wilhelmina but a short time before and it seemed not improbable that the figures and conclusion were in her own imperial hand.

While this subject was under discussion the Prince of Albion sauntered down the walk. He was a handsome man, with blue projecting eyes, somewhat stout, perhaps, but not obese. In his train were two ladies and a few men. As he was about to pass Mrs. Incoul he stopped and raised his hat. It was of soft felt, she noticed, and his coat was tailless. He uttered a few amiable commonplaces and then moved on. The terrace had become very crowded. The little party had found seats near the musicians, and from either side came a hum of voices. A Saxon halted before them, designating with pointing finger the retreating back of the Prince, his companion, a pinguid woman who looked as though she lived on fish, shouted, "*Herr Jesus! ist es ja möglich*," and hurried on for a closer view. Near by was a group of Brazilians and among them a pretty girl in a fantastic gown, whose voice was like the murmur of birds. To the left were some Russians conversing in a hard, cruel French. The girl seemed to have interested them. "But why," asked one, "but why is it that she wears such loud colors?" To which another, presumably the wit of the party, answered idly, "Who knows, she maybe deaf." And immediately behind Mrs. Incoul were two young Americans, wonderfully well dressed, who were exchanging chaste anecdotes and recalling recent adventures with an accompaniment of smothered laughter that was fathomless in its good-fellowship.

Maida paid no attention to the conversation about her. She was thinking of the yellow envelope, and for the first time she began to form some conception of her husband's wealth. Apparently he thought nothing of prices that seemed exorbitant to one whose coffers notoriously overflowed. She had never spoken to him about money, nor he to her; she knew merely that his purse was open; yet, as is usual with one who has been obliged to count the pennies, she had in her recent shopping often hesitated and refused to buy. In Paris she had chaffered over handkerchiefs and been alarmed at Doucet's bill. Indeed at Virot's when she told that poetic milliner what she wished to pay for a bonnet, Virot, smiling almost with condescension, had said to her, "The *chapeau* that madame wants is surely a *chapeau en Espagne*."

And now for the first time she began to understand. She

saw how much was hers, how ungrudgingly it was given, how easy her path was made, how pleasant it might be for the rest of her days, and she half-turned and looked at her husband. If she could only forget, she thought, only forget and begin anew. If she could but tell him all! She moaned to herself. The moon was shining behind the Kursaal and in the air was the usual caress. The musicians, who had just attacked and subdued the Meistersänger, began a sob of Weber's that had been strangled into a waltz, and as the measures flowed they brought her that pacification which music alone can bring.

The past was over and done, ill-done, she knew, but above it might grow such weeds of forgetfulness as would hide it even from herself. In a semi-unconsciousness of her surroundings she stared like a pretty sphinx into the future. The waltz swooned in its ultimate accords, but she had ceased to hear; it had lulled and left her; her thoughts roamed far off into distant possibilities; she was dreaming with eyes wide open.

Abruptly the orchestra attacked a score that was seasoned with red pepper—the can-can of an opéra-bouffe; the notes exploded like fire crackers, and in the explosion brought vistas of silk stockings, whirlwinds of disordered skirts, the heat and frenzy of an orgy. And then, as the riot mounted like a flame, suddenly in a clash and shudder of brass the uproar ceased.

Maida, aroused from her revery by the indecency of the music, looked idly about her. The Russians were drinking beer that was as saffron as their own faces. The Brazilians had departed. The young Americans were smoking Bond street cigarettes which they believed to be Egyptian, and discussing the relative merits of Hills and Poole.

"While I was getting measured for that top-coat you liked so much," said one, "Leigh came in."

"Lee? What Lee? Sumpter?"

"No; Lenox Leigh."

"Did he, though? How was he?"

"Finest form. Said he would take in Paris and Baden. He may be here now for all I know. Let's ask the waiter for a Fremden-List."

Maida had heard, and with the hearing there had come to her an enveloping dread. She felt that, did she see him, the love which she had tried to banish would return unfettered from its exile. Strength was not yet hers; with time, she knew, she could have sworn it would come; but, for the moment, she was helpless, and into the dread a longing mingled. At once, as though in search of a protection that should guard her against herself, she turned to her husband. To him, the Russians, Brazilians, and other gentry had been part of the landscape. He had little taste for music, and Blydenburg had bored him as that amiable gentleman was accustomed to bore every one with whom he conversed, yet, nevertheless, through that spirit of paradox which is common to us all, Mr. Incoul liked the man, and for old association's sake took to the boredom in a kindlier fashion than had it come from a newer and more vivacious acquaintance. Blydenburg had been explaining the value of recent excavations in Tirynth, a subject which Mr. Incoul understood better than the informist, but he noticed Maida's movement and stopped short.

"Come, Milly," he said to his daughter, "let's be going."

Milly had sat by his side the entire evening, in stealthy enjoyment of secular music, performed for the first time in her hearing on the Lord's day. She was a pale, freckled girl, with hair of the shade of Bavarian beer. She was not beautiful, but then she was good —a sort of angel bound in calf.

When Milly and her father had disappeared, Maida turned to her husband again. "Do you mind leaving Baden?" she asked.

Mr. Incoul eyed her a moment. "Why?" he asked. He had a trick of answering one question with another, yet for the moment she wondered whether he too had heard the conversation behind them, and then comforted by the thought that in any case the name of Lenox Leigh could convey but little to him, she shrugged her shoulders. "Oh, I don't know," she said; "I don't like it; it's hot and crowded. I think I would like the seashore better."

"Very good," he answered; "whatever you prefer. I will speak to Karl to-night." (Karl was the courier.) "I don't suppose," he added, reflectively, "that you would care for Trouville—I know I should not."

He had risen, and Maida, who had risen with him, was looking down at the gravel, which she toyed nervously with her foot. The opera that had been given that evening was evidently over. A stream of people were coming from the direction of the theatre, and among them was the Prince. He was chatting with his companions, but his trained eye had marked Mrs. Incoul, and when he reached the place where she stood he stopped again.

"You didn't go in to-night," he said, collectively. "It was rather good, too." And then, without waiting for an answer, he continued: "Won't you both dine with us to-morrow?"

"Oh, we can't," Maida answered. She was tormented with the thought that at any moment Lenox might appear. "We can't; we are going away."

The Prince smiled in his brown beard. Americans were

popular with him. He liked their freedom. There was, he knew, barely one woman in Baden, not utterly bedridden, who would have taken his invitation so lightly. "I am sorry," he said, and he spoke sincerely. Like any other sensible man, he liked beauty and he liked it near him. He knew that Mrs. Incoul had been recently married, and in his own sagacious way, *il posait des jalons.* "You are to be at Ballaster in the autumn, I hear." Ballaster was a commodious shooting-box in Scotland, the possession of an hospitable peer.

"Yes, I believe we are," Maida answered.

"I hope to see you there," and with these historic words, Prince Charming departed.

VI.
BIARRITZ

After a frühstück of coffee and honey, to which the inn-keeper, out of compliment to the nationality of his guest, had added an ear of green corn—a combination, be it said, that no one but a German could have imagined—Mr. Incoul went in search of his friend.

He had questioned Karl, and the courier had spoken of Ostend with such enthusiasm that his employer suspected him of some personal interest in the place and struck it at once from the list of possible resorts which he had been devising. On the subject of other *bains de mer* the man was less communicative. There was, he said, nothing attractive about Travemunde, except the name; Scheveningen was apt to be chilly; Trouville he rather favored, but to his thinking Ostend was preferable.

When the courier had gone Mr. Incoul ran his eye down a mental map of the coast of France, and just as it reached the Spanish frontier he remembered that some one in his hearing had recently sounded the attractions of Biarritz. On that seaboard he ultimately decided, and it was with the idea that Blydenburg might go further and fare worse that he sought his friend and suggested the advantages of a trip to the Basque country.

Mr. Blydenburg had few objections to make. He had

taken very kindly to the consumption of beer, but beer had not agreed with him, and he admitted, did he stay in Baden, that, in spite of the ill effects, he would still be unable to resist the allurements of that insidious beverage. "Act like a man, then," said Mr. Incoul, encouragingly; "act like a man and flee from it."

There was no gainsaying the value of this advice, but between its adoption and a journey to Biarritz the margin was wide. "It is true," he said, reflectively, "I could study the language at the fountain-head" (Mr. Blydenburg, it may be explained, was a gentleman who plumed himself on his familiarity with recondite tongues, but one whose knowledge of the languages that are current in polite society was such as is gleaned from the appendices of guide-books).

Mr. Incoul nodded approvingly, "Certainly there would be no difficulty about that."

Blydenburg looked at him musingly for a moment and nodded, too. "The name Biarritz," he said, "comes, I am inclined to believe, from bi haritz—two oaks. Minucius thinks that it comes from bi harri—two rocks; but I have detected Minucius in certain errors which has made me wary of accepting his opinion. For instance, he claims that the Basques are descendants of the Phoenicians. Nothing could be more preposterous. They are purely Iberian, and probably the most ancient race in Europe. Why, you would be surprised " —

Mr. Incoul interrupted him cruelly—"I often am," he said; "now tell me, will you be ready this afternoon?"

"The laundress has just taken my things."

"Send after them, then. I make no doubt that there you can find another on the Bay of Biscay."

"I wonder what Biscay comes from? bi scai, two currents,

perhaps. Yes, of course, I will be ready." And as his friend moved away, he pursed his lips abstractedly and made a note of the derivation.

A courier aiding, the journey from Baden to Biarritz can be accomplished without loss of life or reason. It partakes something of the character of a zigzag, the connections are seldom convenient, the wayside inns are not of the best, but if people go abroad to be uncomfortable, what more can the heart desire? The Incoul-Blydenburg party, impeded by Karl, a body-servant, and two maids, received their alloted share of discomfort with the very best grace in the world. They reached Bayonne after five days, not, it is true, of consecutive motion, but of such consecutive heat that they were glad to descend at the station of that excitable little city and in the fresh night air drive in open carriages over the few kilometres that remained to be traversed.

It was many hours before the journey was sufficiently a part of the past to enable the travelers to look about them, but on the evening succeeding their arrival, after a dinner on the verandah of the Continental, they sat with much contentment of spirit enjoying the intermittent showers of summer stars and the boom and rustle of the waves. Baden was unregretted. To the left, high above, on the summit of a projecting eminence, the white and illuminated Casino glittered like an aerian palace. To the right was the gardened quadrangle of the former Empress of the French, in the air was the scent of seaweed and before them the Infinite.

"It's quite good enough for me," Blydenburg confided to his companions, and the confidence in its inelegant terseness conveyed the sentiments of them all.

A week passed without bringing with it any incident worthy of record. In the mornings they met at the Moorish Pavilion which stands on the shore and there lounged or bathed. Maida's beauty necessarily attracted much attention, and when she issued in a floating wrapper from the sedan-chair in which she allowed herself to be carried from the Pavilion to the sea, a number of amateurs who stood each day just out of reach of the waves, expressed their admiration in winning gutturals.

She was, assuredly, very beautiful, particularly so in comparison with the powdered sallowness of the ladies from Spain, and when, with a breezy gesture of her own, she tossed her wrap to the bather and with sandaled feet and a white and clinging costume of serge she stepped to the water there was one on-looker who bethought him of a nymph of the Ægean Sea. She was a good swimmer, as the American girl often is, and she breasted and dived through the wonderful waves with an intrepidity such as the accompanying *baigneur* had been rarely called upon to restrain.

From the shade of beach chairs, large and covered like wicker tents, her husband and the Blydenburgs would watch her prowess, and when, after a final ride on the crest of some great billow, she would be tossed breathless and deliciously disheveled into the steadying arms of the bather, the amateurs were almost tempted to applaud.

In the afternoons there were drives and excursions. One day to Bayonne along the white, hard road that skirts the Chambre d'Amour, through the peace and quiet of Aiglet and on through kilometres of pines to the Adour, a river so beautiful in itself that all the ingenuity of man has been unable to make it wholly hideous, and thence by its banks to the outlying gardens of the city.

On other days they would loiter on the cliffs that overhang the Côte des Basques, or push on to Bidart, a chromatic village where the inhabitants are so silent that one might fancy them enchanted by the mellow marvels of their afternoons.

But of all other places Maida preferred Saint Jean-de-Luz. It lies near the frontier on a bay of the tenderest blue, and for background it has the hazy amethyst of the neighborly Pyrenees. The houses are rainbows of blended colors; from the open doorways the passer, now and then, catches a whiff of rancid oil, the smell of victuals cooked in fat, from a mouldering square a cathedral casts an unexpected chill, but otherwise the town is charming, warm and very bright. On the shore stands an inn and next to it a toy casino.

To this exotic resort the little party drove one afternoon. It had been originally arranged to pass the day there, but on the day for which the excursion was planned, a *Course Landaise* was announced at Biarritz, and it was then decided that they should first view the *course* and dine afterwards at Saint Jean. At first both Maida and Miss Blydenburg refused to attend the performance and it was not until they were assured that it was a bullfight for ladies in which there was no shedding of blood that they consented to be present. The spectacle which they then witnessed was voted most agreeable. The bulls, which turned out to be heifers, very lithe and excitable, were housed in boxed stalls, which bore their respective names: Isabel, Rosa, Paquita, Adelaide, Carlota and Sofia. The ring itself was an improvised arrangement constructed in a great racquet court. The spectators, according to their means, found seats on either side, the poorer in the sun and the more wealthy in the shaded Tribune d'Honneur. After a premonitory blare from municipal brass the quadrille entered the arena. They were a good-looking set of men, more plainly dressed than their bloodier brothers of Spain, and very agile. Two of them carrying long poles stationed themselves at the sides, one, armed with a barb laid himself down a few feet from Isabel's door, and a fourth threw his soft hat in the middle of the ring, put his feet in it and stood expectant. In a moment a latch was drawn, Isabel leaped from her stall, bounded over the prostrate form that pricked her on the way and made a straight rush for the motionless figure in the centre of the ring. When she reached him he was in the air and over her with his feet still in the hat. Isabel was bewildered, instead of goring a man she had run her horns into empty space and in her annoyance she turned viciously at one of the pole-bearing gentlemen who vaulted over her as easily as were he crossing a gutter, but in vaulting the pole slipped from him, and amid the applause of the audience Isabel chased him across the ring to a high fence opposite, and to which he rose like a bird with Isabel's horns on his heels. There was more of this amusement, and then Isabel, a trifle tired, was lured back to her box; Rosa was loosed and the performance repeated.

The escapes seemed so hairbreadth that Mr. Blydenburg announced his intention of witnessing a genuine bullfight, and on the way to Saint Jean urged his companions to accompany him over the border and view the real article. "There is one announced for next Sunday," he said, "at San Sebastian, a stone's throw from here." The appetite of all had been whetted, and during the rest of the drive, Mr. Blydenburg discoursed on the subject with such learning and enthusiasm that even his daughter consented to forget her Sabbath principles and make one of the projected party.

When the meal was done, they went into the toy casino. There was a band playing at one end of the hall, the which was so narrow that the director had been obliged to select thin musicians, and beyond was a paperless reading-room, a vague café, a dwarf theatre, and a salle-de-jeu in white and gamboge. In the latter division, where the high life of Saint Jean had assembled, stood a table that resembled a roulette. In its centre were miniature revolving bulls, which immediately attracted Mr. Blydenburg's attention, and on the green baize were painted the names of cities.

"Banderilla! Ruego! Sevilla!" the croupier called, as the party entered. In one hand he held a rake, with which he possessed himself of the stakes of those who had lost, and with the other hand he tossed out coin to those who had won. The machinery was again set in motion, and when the impulse had ceased to act he called out anew, "Espada! Nero! Madrid!"

Mr. Blydenburg was thoroughly interested. In the residue of twenty-five French lessons, which he had learned in his boyhood from a German, he made bold to demand information.

"It's the neatest game in the world," the croupier replied; "six for one on the cities, even on the colors, even on banderilla or espada, and twenty for one on Frascuelo." And, as he gave the latter information, he pointed to a little figure armed with a sword, which was supposed to represent that famous matador. "The minimum," he added, obligingly, "is fifty centimes; the maximum, forty sous."

"I'll go Frascuelo," said Blydenburg, and suiting the action to the word, he placed a coin on the table. Maida, meanwhile, had put money on everything—cities, colors, banderilla, espada, and Frascuelo as well. To the surprise of every one, but most to that of the croupier, Frascuelo won. Maida saw twenty francs swept from her and forty returned. Blydenburg, who had played a closer game, received forty also, but he lost nothing, and he beamed as joyously as had the University of Copenhagen crowned an essay of his own manufacture.

It was by means of these mild amusements that the first week of their sojourn was helped away. Through the kindness of an international acquaintance, Mr. Incoul had been made welcome at the Cercle de Biarritz, and in that charming summer club, where there is much high play and perfect informality, he had become acquainted with a Spaniard, the Marquis of Zunzarraga.

One day when the latter gentleman had wearied of the columns of the *Epoca* and Mr. Incoul, and sought in vain for some refreshment from *Galignani*, they drew their chairs together and exchanged cigarettes.

In answer to the question which is addressed to every new-comer, Mr. Incoul expressed himself pleased with the country, adding that were not hotel life always distasteful he would be glad to remain on indefinitely.

"You might take a villa," the marquis suggested. To this Mr. Incoul made no reply. The nobleman fluttered his fingers a moment and then said, "take mine, you can have it, servants and all."

The Villa Zunzarraga was near the hotel and its airy architecture had already attracted Mr. Incoul's eye. It was a modern improvement on a feudal château, there were turreted wings in which the matchicoulis were replaced by astrogals and a broad and double stairway of marble led up to the main entrance.

"If you have nothing better to do to-day," the marquis continued, "go in and take a look at it. I have never rented it before, but this summer the marquesa is with the queen, my mistress, and I would be glad to have it off my hands."

After consulting Maida in regard to her wishes, Mr. Incoul determined to act on the suggestion, and that afternoon they went together to view the villa. In its appointments there was little fault to be found. There was no vestibule, unless, indeed, the entrance hall, which was large enough to accommodate a small cotillon, could be so considered; on the right were reception-rooms, to the left a dining-room, all facing the sea, while at the rear, overlooking a quiet garden that seemed to extend indefinitely and lose itself in the lilac fringes of the tamaris, was a library. On the floor above were bed and sitting rooms. In one wing were the offices, kitchen and servants' quarters, in another was the coachhouse and stables.

Under the guidance of the host, Mr. Incoul went to explore the place, while Maida remained in the library. It was a satisfactory room, lined on three sides with low, well-filled book-cases, the windows were doors and extended nearly to the ceiling, but the light fell through pink awnings under which was a verandah with steps that led to the garden below. From the walls hung selections of Goya's Proverbios and Tauromaquia, a series of nightmares in black and white. Among them was a picture of a lake of blood haunted by evil spirits; a vertiginous flight of phantoms more horrible than any Doré ever saw; a reunion of sorcerers with cats for steeds; women tearing teeth from the mouths of the gibbeted; a confusion of demons and incubes; a disordered dance of delirious manolas; caricatures that held the soul of Hoffmann; the disembowelment of fantastic chulos; horses tossed by bulls with chimerical horns; but best of all, a skeleton leaning with a leer from the tomb and scrawling on it the significant legend, *Nada*, nothing.

In one corner, on a pedestal, there glittered a Buddha,

the legs crossed and a smile of indolent apathy on its imbecile features. Behind it was a giant crucifix with arms outstretched like the wings of woe.

Maida wandered from book-case to book-case, examining the contents with incurious eye. The titles were strange to her and new. In one division were the works of Archilaus, Albert le Grand, Raymond Lulle, Armand de Villenova, Nostradamus, and Paracelsus, the masters of occult science. Another was given up to Spanish literature. There were the poems of Berceo, the romancero of the church; the codex of Alphonso X., the Justinian of mediæval Spain; El Tesoro, a work on alchemy by the same royal hand and the Conquista d'ultramar. There was the Libro de consejos, by Sanchez IV.; and Bicerro, the armorial of the nobility, by his son, Alphonso XI. Therewith was a collection of verse of the troubadours, the songs of Aimeric de Bellinsi, Foulque de Lunel, Carbonel, Nat de Tours, and Riquier, the last of the knight-errants. Then came the poems of Juan de Mena, the Dante of Castille; the Rabelaisian relaxations of the Archbishop of Hita; the cancionero of Ausias March, that of Baena, of Stuniga, and that of Ixar.

Another book-case was filled with the French poets, from Villon to Soulary. The editions were delicious, a pleasure to hold, and many of them bore the imprint of Lemerre. Among them was the Fleurs du Mai, an unexpurgated copy, and by it were the poems of Baudelaire's decadent descendants, Paul Verlaine and Mallarmé.

There were other book-cases, and of these there was one of which the door was locked. In it were Justine and Juliette, by the Marquis de Sade; the works of Piron; the works of Beroalde de Verville; a copy of Mercius; a copy of Thérèse Philosophe; the De Arcanis Amoris; Mirabeau's Ride-au-levé; Gamaini, by Alfred de Musset and George Sand; Boccaccio; the Heptameron; Paphian Days; Crébillon's Sopha; the Erotika Biblion; the Satyricon of Petronius; an illustrated catalogue of the Naples Museum; Voltaire's Pucelle; a work or two of Diderot's; Maiseroy's Deux Amies; the Clouds; the Curée; everything, in fact, from Aristophanes to Zola.

The collection was meaningless to Maida, and she turned aside and went out on the verandah. Below, on the gravel walk, was a cat with a tail like a banner, and a neck furred like a ruff. Maida crumpled a bit of paper and threw it down. The cat jumped at it at once, toyed with it for a moment, and then, sliding backwards with a crab-like movement, its back arched, and its ears drawn down, it caught a glimpse of Maida's unfamiliar figure, and fled to the bushes with a shriek of feigned terror. A servant passed, and ignorant of Maida's presence, apostrophized the retreating feline as a loafer and a liar.

A moment later Mr. Incoul and the marquis reappeared.

"I have been admiring your Angora," Maida said, "but I fear I startled it."

The marquis rubbed his hands together thoughtfully. "It is a wonderful animal," he answered, "but it is not an Angora, it is a Thibetian cat, and though it does not talk, at least it converses. It is so odd in its ways that I called it Mistigris, as one might a familiar spirit, but my children prefer Ti-Mi; they think it more Thibetian, I fancy." He coughed slightly and looking at the points of his fingers, he added, "I will leave it with you of course."

And then Maida understood that the matter was settled and that the house was hers.

VII.
WHAT MAY BE SEEN FROM A PALCO

The installation was accomplished without difficulty. The marquis migrated to other shores and it took Maida but a short time to discover the pleasures of being luxuriously housed. The apartment which she selected for herself was composed of four rooms: there was a sitting-room in an angle with windows overlooking the sea and others that gave on a quiet street which skirted one wing of the villa. Next to it was a bed-room also overlooking the street, while back of that, on the garden side, was a bath and a dressing-room. A wide hall that was like a haunt of echoes separated these rooms from those of her husband.

Through the street, which was too steep to be much of a thoroughfare, there came each morning the clinging strain of a pastoral melody, and a pipe-playing goat-herd would pass leading his black, long-haired flock to the doors of those who bought the milk. When he had gone the silence was stirred by another sound, a call that rose and fell with exquisite sweetness and died away in infinite vibrations: it came from a little old woman, toothless and bent, who, with summer in her voice, hawked crisp gold bread of crescent shape, vaunting its delicacy in birdlike trills. There were other venders who announced their wares in similar ways, and one, a fisher, chaunted a low and mournful measure which he must have caught from the sea.

It was pleasant to be waked in this wise, Maida thought, and as she lay in her great bed of odorous wood, she listened to the calls, and when they had passed, the boom and retreating rustle of the waves occupied and lulled her. In such moments the thoughts that visited her were impermanent and fleeting. She made no effort to stay them, preferring the vague to the outlined, watching the changes and transformations of fancy as though her soul and she were separate, as were her mind a landscape, some

> Paysage choisi,
> Que vont charmant masques et bergamasques
> Jonant du luth et dansant et quasi
> Tristes sous leurs déguisements fantasques.

The room was an accomplice of her languor. The windows were curtained with filmy yellow. Before them were miniature balconies filled with flowers, and as the sun rose the light filtered through flesh-colored awnings striated with ochre. The floor was a mosaic of variegated and lacquered wood. On either side of the bed were silk rugs, sea green and pink, seductive to the foot; the ceiling was a summer sky at dawn, a fresco in cinnabar and smalt.

The Blydenburgs, less luxuriously inclined, remained at the hotel. Mr. Blydenburg had not as yet enjoyed an opportunity of conversing in Basque; he had indeed attempted to address a mildewed little girl whom he encountered one day when loitering on the cliffs, but the child had taken flight, and a mule that was pasturing on a bramble, threw back its ears, elongated its tail and curving its lips, brayed with such anguish that Mr. Blydenburg was fain to delay his studies until fortune offered a more favorable opportunity.

It was at San Sebastian, he thought, that such an opportunity would be found ready made, and on the morning of the projected excursion he was in great and expectant spirits.

The morning itself was one of those delicious forenoons that reminded one of Veronese. In the air was a caress and in the breeze an exhilaration and a tonic. In the streets and about the squares there was an unusual liveliness, much loud talking, a great many oaths, and the irritation and excitement which is the prelude to a festival. The entire summer colony seemed to be on its way to Spain.

In the court-yard of the Villa Zunzarraga four horses harnessed to a landau stood in readiness. On the box the driver glistened with smart buttons and silver braid. His coat was short, his culottes were white, his waistcoat red, and he had made himself operatic with the galloons and trappings of an eighteenth-century postilion. It was not every day in the year that he drove to a corrida. By way of preparation for the coming spectacle, Karl, who stood at the carriage door, had already engaged a palco.

When Blydenburg and Milly arrived, and the party had entered the landau, there was a brisk drive through the town and a long sweep down the Route d'Espagne than which even the Corniche is not more lovely. The vaporous Pyrenees seemed near enough to be in reach of the hand, the elms that lined the roadside were monstrous, like the elms in a Druid forest, the fields were as green as had they been painted. There were pink villas with blinds of pale yellow, white houses roofed with tiles of mottled red, gardens splendid with the scent of honeysuckle, and children, bright-eyed, clear-featured, devoured by vermin and greed, ran out in a bold, aggressive way and called for coin.

"Estamos en España!" The carriage had come to a sudden

halt. In the beauties of the landscape the journey had been forgotten. But at the driver's word there came to each of them that sudden thrill which visits every one that crosses a new frontier. Blydenburg looked eagerly about him. He had expected to be greeted by alcaldes and alguacils, he had fancied that he would view a jota, or at the very least a road-side bolero. "Are we really in Spain?" he wondered. In places of ladies in mantillas and short skirts there was a group of mangy laborers, the alcaldes and alguacils were represented by a sullen aduenaro, and the only trace of local color was in a muttered *"Coño de Dios"* that came wearily from a by-stander. Certainly they were in Spain.

The custom-house officer made a motion, and the carriage swept on. To the left was Fuenterrabia, dozing on its gulf of blue, and soon they were in Irun. There was another halt for lunch and a change of horses, and then, on again. The scenery grew wilder, and the carriage jolted, for the road was poor. They passed the Jayzquibel, the Gaïnchurisqueta, the hamlet of Lezo, Passaje, from whence Lafayette set sail; Renteria, a city outside of the year of our Lord; they crossed the Oyarzun, they passed Alza, another stream was bridged and at last the circus hove in sight.

The bull-ring of San Sebastian is sufficiently vast for a battalion to manoeuvre in at its ease. It is circled by a barrier some five feet high, back of which is another and a higher one. Between the two is a narrow passage. Above the higher barrier rise the tendidos—the stone benches of the amphitheatre—slanting upwards until they reach a gallery, in which are the gradas—the wooden benches—and directly over these, on the flooring above, are the palcos or boxes. Each box holds twenty people. They are all alike save that of the President's, which is larger, decorated with hangings and furnished with chairs, the other boxes having only seats of board. Under the President's box, and beneath the tendidos, is the toril from which the bulls are loosed. Opposite, across the arena, is the matedero, the gateway through which the horses enter and the dead are dragged out. In the passage between the two barriers are stationed the "supes," who cover up the blood, unsaddle dead horses, and attend to other matters of a similar and agreeable nature. There, too, the carpenters stand ready to repair any injury to the woodwork, and among them is a man in black, who at times issues furtively and gives a *coup de grace* to a writhing beast. There also are usually a few privileged amateurs who seek that vantage ground much as the dilettanti seek the side scenes of the theatre.

These arrangements, which it takes a paragraph to describe, are absorbed at a glance, but with that glance there comes an aftershock—a riot of color that would take a library to convey. For the moment the eye is dazzled; a myriad of multicolored fans are fluttering like fabulous butterflies; there are unimagined combinations of insolent hues; a multitude of rainbows oscillating in a deluge of light. And while the eye is dazzled the ear is bewildered, the pulse is stirred. The excitement of ten thousand people is contagious; the uproar is as deafening as the thunder of cannon. And then, at once, almost without transition, a silence. The President has come, and the most magnificent of modern spectacles is about to begin.

Almost simultaneously with the appearance of the chief magistrate of the town, the Incouls and Blydenburgs entered their box. There was a blast from a trumpet and an official in the costume known as that of Henri IV issued on horseback from the matedero. The ring which a moment before had been peopled with amateurs was emptied in a trice. The principal actor, the espada, Mazzantini, escorted by his cuadrilla and followed by the picadors, advanced to the centre of the arena and there amid an explosion of bravos, bowed with a grace like that which Talma must have possessed, first to the President, who raised his high hat in return, and then in circular wise to the spectators.

He was young and exceedingly handsome, blue of eye and clear-featured; he smiled in the contented way of one who is sure of his own powers, and the applause redoubled. The Basques have made a national idol of him, for by birth he is one of them and very popular in Guipuzcoa. He was dressed after the fashion of Figaro in the "Barbiere," his knee breeches were of vermilion silk seamed with a broad spangle, his stockings were of flesh color, he wore a short, close-fitting jacket, richly embroidered; the vest was very low but gorgeous with designs; about his waist was a scarlet sash; his shoulders were heavy with gold and on his head was a black pomponed turban, the torero variety of the Tam O'Shanter. His costume had been imitated by the chulos and banderilleros. Nothing more seductive could be imagined. They were all of them slight, lithe and agile, and behind them the picadors in the Moorish splendor of their dress looked like giants on horseback.

The President dropped from his box the key of the toril. The alguacil is supposed to catch it in his hat, but in this instance he muffed it; it was picked up by another; the alguacil fled from the ring, the picadors stationed themselves lance in hand at equal distances about the barrier, the chulos prepared their mantles, there was a ringing fanfare, the doors of the toril flew open, and a black monster with the colors of his *ganaderia* fastened to his neck shot into the arena.

If he hesitated no one knew it. There was a confused

mass of horse, bull and man, he was away again, another picador was down, and then attracted by the waving cloak of a chulo he turned and chased it across the ring. The chulo was over the fence in a second, and the bull rose like a greyhound and crossed it, too. Truly a magnificent beast. The supes and amateurs were in the ring in an instant and back again when the bull had passed. A door was opened, and surging again into the ring he swept like an avalanche on a picador, and raising him horse and all into the air flung him down as it seemed into the very pits of death. The picador was under the horse and the bull's horns were seeking him, but the brute reckoned without the espada. Mazzantini had caught him by the tail, which he twisted in such exquisite fashion that he was fain to turn, and as he turned the espada turned with him. The chulos meanwhile raised the picador over the barrier, for his legs and loins were so heavy with iron that once down he could not rise unassisted. Across the arena a horse lay quivering in a bath of gore, his feet entangled in his entrails, and another, unmounted, staggered along dyeing the sand with zigzags of the blood that spouted, fountain-like, from his breast. And over all was the tender blue of the sky of Spain.

When Mazzantini loosed his hold, he stood a moment, folded his arms, gave the bull a glance of contempt, turned on his heel and sauntered away. The applause was such as no *cabotin* has ever received. It was the delirious plaudits of ten thousand people drunk with the sun, with excitement—intoxicated with blood. Mazzantini bowed as calmly as were he a tenor, whose *ut de poitrine* had found appreciation in the stalls. And while the applause still lasted, the bull caught the staggering, blindfolded, unprotected horse and tossed him sheer over the barrier, and would have jumped after him had he not perceived a fourth picador ambling cautiously with pointed lance. At him he made a fresh rush, but the picador's lance was in his neck and held him away. He broke loose, however, and with an under lunge disemboweled the shuddering horse.

There was another blast of the trumpets, the signal for the banderilleros whose office it is to plant barbs in the neck of the bull—a delicate operation, for the banderillero must face the bull, and should he trip he is dead. This ceremony is seldom performed until the bull shows signs of weariness; then the barbs act like a tonic. In this instance the bull seemed as fresh as were he on his native heath, and the spectators were clamorous in their indignation. They called for more horses; they accused the management of economy; men stood up and shook their fists at the President; it was for him to order out fresh steeds, and, as he sat impassible, *pollice verso*, as one may say, they shouted *"Fuego al presidente, perro de presidente"* —dog of a president; set him on fire. And there were cat-calls and the screech of tin horns, and resounding and noisy insults, until the general attention was diverted by the pose of the banderilleros and the leaping and kicking of the bull, seeking to free his neck from the torturing barbs. At last, when he had been punctured eight times, he sought the centre of the ring, and stood there almost motionless, his tufted tail swaying nervously, his tongue lolling from his mouth, a mist of vapor circling from his nostrils, seething about his splendid horns and wrinkled neck, and in his great eyes a look of wonder, as though amazed that men could be cruder than he.

Again the trumpets sounded. Mazzantini, with a sword concealed in a muleta of bright scarlet silk, and accompanied by the chulos, approached him. The chulos flaunted their vivid cloaks, and when the bull, roused by the hated colors to new indignation, turned to chase them, they slipped aside and in the centre of the ring stood a young man dressed as airily as a dancer in a ballet, in a costume that a pin would have perforated, and before him a maddened and a gigantic brute.

In a second the bull was on him, but in that second a tongue of steel leaped from the muleta, glittered like a silver flash in the air, and straight over the lowered horns it swept and then cleaved down through the parting flesh and touched the spring of life. At the very feet of the espada the bull fell; he had not lost a drop of blood; it was the supreme expression of tauromaquia, the recognition that skill works from force.

And then the applause! There was a whirl of hats and cigars and cigarettes, and had San Sebastian been richer there would have been a shower of coin. Women kissed their hands and men held out their arms to embrace him. It was the delirium of appreciation. And Mazzantini saluted and bowed and smiled. He was quite at home, and calmer and more tranquil than any spectator. Suddenly there was a rush of caparisoned mules, ropes were attached to the dead horses, the bull was dragged out, the blood was concealed with sand, the toilet of the ring was made, the trumpets sounded and the last act of the first of the wonderful cycle of dramas was done.

There were five more bulls to be killed that day, but with their killing the action with which these pages have to deal need not be further delayed. From the box in the sombra Mr. Incoul had watched the spectacle with unemotional curiosity. Blydenburg, who had fortified himself with the contents of a pocket flask, manifested his earliest delight by shouting Bravo, but with such a disregard of the first syllable, and such an explosion of the second, that Mr. Incoul mistaking the applause for an imitation of the bark of a dog had at last begged him to desist.

The adjoining box was crowded, and among the occupants was a delicious young girl, with the Orient in her eyes, and lips that said Drink me. To her the spectacle was evidently one of alluring pathos. *"Pobre caballo,"* she would murmur when a horse fell, and then with her fan she would hide the bridge of her nose as though that were her organ of vision. But no matter how high the fan might be raised she always managed to see, and with the seeing there came from her compassionate little noises, a mingling of *"ay"* and *"Dios mio,"* that was most agreeable to listen to. Miss Blydenburg, who sat so near her that she might have touched her elbow, took these little noises for signals and according to their rise and fall learned when and when not to look down into the terrible ring below.

In the momentary intermission that occurred after the duel between the espada and the first bull, a mozo, guided by Karl, appeared in the box bearing with him cool liquids from the caverns beneath. Blydenburg, whose throat was parched with brandy and the strain of his incessant shouts, swallowed a naranjada at a gulp. Mr. Incoul declined to take anything, but the ladies found much refreshment in a concoction of white almonds which affects the tonsils as music affects the ear.

It was not until this potion had been absorbed that Maida began to take any noticeable interest. She had been fatigued by the drive, enervated by the heat, and the noise and clamor was certainly not in the nature of a sedative. But the almonds brought her comfort. She changed her seat from the rear of the box to the front, and sat with one arm on the balustrade, her hand supporting her delicate chin, and as her eyes followed the prowess of the bull she looked like some fair Pasiphae in modern guise.

It must have been the novelty of the scene that interested her. The light, the unusual and brilliant costumes, the agility of the actors, and the wonder of the sky, entered, probably, as component parts into any pleasure that she experienced. Certainly it could have been nothing else, for she was quick to avert her eyes whenever blood seemed imminent. The second bull, however, was far less active than the first. He had indeed accomplished a certain amount of destruction, but his attacks were more perfunctory than angered, and it was not until he had been irritated by the colored barbs that he displayed any lively sense of resentment. Then one of the banderilleros showed himself either awkward or timid; he may have been both; in any event his success was slight, and as the Spanish audience is not indulgent, he was hissed and hooted at. "Give him a pistol," cried some—the acme of sarcasm—*"Torero de las marinas,"* cried others. He was offered a safe seat in the tendidos. One group adjured the President to order his instant imprisonment. One might have thought that the tortures of the Inquisition could not be too severe for such a lout as he.

Maida, who was ignorant of the duties of a banderillero, looked down curiously at the gesticulating crowd below. The cause of their indignation she was unable to discover, and was about to turn to Mr. Blydenburg for information, when there came a singing in her ears. The question passed unuttered from her thoughts. The ring, the people, the sky itself had vanished. Near the toril, on a bench of stone, was Lenox Leigh.

VIII.
An Unexpected Guest

Gradually the whirling ceased, the singing left her ears. Leigh raised his hat and Maida bowed in return. His eyes lingered on her a moment, and then he turned and disappeared.

"A friend of mine, Mr. Leigh, is down there," the girl announced. Her husband looked over the rail. "He's gone," she added. "I fancy he is coming up here."

"Who's coming?" Blydenburg inquired, for he had caught the words.

"A friend of my wife's," Mr. Incoul answered. "A man named Leigh—do you know him?"

"Mrs. Manhattan's brother, isn't he? No, I don't know him, but Milly does, I think. Don't you, Milly?"

Milly waved her head vaguely. She indeed knew the young man in question, but she was not overconfident that he had ever been more than transiently aware of her maidenly existence. She had, however, no opportunity to formulate her uncertainty in words. There was a rap on the door and Leigh entered.

Mr. Incoul rose as becomes a host. The young man bowed collectively to him and the Blydenburgs. He touched Maida's hand and found a seat behind her. A bull-fight differs from an opera in many things, but particularly in this, that there may be exclamations, but there is no attempt at continuous conversation. Lenox Leigh, though not one to whom custom is law, said little during the rest of the performance. Now and then he bent forward to Maida, but whatever he may have said his remarks were fragmentary and casual. This much Miss Blydenburg noticed, and she noticed also that Maida appeared more interested in her glove than in the spectacle in the ring.

When the sixth and last bull had been vanquished and the crowd was leaving the circus, Mr. Incoul turned to his guest, " We are to dine at the Inglaterra, will you not join us?"

"Thank you," Lenox answered, "I shall be glad to. I came here in the train and I have had nothing since morning. I have been ravenous for hours, so much so," he added lightly, "that I have been trying to poison my hunger by thinking of the dishes that I dislike the most, beer soup, for instance, stewed snails, carp cooked in sweetmeats or unseasoned salads of cactus hearts."

"I don't know," Mr. Incoul answered gravely, "I don't know what we will have to-night. The dinner was ordered last week. They may have cooked it then."

"Possibly they did. On a *fiesta* San Sebastian is impossible. There are seven thousand strangers here to-day and the accommodations are insufficient for a third of them."

"I want to know—" exclaimed Blydenburg, always anxious for information. They had moved out of the box and aided by the crowd were drifting slowly down the stair.

At the *salida* Karl stood waiting to conduct them to the carriage.

"If you will get in with the ladies," said Mr. Incoul, "Blydenburg and myself will walk. The hotel can't be far."

To this proposal the young man objected. He had been

sitting all day, he explained, and preferred to stretch his legs. He may have had other reasons, but if he had he said nothing of them. At once, then, it was arranged that the ladies, under Karl's protection, should drive to the Inglaterra, and that the others should follow on foot.

Half an hour later the entire party were seated at a table overlooking the Concha. The sun had sunk into the ocean as though it were imbibing an immense blue syrup. On either side of the bay rose miniature mountains, Orgullo and Igueldo tiara'd with fortresses and sloped with green. To the right in the distance was a great unfinished casino, and facing it, beneath Orgullo, was a cluster of white ascending villas. The dusk was sudden. The sky after hesitating between salmon and turquoise had chosen a lapis lazuli, which it changed to indigo, and with that for flooring the stars came out and danced.

The dinner passed off very smoothly. In spite of his boasted hunger, Lenox ate but sparingly. He was frugal as a Spaniard, and in the expansion which the heavy wine of the country will sometimes cause, Mr. Blydenburg declared that he looked like one. Each of the party had his or her little say about the corrida and its emotions, and Blydenburg, after discoursing with much learning on the subject, declared, to whomsoever would listen, that for his part he regretted the gladiators of Rome. As a topic, the bull-fight was inexhaustible. Every thread of conversation led back to it, and necessarily, in the course of the meal, Lenox was asked how it was that he happened to be present.

"I arrived at Biarritz from Paris last night," he explained, "and when I learned this morning that there was to be a bull-fight, I was not in a greater hurry to do anything else than to buy a ticket and take the train."

"Was it crowded?" Blydenburg asked in his florid way.

"Rather. It was comfortable enough till we reached Irun, but there I got out for a Spanish cigar, and when I returned, the train was so packed that I was obliged to utilize a first-class ticket in a third-class car. None of the people who lunched at the buffet were able to get back. I suppose three hundred were left. There was almost a riot. The station master said that Irun was the head of the line, and to reserve a seat one must sit in it. Of course those who had seats were hugely amused at those who had none. One man, a Frenchman, bullied the station-master dreadfully. He said it was every kind of an outrage; that he ought to put on more cars; that he was incompetent; that he was imbecile; that he didn't know his business. 'It's the law,' said the station-master. 'I don't care that for your law!' cried the Frenchman. 'But the Préfet, sir.' 'To blazes with your Préfet!;' But that was too strong. The Frenchman might abuse what he saw fit, but the Préfet evidently was sacred. I suppose it was treasonable to speak of him in that style. In any event, the station-master called up a file of soldiers and had the Frenchman led away. The onlookers were simply frantic with delight. If the Frenchman had only been shot before their eyes it would indeed have been a charming prelude to a bullfight." And then with an air that suggested retrospects of unexpressed regret, he added pensively, "I have never seen a man shot."

"No?" said Milly, boldly; "no more have I. Not that I want to, though," she hastened to explain. "It must be horrid."

Lenox looked up at her and then his eyes wandered to Maida, and rested caressingly in her own. But the caress was transient. Immediately he turned and busied himself with his plate.

"Are you to be in Biarritz long?" Mr. Incoul asked. The

tone was perfectly courteous, friendly, even, but at the moment from the very abruptness of the question Lenox feared that the caress had been intercepted and something of the mute drama divined. Mentally he arranged Mr. Incoul as one constantly occupied in repeating *J'ai de bon tabac, tun'n auras pas*, and it was his design to disarm that gentleman of any suspicion he might harbor that his good tobacco, in this instance at least, was an envied possession or one over which he would be called to play the sentinel. The rôle of *mari sage* was frequent enough on the Continent, but few knew better than Lenox Leigh that it is rarely enacted in the States, and his intuitions had told him long before that it was one for which Mr. Incoul was ill adapted. Yet between the mart sage and the suspicionless husband there is a margin, and it was on that margin that Lenox determined that Mr. Incoul should tread. "No," he answered at once, and without any visible sign of preoccupation. "No, a day or two at most; I am on my way to Andalucia."

BIydenburg, as usual, was immediately interested. "It's very far, isn't it? " he panted.

"Not so far as it used to be. Nowadays one can go all the way in a sleeping car. Gautier, who discovered it, had to go in a stage-coach, which must have been tedious. But in spite of the railways the place is pretty much the same as it has been ever since the Middle Ages. Even the cholera has been unable to banish the local color. There are trains in Seville precisely as there are steamboats on the Grand Canal. But the sky is the same, and in the Sierra Morena there are still Moors and as yet no advertisements."

"You have been there then?"

"Yes, I was there some years ago. You ought to go yourself. I know of nothing so fabulous in its beauty. It is true I was there in the spring, but the autumn ought not to be a bad time to go. The country is parched perhaps, but then you would hardly camp out."

"What do you say, Incoul?" Blydenburg asked. "Wouldn't you like it?" he inquired of Maida.

"I could tell better when we get there," she answered; "but we might go," she added, looking at her husband.

"Why," said Blydenburg, "we could see Madrid and Burgos and Valladolid. It's all in the way."

Lenox interrupted him. "They are tiresome cities though, and gloomy to a degree. Valladolid and Burgos are like congeries of deserted prisons, Madrid is little different from any other large city. Fuenterrabia, next door here, is a thousand times more interesting. It is Cordova you should visit and Ronda and Granada and Sevilla and Cadix." And, as he uttered the names of these cities, he aromatized each of them with an accent that threw Blydenburg into stupors of admiration. Pronounced in that way they seemed worth visiting indeed.

"Which of them do you like the best?"

"I liked them all," Lenox answered, " I liked each of them best."

"But which is the most beautiful?"

"That depends on individual taste. I prefer Ronda, but Granada, I think, is most admired. If you will let me, I will quote a high authority:

> "'Grenade efface en tout ses rivales; Grenade
> Chante plus mollement la molle sérénade:
> Elle peint ses maisons des plus riches couleurs,
> Et l'on dit, que les vents suspendent leurs haleines,
> Quand, par un soir d'été, Grenade dans ses plaines,
> Répand ses femmes et ses fleurs.'"

In private life, verse is difficult of recitation, but Lenox recited well. He made such music of the second line that there came with his voice the sound of guitars; the others he delivered with the vowels full as one hears them at the Comedie, and therewith was a little pantomime so explanatory and suggestive that Blydenburg, whose knowledge of French was of the most rudimentary description, understood it all, and, in consequence, liked the young man the better.

The dinner was done, and they moved out on the terrace. The moon had chased the stars, the Concha glittered with lights, and before the hotel a crowd circled in indolent coils as though wearied with the holiday. There were many people, too, on the terrace, and in passing from the dining-room the little party, either by accident or design, got cut in twain. For the first time since the spring evening, Maida and Lenox were alone. Their solitude, it is true, was public, but that mattered little.

Maida utilized the earliest moment by asking her companion how he got there. "You should not have spoken to me," she added, before he could have answered.

"Maida!"

"No, you must go, you —"

"But I only came to find you," he whispered.

"To find me? How did you know where I was?"

"The *Morning News* told me. I was in Paris, on my way to Baden, for I heard you were there, and then, of course, when I saw in the paper that you were here, I followed after."

"Then you are not going to Andalucia?"

"No, not unless you do."

The girl wrung her hand. "Oh, Lenox, do go away!"

"I can't, nor do you wish it. You must let me see you. I

will come to you tomorrow—he has an excellent voice, not so full as Gayarre's, but his method is better."

Mr. Incoul had suddenly approached them, and as suddenly Lenox's tone had changed. To all intents and purposes he was relating the merits of a tenor.

"The carriage is here," said Maida's husband, "we must be going; I am sorry we can't offer you a seat, Mr. Leigh, we are a trifle crowded as it is."

"Thank you, you are very kind. The train will take me safely enough."

He walked with them to the carriage, and aided Maida to enter it. Karl, who had been standing at the door, mounted to the box. When all were seated, Mr. Incoul added: "You must come and see us."

"Yes, come and see us, too," Blydenburg echoed. "By the way, where are you stopping?"

"I shall be glad to do so," Lenox answered; "I am at the Grand." He raised his hat and wished them a pleasant drive. The moon was shining full in his face, and Miss Blydenburg thought him even handsomer than Mazzantini. His good wishes were answered in chorus, Karl nudged the driver, and in a moment the carriage swept by and left him standing in the road.

"What a nice, frank fellow he is," Blydenburg began; "so different from the general run of young New Yorkers. There, I forgot to tell him I knew his sister; I am sorry, it would have seemed sort of friendly, made him feel more at home, don't you think? Not but that he seemed perfectly at his ease as it was. I wonder why he doesn't marry? None of those Leighs have money, have they? He could pick up an heiress, though, in no time, if he wanted to. Perhaps he prefers to be a bachelor. If he does I don't blame him a bit, a good-looking young fellow—"

And so the amiable gentleman rambled on. After a while finding that the reins of conversation were solely in his own hands, he took the fullest advantage of his position and discoursed at length on the bullfight, its history, its possibilities, the games of the Romans, how they fared under the Goths, what improvements came with the Moors, and wound up by suggesting an immediate visit to Fuenterrabia.

For the moment no enthusiasm was manifested. Mr. Incoul admitted that he would like to go, but the ladies said nothing, and presently the two men planned a little excursion by themselves.

Miss Blydenburg had made herself comfortable and fallen into a doze, but Maida sat watching the retreating uplands with unseeing eyes. Her thoughts had wandered, the visible was lost to her. Who knows what women see or the dreams and regrets that may come to the most matter-of-fact? Not long ago at the opera, in a little Italian town, the historian noticed an old lady, one who looked anything but sentimental, for that matter rather fierce than otherwise, but who, when Cherubino had sung his enchanting song, brushed away a furtive and unexpected tear. *Voi che sapete* indeed! Perhaps to her own cost she had learned and was grieving dumbly then over some ashes that the strain had stirred, and it is not impossible that as Maida sat watching the retreating uplands her own thoughts had circled back to an earlier summer when first she learned what Love might be.

IX.
MR. INCOUL DINES IN SPAIN.

On the morrow Mr. Blydenburg consulted his guide-books. The descriptions of Fuenterrabia were vague but alluring. The streets, he learned, were narrow; the roofs met; the houses were black with age; the doors were heavy with armorials; the windows barred—in short, a mediæval burg that slept on a blue gulf and let Time limp by unmarked. Among the inhabitants were some, he found, who accommodated travelers. The inns, it is true, were unstarred, but the names were so rich in suggestion that the neglect was not noticed. Mr. Blydenburg had never passed a night in Spain, and he felt that he would like to do so. This desire he succeeded in awakening in Mr. Incoul, and together they agreed to take an afternoon train, explore the town, pass the evening at the Casino and return to Biarritz the next morning. The programme thus arranged was put into immediate execution; two days after the bullfight they were again on their way to the frontier, and, as the train passed out of the station on its southern journey, Maida and Lenox Leigh were preparing for a stroll on the sands.

There is at Biarritz a division of the shore which, starting from the ruins of a corsair's castle, extends on to Saint-Jean-de-Luz. It is known as the Cote des Basques. On one side are the cliffs, on the other the sea, and between the two is a broad avenue which almost disappears when the tide is high. The sand is fine as face powder, *nuance* Rachel, packed hard. From the cliffs the view is delicious: in the distance are the mountains curving and melting in the haze; below, the ocean, spangled at the edges, is of a milky blue. Seen from the shore, the sea has the color of absinthe, an opalescent green, entangled and fringed with films of white; here the mountains escape in the perspective, and as the sun sinks the cliffs glitter. At times the sky is flecked with little clouds that dwindle and fade into spirals of pink; at others great masses rise sheer against the horizon, as might the bastions of Titan homes; and again are gigantic cathedrals, their spires lost in azure, their turrets swooning in excesses of vermilion grace. The only sound is from the waves, but few come to listen. The Côte des Basques is not fashionable with the summer colony; it is merely beautiful and solitary.

It was on the downs that Maida and Lenox first chose to walk, but after a while a sloping descent invited them to the shore below. Soon they rounded a projecting cliff, and Biarritz was hidden from them. The background was chalk festooned with green; afar were the purple outlines of the Pyrenees, and before them the ocean murmured its temptations of couch and of tomb.

They had been talking earnestly with the egotism of people to whom everything save self is landscape. The encircling beauty in which they walked had not left them unimpressed, yet the influence had been remote and undiscerned; the effect had been that of accessories. But now they were silent, for the wonder of the scene was upon them.

Presently Maida, finding a stone conveniently placed, sat down on the sand and used the stone for a back. Lenox threw himself at her feet. From the downs above there came now and then the slumberous tinkle of a bell, but so faintly that it fused with the rustle of the waves; no one heard it save a little girl who was tending cattle and who knew by the tinkle where each of her charges browsed. She was a ragged child, barefooted and not very wise; she was afraid of strangers with the vague fear that children have. And at times during the summer, when tourists crossed the downs where her cattle were, she would hide till they had passed.

On this afternoon she had been occupying herself with blades of grass, which she threw in the air and watched float down to the shore below, but at last she had wearied of this amusement and was about to turn and bully the cows in the shrill little voice which was hers, when Maida and her companion appeared on the scene. The child felt almost secure; nothing but a bird could reach her from the shore and of birds she had no fear, and so, being curious and not very much afraid, she watched the couple with timid, inquisitive eyes.

For a long time she watched and for a long time they remained motionless in the positions which they had first chosen. At times the sound of their voices reached her. She wished she were a little nearer that she might hear what they said. She had never seen people sit on the beach before, though she had heard that people sometimes did so, all night, too, and that they were called smugglers. But somehow the people beneath her did not seem to belong to that category. For a moment she thought that they might be guarding the coast, and at that thought an inherent instinctive fear of officials beat in her small breast. She had indeed heard of female smugglers; there was her own aunt, for instance; but no, she had never heard of a coast-guard in woman's clothes. That idea had to be dismissed, and so she wondered and watched until she forgot all about them, and turned her attention to a white sail in the open.

The white sail fainted in sheets of cobalt. The sun which had neared the horizon was dying in throes of crimson and gamboge. It was time she knew to drive the cattle home. She stood up and brushed her hair aside, and as she did so, her eyes fell again on the couple below. The man had moved; he was not lying as he had been with his back to the bluff; he was kneeling by his companion, her head was on his shoulder, her arms were about his neck, and his mouth was close to hers. The little maid smiled knowingly; she had seen others in much the same attitude; the mystery was dissolved; they were neither guards nor smugglers—they were lovers; and she ran on at once through the bramble and called shrilly to the cows.

The excursionists, meanwhile, had reached Hendaye and had been ferried across the stream that flows between it and Fuenterrabia. At the landing they were met by a gentleman in green and red who muttered some inquiry. The boatman undid the straps of the valise which they bore, and this rite accomplished, the gentleman in green and red looked idly in them and turned as idly away. The boatman shouldered the valises again, and started for the inn.

Mr. Incoul and his friend were both men to whom the visible world exists and they followed with lingering surprise. They ascended a sudden slope, bordered on one side by a high white wall in which lizards played, and which they assumed was the wall of some monastery, but which they learned from the boatman concealed a gambling-house, and soon entered a small grass-grown plaza. To the right was a church, immense, austere; to the left were some mildewed dwellings; from an upper window a man with a crimson turban looked down with indifferent eyes and abruptly a bird sang.

From the plaza they entered the main street and soon were at the inn. Mr. Incoul and Blydenburg were both men to whom the visible world exists, but they were also men to whom the material world has much significance. In the hall of the inn a chicken and two turkeys clucked with fearless composure. The public room was small, close and full of insects. At a rickety table an old man, puffy and scornful, was quarreling with himself on the subject of a *peseta* which he held in his hand. The inn-keeper, a frowsy female, emerged from some remoter den, eyed them with unmollifiable suspicion and disappeared.

"We can't stop here," said Blydenburg with the air of a man denying the feasibility of a trip to the moon.

On inquiry they learned that the town contained nothing better. At the Casino there were roulette tables, but no beds. Travelers usually stopped at Hendaye or at Irun.

"Then we will go back to Biarritz."

They sent their valises on again to the landing place and then set out in search of Objects of Interest. The palace of Charlemagne scowled at them in a tottering, impotent way. When they attempted to enter the church, a chill caught them neck and crop and forced them back. For some time they wandered about in an aimless, unguided fashion, yet whatever direction they chose that direction led them firmly back to the landing place. At last they entered the Casino.

The grounds were charming, a trifle unkempt perhaps, the walks were not free from weeds, but the air was as heavy with the odor of flowers as a perfumery shop in Bond street. In one alley, in a bower of trees, was a row of tables; the covers were white and the glassware unexceptionable.

"We could dine here," Blydenburg said in a self-examining way. A pretty girl of the manola type, dressed like a soubrette in a vaudeville, approached and decorated his lapel with a tube-rose. "We certainly can dine here," he repeated.

The girl seemed to divine the meaning of his words. "*Ciertamente, Caballero*," she lisped.

Mr. Blydenburg had never been called *Caballero* before, and he liked it. "What do you say, Incoul?" he asked.

"I am willing, order it now if you care to."

But the ordering was not easy. Mr. Blydenburg had never studied pantomime, and his gestures were more indicative of a patient describing a toothache to a dentist than of an American citizen ordering an evening meal. "*Kayry-Oostay*," he repeated, and then from some abyss of memory he called to his aid detached phrases in German.

The girl laughed blithely. Her mouth was like a pomegranate cut in twain. She took a thin book bound in morocco from the table and handed it to the unhappy gentleman. It was, he found, a list of dishes and of wines. In his excitement, he pointed one after another to three different soups, and then waving the book at the girl as who should say, "I leave the rest to you," he dared Mr. Incoul to go into the Casino and break the bank for an appetizer.

The Casino, a low building of leprous white, stood in the centre of the garden. At the door, a lackey, in frayed, ill-fitting livery, took their sticks and gave them numbered checks in exchange. The gambling-room was on the floor above, and occupied the entire length of the house. There, about a roulette table, a dozen men were seated playing in a cheap and vicious way for small stakes. They looked exactly what they were, and nothing worse can be said of them. "A den of thieves in a miniature paradise," thought Mr. Blydenburg, and his fancy was so pleasured with the phrase that he determined to write a letter to the *Evening Post*, in which, with that for title, he would give a description of Fuenterrabia. He found a seat and began to play. Mr. Incoul looked on for a moment and then sought the reading-room. When he returned Blydenburg had a heap of counters before him.

"I have won all that!" he exclaimed exultingly. He looked at his watch, it was after seven. He cashed the counters and together they went down again to the garden.

The dinner was ready. They had one soup, not three, and other dishes of which no particular mention is necessary. But therewith was a bottle of Val de Penas, a wine so delicious that a temperance lecturer suffering from hydrophobia would have drunk of it. The manola with the pomegranate mouth fluttered near them, and toward the close of the meal Mr. Blydenburg chucked her under the chin. "Nice girl that," he announced complacently.

"I dare say," his friend answered, "but I have never been able to take an interest in women of that class."

Blydenburg was flushed with winnings and wine. He did not notice the snub and proceeded to relate an after-dinner story of that kind in which men of a certain age are said to luxuriate. Mr. Incoul listened negligently.

"God knows," he said at last, "I am not a Puritan, but I like refinement, and refinement and immorality are incompatible."

"Fiddlesticks! Look at London, look at Paris, New York even; there are women whom you and I both know, women in the very best society, of whom all manner of things are said and known. You may call them immoral if you want to, but you cannot say that they are not refined."

"I say this, were I related in any way, were I the brother, father, the husband of such a woman, I would wring her neck. I believe in purity in women, and I believe also in purity in men."

"Yes, it's a good thing to believe in, but it's hard to find."

Mr. Incoul had spoken more vehemently than was his wont, and to this remark he made no answer. His eyes were green, not the green of the cat but the green of a tiger, and as he sat with fingers clinched, and a cheerless smile on his thin lips, he looked a modern hunter of the Holy Grail.

The night train leaves Hendaye a trifle after ten, and soon a *sereno* was heard calling the hour, and declaring that all was well. It was time to be going, they knew, and without further delay they had themselves ferried again across the stream. The return journey was unmarked by adventure or incident. Mr. Blydenburg fell into a doze, and after dreaming of the pomegranate mouth awoke at Biarritz, annoyed that he had not thought to address the manola in Basque. At the station they found a carriage, and, as Blydenburg entered it, he made with himself a little consolatory pact that some day he would go back to Fuenterrabia alone.

The station at Biarritz is several miles from the town, and as the horses were slow it was almost twelve o'clock before the Continental was reached. Blydenburg alighted there and Mr. Incoul drove on alone to the villa. As he approached it he saw that his wife's rooms were illuminated. For the moment he thought she might be waiting for him, but at once he knew that was impossible, for on leaving he had said he would pass the night in Spain.

The carriage drew up before the main entrance. He felt for small money to pay the driver, but found nothing smaller than a louis. The driver, after a protracted fumbling, declared that in the matter of change he was not a bit better of. Where is the cabman who was ever supplied? Rather than waste words Mr. Incoul gave him the louis and the man drove off, delighted to find that the old trick was still in working order.

Mr. Incoul looked up again at his wife's window, but during his parley with the driver the lights had been extinguished. He entered the gate and opened the door with a key. The hall was dark; he found a match and lit it. On the stair was Lenox Leigh. The match flickered and went out, but through the open door the moon poured in.

The young man rubbed his hat as though uncertain what to do or say. At last he reached the door, "I am at the Grand, you know," he hazarded.

"Yes, I know," Mr. Incoul answered, "and I hope you are comfortable."

Leigh passed out. Mr. Incoul closed and bolted the door behind him. For a moment he stood very still. Then turning, he ascended the stair.

X.
THE POINT OF VIEW

On leaving the villa Lenox Leigh experienced a number of conflicting emotions, and at last found relief in sleep. The day that followed he passed in chambered solitude; it was possible that some delegate from Mr. Incoul might wish to exchange a word with him, and in accordance with the unwritten statutes of what is seemly, it behooved him to be in readiness for the exchange of that word. Moreover, he was expectant of a line from Maida, some word indicative of the course of conduct which he should pursue, some message, in fact, which would aid him to rise from the uncertainty in which he groped. As a consequence he remained in his room. He was not one to whom solitude is irksome, indeed he had often found it grateful in its refreshment, but to be enjoyable solitude should not be coupled with suspense; in that case it is uneasiness magnified by the infinite. And if fear be analyzed, what is it save the dread of the unknown? When the nerves are unstrung a calamity is often a tonic. The worst that can be has been done, the blow has fallen, and with the falling fear vanishes, hope returns, the healing process begins at once.

The uneasiness which visited Lenox Leigh came precisely from his inability to determine whether or not a blow was impending. As to the blow, he cared, in the abstract, very little. It it were to be given, let it be dealt and be done with; that which alone troubled him was his ignorance of what had ensued after his meeting with Mr. Incoul, and his incapacity to foresee in what manner the consequences of that meeting would affect his relations with Mr. Incoul's wife.

In this uncertainty he looked at the matter from every side, and, that he might get the broadest view, he recalled the incidents connected with the meeting. The facts of the case seemed then to resolve themselves into this: Mr. Incoul had unexpectedly returned to his home after midnight, and had met a friend of his wife's descending the stair. Their greeting, if formal, had been perfectly courteous. The departing guest had informed the returning husband at what hotel he was stopping, and that gentleman had expressed the hope that he was comfortable. Certainly there was nothing extraordinary in that. People who dwelled in recondite regions might see impropriety in a call that extended up to and beyond midnight, whereas others who lived in more liberal centres might consider it the most natural thing in the world. It was, then, merely the point of view, and what was the point of view which Mr. Incoul had adopted? If he considered it an impropriety why had he seemed so indifferent? And, if he considered it natural and proper, why should he have been so damned civil? Why should he have expressed the hope that his wife's guest was comfortable at a hotel? Was the expression of that hope merely a commonplace rejoinder, or was it an intentional slur? Surely, every one possessed of the brain of a medium-sized rabbit feels that it is as absurd to expect an intelligent being to be comfortable in a hotel as it is to suppose that he can find enjoyment in an evening party or amusement in a comic paper. Then again, and this, after all, was the great question: was the return of Mr. Incoul intentional or accidental? If it was intentional, if he had gone away intending that he would be absent all night merely that by an unexpected return he might verify any suspicions which he may have harbored, then in driving to his door in a rumbling coach he had shown himself a very poor plotter. On the other hand, if the return were accidental had it served to turn a suspicionless husband into a suspicious one, and if it had so served, how far did those suspicions extend? Did he think that his wife and her guest had been occupied with aimless chit-chat, or did he believe that their conversation had been of a personal and intimate nature?

As Lenox pondered over these things it seemed to him that, let Mr. Incoul suspect what he might, the one and unique cause for apprehension lay in the attitude which Maida had assumed when her husband, after closing the door, had gone to her in search of an explanation. That he had so gone there was to him no possible doubt. And it was in the expectancy of tidings as to the result of that explanation that he waited the entire day in his room.

But the afternoon waned into dusk and still no tidings came. As the hours wore on his uneasiness decreased. "Bah!" he muttered to himself at last, "in the winter I gave all my mornings to Pyrrho and Ænesidemus, and here six months later during an entire day I bother myself about eventualities."

He sighed wearily with an air of self-disgust, and rising from the sofa on which his meditations had been passed he went to the window. The Casino opposite was already illuminated. "They will be there to-night," he thought. "I have been a fool for my pains. If Maida hasn't written it is because there has been nothing to write. I will look them up after dinner and everything will be as before." He took off his morning suit and got himself into evening dress. He tied his white cravat without emotion, with a precision that was geometric in its accuracy, and to hold the tie in place he ran a silver pin through the collar without so much as pricking his neck. He was thoroughly at ease. The fear of the blow had passed. Pyrrho, Ænesidemus, the whole corps of ataraxists had surged suddenly and rescued him from the toils of the inscrutable.

At a florist's in the street below he found an orchid with which he decked his button-hole, and then in search of dinner he sauntered into Helder's, a restaurant on the main street, a trifle above the Grand Hotel. It was crowded; there did not seem to be a single table unoccupied. He hesitated for a moment, and was about to go elsewhere when he noticed some one signaling to him from the remoter end of the garden. He could not at first make out who it was and it was not until he had made use of a monocle that he recognized a fellow Baltimorean, Mr. Clarence May, with whom in days gone by he had been on terms approaching those of intimacy.

Mr. Clarence May, more familiarly known as Clara, was a pigeon-shooter who for some years past had been promenading the side scenes of continental life. He was well known in the penal colonies of the Riviera, and hand-in-glove with some of the most distinguished *rastaquouères*, yet did he happen in a proscenium it was by accident. In appearance he was not beautiful: he was a meagre little man, possessed of vague features and an allowance of sandy hair so undetermined that few were able to remember whether or not he wore any on his face. When he spoke it was with a slight stutter, a trick of speech which he declared he had inherited from his wet-nurse.

He rose from his seat, and hurrying forward, greeted Lenox as though he had seen him the week before. He was anything but an idealist, yet he treated Time as though it were the veriest fiction of the non-existent, and he bombarded no one with questions as to what had become of them, or where had they been.

"I have just ordered dinner," he said, in his amusing stammer, "you must share it with me." And Lenox, who had not a prejudice to his name, accepted the invitation as readily as it was made.

"I don't know," May continued, when they were seated—"I don't know whether you will like the dinner—I have ordered very little. No soup, too hot, don't you think? No oysters, there are none; all out visiting, the man said; for fish I have substituted a melon; fish, at the seaside, is never good; then we are to have white truffles, with a plain sauce, a chateaubriand, salad, a bit of cheese—*voila!* How will that suit you?"

Lenox nodded, as who should say, had I ordered it myself it could not be more to my taste, and thus encouraged, May offered him a glass of Amer Picon, a beverage that smells like an orange and looks like ink.

The dinner passed off pleasantly enough. The white truffles were excellent, and the Chateaubriand cooked to a turn. The only fault to be found was with the Brie, which May seemed to think was not as flowing as it should be.

"By the way," he said at last when coffee was served, "you know Mirette is here?"

"Mirette? Who is Mirette?"

"Why, good gad! My dear fellow, Mirette is Mirette; the one adorable, unique, divine Mirette. You don't mean to say you never heard of her!"

"I do, though perhaps she may have had the good fortune to hear of me."

"Heavens alive, man! don't you read the papers?"

Lenox smiled. "Why should I? I am not interested in the community. It might be stricken with dry-rot, elephantiasis and plica polonica for ought I care. Besides, there is nothing in them; the English papers are all advertisements and aridity, the French are frivolous and obscene. I mind neither frivolity nor obscenity; both have their uses, as flowers and cesspools have theirs; but I object to them served with my breakfast. I think if once a year a man would read a summary of the twelvemonth, he would get in ten minutes a digest of all that might be necessary to know, and what is more to the point, he would have to his credit a clear profit of two hundred hours at the very least, and two hundred hours rightly employed are sufficient for the acquirement of such a knowledge of a foreign language as will permit a man to make love in it gracefully. No, I seldom read the papers, so forgive my ignorance as to Mirette."

"After such an explanation I shall have to. But if you care to learn by word of mouth that which you decline to read in print, Mirette is *premier sujet.*"

"In the ballet, you mean."

"Yes, in the ballet, and I can't for the life of me think of a ballet without her."

"She must have gone to your head."

"And to every one's who has seen her."

"You say she is here?"

"Yes, she'll be at the Casino to-night; I'll present you if you say so."

"I might take a look at her, but I fancy I shall be occupied elsewhere."

"As you like." May drew out his watch. "It's after nine," he added, "if we are going to the Casino we had better be t-toddling."

On the way there May entered a tobacconist's, and Lenox waited for him without. As he loitered on the curb, Blydenburg rounded an adjacent corner.

"Well," exclaimed the latter, "you didn't see our friends off."

"What friends?"

"The Incouls of course; didn't you know that they had gone?"

Lenox looked at him blankly. "Gone," he echoed.

"Yes, they must have sent you word. Incoul seemed to expect you. They have gone up to Paris. If I had known beforehand—"

Mr. Blydenburg rambled on, but Lenox no longer listened. It was for this then that he had been bothering himself the entire day. The abruptness of the departure mystified him, yet he comforted himself with the thought that had there been anything abnormal, it could not have escaped Blydenburg's attention.

"And you say they expected me?" he asked at last.

"Yes, they seemed to. Incoul left good-bye for you. When you get to Paris look them up."

While he was speaking May came out from the tobacconist's.

"I will do so," Lenox said, and with a parting nod he joined his friend.

As he walked on down the road to the Casino, Mr. Blydenburg looked musingly after him. He would not be a bad match for Milly, he told himself, not a bad match at all; and thinking that perhaps it might be but a question of bringing the two young people together, he presently started off in search of his daughter and led her, lamblike, to the Casino. But once there he felt instinctively that for that evening at least any bringing together of the young people was impossible. Lenox was engaged in an animated conversation with a conspicuously dressed lady, whom, Mr. Blydenburg learned on inquiry, was none other than the notorious Mile. Mirette, of the Theatre National de l'Opéra.

XI.
THE HOUSE IN THE PARC MONCEAU

There had been a crash in Wall street. Two of the best houses had gone under. Of one of these the senior partner had had recourse to the bare bodkin. For several years previous his wife had dispensed large hospitality from a charming hotel just within the gates of the Parc Monceau. At the news of her ruined widowhood she fled from Paris. In a week it was only her creditors that remembered her. The hôtel was sold under the hammer. A speculator bought it and while waiting a chance to sell it again at a premium, offered it for rent, fully furnished, as it stood. This by the way.

After the dinner in Spain, Mr. Incoul passed some time in thought. The next morning he sent for Karl, and after a consultation with him, he went to the square that overhangs the sea, entered the telegraph office, found a blank, wrote a brief message, and after attending to its despatch, returned to the villa. His wife was in the library, and as he entered the room the *maitre d'hôtel* announced that their excellencies were served.

Maida had never been more bewildering in her beauty. Her lips were moist, and under her polar-blue eyes were the faintest of semicircles.

"Did you enjoy your trip to Fuenterrabia?" she asked.

"Exceedingly," he answered. But he did not enter into details and the breakfast was done before either of them spoke again.

At last as Maida rose from the table Mr. Incoul said: "We leave for Paris at five this afternoon. I beg you will see to it that your things are ready."

She steadied herself against a chair, she would have spoken, but he had risen also and left the room.

For the time being her mind refused to act. Into the fibres of her there settled that chill which the garb and aspect of a policeman produces on the conscience of a misdemeanant. But the chill passed as policemen do, and a fever came in its place.

To hypnotize her thoughts she caught up an English journal. She read of a cocoa that was grateful and comforting, the praises of Pear's Soap, an invitation from Mr. Streeter to view his wares, a column of testimonials on the merits of a new pill, appeals from societies for pecuniary aid. She learned that a Doré was on exhibition in New Bond street, that Lady Grenville, The Oaks, Market Litchfield, was anxious to secure a situation for a most excellent under-housemaid, that money in large amounts or small could be obtained without publicity on simple note of hand by applying personally or by letter to Moss & Lewes, Golden Square. She found that a harmless, effective and permanent cure for corpulency would be sent to any part of the world, post-paid, on receipt of twelve stamps, and that the Junior Macready Club would admit a few more members without entrance fee. She read it all determinedly, by sheer effort of will, and at last in glancing over an oasis her eye fell upon a telegram from Madrid which stated cholera had broken out afresh.

She took the paper with her and hurried from the room.

In the hall her husband stood talking to Karl. She went to him and pointed to the telegram. "Is it for this we are to leave? " she asked.

He read the notice and returned it. "Yes," he answered, "it is for that." And then it was that both chill and fever passed away.

The journey from Biarritz was accomplished without incident. On their previous visit to Paris, they had put up at the Bristol and to that hostelry they returned. The manager had been notified and the yellow suite overlooking the Place Vendome was prepared for their reception. On arriving, Maida went at once with her maid to her room. Mr. Incoul changed his clothes, passed an hour at the Hamman, breakfasted at Voisin's, and then had himself driven to a house-agent.

The clerk, a man of fat and greasy presence, gave him a list of apartments, marking with a star those which he thought might prove most suitable. Mr. Incoul visited them all. He had never lived in an apartment in Paris and the absence of certain conveniences perplexed him. The last apartment of those that were starred was near the Arc de Triomphe. When he had been shown it over he found a seat, and heedless of the volubility of the concierge, rested his head in his hand and thought. For the moment it seemed to him as though it would be best to return to New York, but there were objections to that, and reflecting that there might be other and better arranged apartments, he left the chattering concierge and drove again to the agent's.

"I have seen nothing I liked," he said simply.

At this the clerk expressed his intense surprise. The apartment in the Avenue Montaigne was everything that there was of most fine, and wait, the Hospodar of Wallachia

had just quitted the one in the Rue de Presbourg. "It aston-
ishes me much," he said.

The astonishment of the clerk was to Mr. Incoul a matter
of perfect indifference. "Have you any private houses?" he
asked.

"Ah, yes, particular hotels." Yes, there was one near the
Trocadero, but for his part he found that the apartment in
the Avenue Montaigne would fit him much better. "But
now that I am there," he continued, "I recall myself of one
that is enchanter as a subjunctive. I engage you to visit it."
And thereupon he wrote down the address of the house in
the Parc Monceau.

It was not, Mr. Incoul discovered, a large dwelling,
but the appointments left little to be desired. In the dressing-rooms was running water, and each of the bed-rooms
was supplied with gas-fixtures. He touched one to see if it
were in working order, and immediately the escaping ether
assured him that it was. He sniffed it with a feeling akin to
pleasure. One would have thought that since he left Madison avenue he had not enjoyed such a treat. There was gas
to be found in the dining-room, but the reception-rooms
were furnished with lamps and candelabras. The bed-rooms
were on the floor above. One of these overlooked the park.
There was a dressing-room next to it, but to the two rooms
there was but one entrance, and that from the hall. This
little suite, Mr. Incoul resolved, should be occupied by his
wife. Beyond, across the hall, was a sitting-room, and at the
other end of the house was a second suite, which Mr. Incoul
mentally selected for himself.

He returned to the agent, and informed him that the
house suited him, an announcement which the man received with an air of personal sympathy.

"Is it not!" he exclaimed, "it made the mouth champagne nothing but to think there. And again, one was at home with one's self. Truly, the hotel was beautiful as a boulevard. Monsieur would never regret himself of it. And had Monsieur servants? No, good then. Let Monsieur not disquiet himself. He who spoke knew of a cook, veritably a blue ribbon, and as to masters of hotel, why, anointed name of a dog, not later than yesterday, he had heard that Baptiste— he who had served the family of Cantacuzene—Monsieur knew her, without doubt, came to be free."

In many respects Paris is not what it might be. The shops are vulgar in their ostentation. Were Monte Cristo to return he would find his splendor cheap and commonplace. In a city where Asiatic magnificence is sold from misfit and remnant counters by the ton, where emeralds large as swallows' eggs are to be had in the side-streets at a discount, where agents are ready to provide everything from an operaseria to a shoelace, the *badauds* have lost their ability to be startled. Paris, moreover, is not what it was. The suavity and civility for which it was proverbial have gone the way of other old-fashioned virtues; the wit which used to run about the streets never by any chance enters a salon; save in China a more rapacious set of bandits than the restauranteurs and shop-keepers do not exist; the theatres are haunts of ennui; the boulevards are filled with the worst-dressed set of people in the world. As for Parisian gaiety, there is nothing duller—no, not even a carnival. In winter the city is a tomb; in summer a furnace. In fact, there are dozens and dozens of places far more attractive, but there is not one where housekeeping is easier. The butcher and baker are invisible providers of the best of fare. The servants understand their duties and attend to them, and, given a little forethought and a good bank account, the palace of the White Cat is there the most realizable of constructions.

In a week's time the house in the Parc Monceau ran in grooves. To keep it running the tenants had absolutely nothing to do but to pay the bills. For this function Mr. Incoul was amply prepared, and, that the establishment should be on a proper footing, he furnished an adjacent stable with carriages, grooms and horse.

XII.
MR. INCOUL IS PREOCCUPIED

Mr. Incoul's attitude to his wife had, meanwhile, in no wise altered. To an observer, nay, to Maida herself, he was as silent, methodical and self-abnegatory as he had been from the first. He had indeed caused her to send a regret to Ballister without giving any reason why the regret should be sent, but otherwise he showed himself very indulgent.

He cared little for the stage, yet to gratify Maida he engaged boxes for the season at the Francais and at the Opéra. Now and then in the early autumn when summer was still in the air he took her to dine in the Bois, at Madrid or Armenenville, and drove home with her in the cool of the evening, stopping, perhaps, for a moment at some one of the different concerts that lined the Champs Elysées. And sometimes he went with her to Versailles and at others to Vincennes, and one Sunday to Bougival. But there Maida would never return; it was crowded with a set of people the like of which she had never seen before, with women whose voices were high pitched and unmodulated, and men in queer coats who stared at her and smiled if they caught her eye.

But with the first tingle that accompanies the falling leaves, the open-air restaurants and concerts closed their doors. There was a succession of new plays which Vitu always praised and Sarcey always damned. The verdict of the latter gentleman, however, did not affect Maida in the least. She went bravely to the Odéon and liked it, to the Cluny where she saw a shocking play that made her laugh till she cried. She went to the Nations and saw Lacressonière and shuddered before the art of that wonderful actor. At the Gymnase she saw the "Maître des Forges" and when she went home her eyes were wet; she saw "Nitouche" and would have willingly gone back the next night to see it again; even Mr. Incoul smiled; nothing more irresistibly amusing than Baron could be imagined; she saw, too, Bartet and Delaunay, and for the first time heard French well spoken. But of all entertainments the Opéra pleasured her most. Already, under Mapleson's reign, she had wearied of mere sweetness in music; she felt that she would enjoy Wagner and even planned a pilgrimage to Bayreuth, but meanwhile Meyerbeer had the power to intoxicate her very soul. The septette in the second act of "L'Africaine" affected her as had never anything before; it vibrated from her finger-tips to the back of her neck; the entire score, from the opening notes of the overture to the farewell of Zuleika's that fuses with the murmur of the sea, thrilled her with abrupt surprises, with series and excesses of delight.

There were, of course, many evenings when neither opera nor theatre was attractive, and on such evenings invitations from resident friends and acquaintances were sometimes accepted and sometimes open house was held.

On these occasions, Maida found herself an envied bride. It was not merely that her husband was rich enough to buy a principality and hand it over for charitable purposes, it was not merely that he was willing to give her everything that feminine heart could desire, it was that, however crowded the halls might be, he seemed conscious of the existence of but one woman, and that woman was his wife. There were triflers who said that this attitude was *bourgeois*; there were others—more witty—who said that it was immoral; but, be this as it may, the South American highwaymen, who called themselves generals, the Russian princesses, the Roumanian boyards, the attaches, embassadors, and other accredited bores, the contingent from the Faubourg, the American residents, who, were they sent in a body to the rack, could not have confessed to an original thought among them, all these, together with a sprinkling of Spaniards and English, the Tout-Paris, in fact, agreed, as it was intended they should, on this one point, to wit, that Mr. Incoul was the most devoted of husbands.

And such apparently he was. If Maida had any lingering doubts as to the real reason of their return to Paris, little by little they faded. After her fright she made with herself several little compacts, and that she might carry them out the better she wrote to Lenox a short, decisive note. She determined that he should never enter her life again. It was no longer his, he had let it go without an effort to detain it, and in Biarritz if it had seemed that he still held the key of her heart, it was owing as much to the unexpectedness of his presence as to the languors of the afternoons. In marrying, she had meant to be brave; indeed, she had been so—when there was no danger; and if in spite of her intentions she had faltered, the faltering had at least served as a lesson which she would never need to learn again. Over the cinders of her youth she would write a Requiescat. Her girlhood had been her own to give, but her womanhood she had pledged to another.

As she thought of these things she wondered at her husband. He had done what she had hardly dared to expect—

he had observed their ante-nuptial agreement to the letter. A brother could not have treated her with greater respect. Surely if ever a man set out to win his wife's affection he had chosen the surest way. And why had he so acted if it were not as he had said, that given time and opportunity, he *would* win her affection. He was doing so, Maida felt, and with infinitely greater speed that she had ever deemed possible. Beside, if the mangled remnants of her heart seemed attractive, why should he be debarred from their possession? Yet, that was precisely the point; he did not know of the mangled remnants, he thought her heart-whole and virginal. But what would he do if he learned the truth? And as she wondered, suddenly the consciousness came to her that she was living with a stranger.

Heretofore she had not puzzled over the possible intricacies of her husband's inner nature. She had known that he was of a grave and silent disposition, and as such she had been content to accept him, without question or query. But as she collected some of the scattered threads and memories of their life in common, it seemed to her that latterly he had become even graver and more silent than before. And this merely when they were alone. In the presence of a third person, when they went abroad as guests, or when they remained at home as hosts, he put his gravity aside like a garment. He encouraged her in whatever conversation she might have engaged in, he aided her with a word or a suggestion, he made a point of consulting her openly, and smiled approvingly at any bright remark she chanced to make.

But when they were alone, unless she personally addressed him, he seldom spoke, and the answers that he gave her, while perfectly courteous in tone and couching, struck her, now that she reflected, as automatic, like phrases learned by rote. It is true they were rarely alone. In the mornings he busied himself with his correspondence, and in the afternoons she found herself fully occupied with shops and visits, while in the evenings there was usually a dinner, a play, or a reception, sometimes all three. Since the season had begun, it was only now and then, once in ten days perhaps, that an evening was passed *en tête-à-tête*. On such occasions he would take up a book and read persistently, or he would smoke, flicking the ashes from the cigar abstractedly with his little finger, and so sit motionless for hours, his eyes fixed on the cornice.

It was this silence that puzzled her. It was evident that he was thinking of something, but of what? It could not be archaeology, he seemed to have given it up, and he was not a metaphysician, the only thinker, be it said, to whom silence is at all times permissible.

At first she feared that his preoccupation might in some way be connected with the episodes at Biarritz, but this fear faded. Mr. Incoul had been made a member of the Cercle des Capucines, and now and then looked in there ostensibly to glance at the papers or to take a hand at whist. One day he said casually, "I saw your friend Leigh at the club. You might ask him to dinner." The invitation was sent, but Lenox had regretted. After that incident it was impossible for her to suppose that her husband's preoccupation was in anywise connected with the intimacy which had subsisted between the young man and herself.

There seemed left to her then but one tenable supposition. Her husband had been indulgence personified. He had been courteous, refined and foreseeing, in fact a gentleman, and, if silent, was it not possible that the silence was due to a self-restraining delicacy, to a feeling that did he speak

MR. INCOUL'S MISADVENTURE

he would plead, and that, perhaps, when pleading would be distasteful to her?

To this solution Maida inclined. It was indeed the only one at which she could arrive, and, moreover, it conveyed that little bouquet of flattery which has been found grateful by many far less young and feminine than she. And so, one evening, for the further elucidation of the enigma, and with the idea that perhaps it needed but a word from her to cause her husband to say something of that which was on his mind, and which she was at once longing and dreading to hear—one evening when he had seemed particularly abstracted, she bent forward and said, "Harmon, of what are you thinking?"

She had never called him by his given name before. He started, and half turned.

"Of you," he answered.

But Maida's heart sank. She saw that his eyes were not in hers, that they looked over and beyond her, as though they followed the fringes of an escaping dream.

XIII.
WHAT MAY BE HEARD IN A GREEN ROOM

One evening in November a new ballet was given at the Opéra. Its production had been heralded in the manner which has found most favor with Parisian impressarii. The dead walls of the capital were not adorned with colored lithographs. The advertising sheets held no notice of the coming performance. But for several weeks previous the columns of the liveliest journals had teemed with items and discreet indiscretions.

Through these measures the curiosity of the Tout-Paris had been coerced afresh, and, when the curtain, after falling on the second act of the "Favorite," parted again before the new ballet, there was hardly a vacant seat in the house.

The box which Mr. Incoul had taken for the season was on what is known as the grand tier. It was roomy, holding eight comfortably and twelve if need be. But Maida, who was adverse to anything that suggested crowding, was always disinclined to ask more than five or six to share it with her, and on the particular evening to which allusion is made she extended her hospitality to but four people: Mr. and Mrs. Wainwaring and their daughter, New Yorkers like herself, and the Duc de la Dèche, a nobleman who served as figurehead to the Cercle des Capucines, and who, so ran the gossip, was anxious to effect an exchange of his coroneted freedom for the possession of Miss Wainwaring and a bundle or two of her father's securities.

During the *entr'acte* that preceded the ballet the box was invaded by a number of visitors, young men who were indebted to Maida for a dinner or a cup of tea and by others who hoped that such indebtedness was still in store for them; there came, too, a popular artist who wished to paint Maida's portrait for the coming Salon and an author who may have had much cleverness, but who never displayed it to any one.

As the invasion threatened to continue Mr. Incoul went out in the corridor, where he was presently joined by the duke, who suggested that they should visit the foyer. They made their way down the giant stair and turning through the lobby passed on through the corridor that circles the stalls until they reached a door guarded from non-subscribers by a Suisse about whose neck there drooped a medallioned chain of silver. By him the door was opened wide and the two men passed on through a forest of side scenes till the *foyer de la danse* was reached.

It was a spacious apartment, well lighted and lined with mirrors; the furniture was meagre, a dozen or more chairs and lounges of red plush. It was not beautiful, but then what market ever is? To Mr. Incoul it was brilliant as a café, and equally vulgar. From dressing-rooms above and beyond there came a stream of willowy girls. Few among them were pretty, and some there were whose faces were repulsive, but the majority were young; some indeed, the rats, as they are called, were mere children. Here and there was a mother of the Mme. Cardinal type, armed with an umbrella and prepared to listen to offers. As a rule, however, the young ladies of the ballet were quite able to attend to any little matter of business without maternal assistance. The Italian element was easily distinguishable. There was the ultra darkness of the eye, the faint umber of the skin, the richer vitality, in fact, of which the anemic daughters of Paris were unpossessed. And now and then the Gothic gutturals of the Spanish were heard, preceded by a wave of garlic.

That night the subscribers to the stalls were out in full force. There were Jew bankers in plenty, there were detachments from the Jockey and the Mirletons, one or two foreign representatives, a few high functionaries, the Minister of the Interior, and he of the Fine Arts, a member of the imperial family of Russia, a number of stock brokers and an Arab Shiek flanked by an interpreter.

Before the curtain rose, battalions of ballerines formed on the stage, and after the performance began they were succeeded by others, the first contingent returning to the dressing-rooms or loitering in the foyer. In this way there was a constant coming and going accompanied by the murmur of the spectators beyond and the upper notes of the flute.

Mr. Incoul was growing weary; he would have returned to the box, but he was joined by acquaintances that he had made at the club, Frenchmen mainly, friends of his companion, and presently he found himself surrounded by a group of *viveurs*, men about town, who had their Paris at the end of their gloves, and to whom it held no secrets. They had dined and talked animatedly in ends and remnants of phrases in a sort of verbal telegraphy; an exclamation helped by a gesture sufficing as often as not for the full conveyance of their thought.

Mr. Incoul spoke French with tolerable ease, but having nothing of moment to say, he held his tongue, contenting himself with listening to the words of those who stood about him. And as he listened, the name of Mirette caught his ear. The programme had already informed him that it was she who was to assume the principal rôle in the new ballet, consequently he was not unfamiliar with it, but of the woman herself he knew nothing, and he listened idly, indifferent to ampler information. But at once his interest quickened; his immediate neighbor had mentioned her in connection with one whom he knew.

"They came up from Biarritz together," he heard him say. "She went there with Chose, that Russian."

"Balaguine?"

"Precisely."

"What did she do with him?"

"Found the Tartar, I fancy."

"And then?"

"*Voilà*, this young American is mad about her."

"He is rich then?"

"What would you? An American! They are it all."

"Yes, a rich one always wins."

"How mean you?"

"This: he plays bac at the Capucines. His banks are fructuous."

"Ah, as to that—" And the first speaker shrugged his shoulders.

A rustle circled through the foyer, men stood aside and nodded affably. The light took on a fairer glow. "Stay," murmured the second speaker, "she is there."

Through the parting crowd Mirette passed with a carriage such as no queen, save perhaps Semiramis, ever possessed. She moved from the hips, her body was erect and unswayed. It was the perfection of artificial grace. Her features were not regular, but there was an expression in them that stirred the pulse. *"Je suis l'Amour,"* she seemed to say, and to add *"prends garde à toi."* As she crossed the room men moistened their lips, and when she had gone they found them still parched.

Mr. Incoul followed her with his eyes. She had not left him unimpressed, but his impression differed from that of his neighbors. In her face his shrewdness had discerned nothing but the animal and the greed of unsatiated appetites. He watched her pass, and stepped from the group in which he had been standing that he might the better follow her movements.

From the foyer she floated on into a side scene, yet not near enough to the stage to be seen by the audience. A few machinists moved aside to let her pass, and as they did so Mr. Incoul saw Lenox Leigh. It was evident that he had been waiting there for her coming. There was a scarf about her neck, and as the young man turned to greet her, she took it off and gave it into his keeping. They whispered together. Beyond, Mr. Incoul could see the tulle of the ballet rising and subsiding to the rhythm of the orchestra. Then came a sudden blare of trumpets, the measure swooned, and as it recovered again the ballet had faded to the back of the stage. Abruptly, as though sprung from a trapdoor, a *régisseur* appeared, and at a signal from him Mirette, with one quick backward stroke to her skirt, bounded from the side scene and fluttered down to the footlights amid a crash and thunder of applause.

Mr. Incoul had heard and seen enough. His mind was busy. He felt the need of fresh air and of solitude. He turned into the corridor and from there went through the vestibule until he reached an outer door, which he swung open and passed out into the night. He was thinly clad, in evening dress, and the air was chilly, but he thought nothing of his dress nor of the warmth or chill of the air. He walked up and down before the building with his head bent and his hands behind his back. A *camelot* offered him a pack of transparent cards, a vender of programmes pestered him to buy, but he passed them unheeding. For fully half an hour he continued his walk, and when he reentered the box, Maida, who of late had given much attention to his moods, noticed that his face was flushed, and that about his lips there played the phantom of a smile.

XIV.
KARL GROWS A MOUSTACHE

For several days Mr. Incoul was much occupied. He left the house early and returned to it late. One afternoon he sent for Karl. Since the return to Paris the courier's duties had not been arduous; they consisted chiefly in keeping out of the way. On this particular afternoon he was not immediately discoverable, and when at last he presented himself it was in the expectation that the hour of his dismissal had struck. He bowed, nevertheless, with the best grace in the world, and noticing that his employer's eyes were upon him, gazed deferentially at the carpet.

Mr. Incoul looked at him in a contemplative way for a moment or two. "Karl," he said at last, and Karl raised his eyes.

"Yes, sir."

"Have you any objections to shaving your whiskers?"

"I, sir? not the slightest."

"I will be obliged if you will do so. This afternoon you might go to Cumberland's and be measured. I have left orders there. Then take a room at the Meurice; you have money, have you not? Very good, keep an account of your expenditures. In a week I will send you my instructions. That will do for to-day."

An hour later Mr. Incoul was watching a game of baccarat at the Cercle des Capucines.

Meanwhile Lenox Leigh had given much of his time to the pleasures of Mirette's society. In making her acquaintance at Biarritz he had been actuated partly by the idleness of the moment and partly by the attracting face of celebrity. He had never known a danseuse; indeed, heretofore, his acquaintance with women had been limited to those of his own *monde*, and during the succeeding days he hovered about her more that he might add a new photograph to a mental album than with any idea of conquest. She amused him extremely. In her speech she displayed a recklessness of adjective such as he had never witnessed before. It was not that she was brilliant, but she possessed that stereotyped form of repartee which is known as *bagou*, and which the Parisian takes to naturally and without effort. Mirette seemed to have acquired it in its supremest expression. One day, for instance, the curiosity of her circle of admirers was aroused by a young actress who, while painfully plain, squandered coin with remarkable ease. "Whom do you suppose she gets the money from?" some one asked, and Mirette without so much as drawing breath answered serenely, "A blind man." In spite of the *bagou* Mirette was not a Parisian. She was born in the provinces, at Orléans, and was wont to declare herself a lineal descendant of Joan of Arc. She lied with perfect composure; if reproached she curled her lips. "Lies whiten the teeth," she would say, an argument which it was impossible to refute.

Under the empire she would have been a success; under a republic she complained of the difficulty of making two ends meet. Now Lenox was not rich, but he was an American, and the Americans have assumed in Paris the position which the English once held. Their coffers are considered inexhaustible. On this subject, thanks to Mrs. Mackay, Mr. Incoul, the Vanderbilts, the Astors and a dozen others, there is now no doubt in the mind of the French. To be an American is to be a Vesuvius of gold pieces.

As a native of the land of millions, Lenox found that his earliest attentions were received with smiles, and in time when a Russian became so scratched that the Tartar was visible, Mirette welcomed him with undisguised favor.

Like many another, Lenox had his small vanities; he would have liked to have thought himself indispensable to Maida's happiness, but in her absence he did not object to being regarded as the *cavaliere servente* of the first lady of the ballet. Between the two women the contrast was striking. Mirette, as has been hinted, was reckless of adjective; she was animal, imperious, and at times frankly vulgar. Maida was her antithesis. She shrank from coarseness as from a deformity. Both represented Love, but they represented the extremes. One was as ignorant of virtue as the other was unconscious of vice. One was Mylitta, the other Psyche. Had the difference been less accentuated, it would have jarred. But the transition was immeasurable. It was like a journey from the fjords of Norway to the jungles of Hindustan. That Psyche was regretted goes without the need of telling, but Mylitta has enchantments which are said to lull regret.

In the second week of October the bathing was still delicious. The waves encircled one in a large, abrupt embrace. Mirette would have liked to remain, the beach was a daily triumph for her. There was not a woman in the world who could have held herself in the scantiest of costumes, under the fire of a thousand eyes, as gracefully as she. No sedan-chair for her indeed. No hurrying, no running, no enveloping wrap. No pretense or attempt to avoid the scrutiny of the bystanders. There was nothing of this for her. She crossed the entire width of sand, calmly, slowly, an invitation on her lips and with the walk and majesty of a queen. The amateurs as usual were tempted to applaud. It was indeed a triumph, an advertisement to boot, and one which she would have liked to prolong. But she was needed at the Opéra and so she returned to Paris accompanied by Lenox Leigh.

In Paris it is considered inconvenient for a pretty woman to go about on foot, and as for cabs, where is the self-respecting chorus-girl who would consent to be seen in one? Mirette was very positive on this point and Lenox agreed with her thoroughly. He did not, however, for that reason offer to provide an equipage. Indeed the wherewithal was lacking. He had spent more money at Biarritz than he had intended, perhaps ten times the amount that he would have spent at Newport or at Cowes, and his funds were nearly exhausted.

As every one is aware a banker is the last person in the world to be consulted on matters of finance. If a client has money in his pocket a banker can transfer it to his own in an absolutely painless manner, but if the client's pocket is empty what banker, out of an opera-bouffe, was ever willing to fill it? Lenox reflected over this and was at a loss how to act. The firm on whom his drafts were drawn held nothing on their ledgers to his credit. He visited them immediately on arriving and was given a letter which for the moment he fancied might contain a remittance. But it bore the Paris postmark and the address was in Maida's familiar hand. As he looked at it he forgot his indigence, his heart gave an exultant throb. He had promised himself that when he met her again matters should go on very much as they had before, and he had further promised himself that so soon as his former footing was re-established he would give up Mirette. He was therefore well pleased when the note was placed in his hands. It had a faint odor of orris, and he opened it as were he unfolding a lace handkerchief. But from what has gone before it will be understood that his pleasure was short lived. The note was brief and categoric, he read it almost at a glance, and when he had possessed himself of the contents he felt that the determination conveyed was one from which there was no appeal, or rather one from which any appeal would be useless. He looked at the note again. The handwriting suggested an unaccustomed strength, and in the straight, firm strokes he read the irrevocable. "It is done," he muttered, "I can write Finis over that." He looked again at the note and then tore it slowly into minute scraps, and watched them flutter from him.

He went out to the street and there his earlier preoccupation returned. It would be a month at least before a draft could be sent, and meanwhile, though he had enough for his personal needs, he had nothing with which to satisfy Mirette's caprices. *Et elle en avait, cette dame!* The thought of separating from her did not occur to him, or if it did it was in that hazy indistinguishable form in which eventualities sometimes visit the perplexed. If Maida's note had been other, he would have washed his hands of Mirette, but now apparently she was the one person on the Continent who cared when he came and when he went. In his present position he was like one who, having sprained an ankle, learns the utility of a crutch. The idea of losing it was not agreeable. Beside, the knowledge that his intimacy with the woman had been envied by grandees with unnumbered hats was to him a source of something that resembled consolation.

Presently he reached the boulevard. He was undecided what to do or where to turn, and as he loitered on the curb the silver head of a stick was waved at him from a passing cab; in a moment the vehicle stopped. May alighted and shook him by the hand.

"I am on my way to the Capucines," he explained, in his blithesome stutter. "There's a big game on; why not come, too?"

"A big game of what?"

"B-b, why baccarat of course. What did you suppose? M-marbles?"

Lenox fumbled in his waistcoat pocket. "Yes, I'll go," he said.

Five minutes later he was standing in a crowded room before a green table. He had never gambled, and hardly knew one card from another but baccarat can be learned with such facility that after two deals a raw recruit can argue with a veteran as to whether it is better to stand on five or to draw. Lenox watched the flight of notes, gold and counters. He listened to the monotonous calls: *J'en donne! Carte! Neuf!* The end of the table at which he stood seemed to be unlucky. He moved to the other, and presently he leaned over the shoulder of a gamester and put down a few louis. In an hour he left the room with twenty-seven thousand francs.

A fraction of it he put in his card-case, the rest he handed to Mirette. It was not a large sum, but its dimensions were satisfactory to her. *"Ce p'tit chat,"* she said to herself, *"je savais bien qu'il ne ferait pas le lapin."* And of the large azure notes she made precisely one bite.

Thereafter for some weeks things went on smoothly enough. Mirette's mornings were passed at rehearsals, but usually the afternoons were free, and late in the day she would take Lenox to the Cascade, or meet him there and drive back with him to dinner. In the evenings there was the inevitable theatre, with supper afterwards at some *cabaret à la mode*. And sometimes when she was over-fatigued, Lenox would go to the club and try a hand at baccarat.

He was not always so fortunate as on the first day, but on the whole his good luck was noticeable. It is possible, however, that he found the excitement enervating. He had been used to a much quieter existence, one that if not entirely praiseworthy was still outwardly decorous, and suddenly he had been pitchforked into that narrowest of circles which is called Parisian life. He may have liked it at first, as one is apt to like any novelty, but to nerves that are properly attuned a little of its viciousness goes a very great way.

It maybe that it was beginning to exert its usual dissolvent effect. In any event Lenox, who all his life had preferred water to wine, found absinthe grateful in the morning.

One afternoon, shortly after the initial performance of the new ballet, he went from his hôtel to the apartment which Mirette occupied in the Rue Pierre-Charon. He was informed that she was not at home. He questioned the servant as to her whereabouts, but the answers he received were vague and unsatisfactory. He then drove to the Cascade, but Mirette did not appear. After dinner he made sure of finding her. In this expectation he was again disappointed.

The next day his success was no better. He questioned the servant uselessly. "Madame was not at home, she had left no word." To each of his questions the answer was invariable. It was evident that the servant had been coached, and it was equally evident that at least for the moment his companionship was not a prime necessity to the first lady of the ballet.

As he left the house he bit his lip. That Mirette should

be capricious was quite in the order of things, but that she should treat him like the first comer was a different matter. When he had last seen her, her manner had left nothing to be desired, and suddenly, without so much as a p. p. c., her door was shut, and not shut as it might have been by accident; no, it was persistently, purposely closed.

Presently he reached the Champs Elysées. It was Sunday. A stream of carriages flooded the avenue, and the sidewalks were thronged with ill-dressed people. The crowd increased his annoyance. The possibility of being jostled irritated him, the spectacle of dawdling shop-keepers filled him with disgust. He hailed a cab in which to escape; the driver paid no attention; he hailed another; the result was the same, and then in the increasing exasperation of the moment he felt that he hated Paris. A fat man with pursed lips and an air of imbecile self-satisfaction brushed against him. He could have turned and slapped him in the face.

Without, however, committing any overt act of violence, he succeeded in reaching his hotel. There he sought the reading-room, but he found it fully occupied by one middle-aged Englishwoman, and leaving her in undisturbed possession of the *Times*, he went to his own apartment. A day or two before he had purchased a copy of a much applauded novel, and from it he endeavored to extract a sedative. Mechanically he turned the pages. His eyes glanced over and down them, resting at times through fractions of an hour on a single line, but the words conveyed no message to his mind, his thoughts were elsewhere, they surged through vague perplexities and hovered over shadowy enigmas, until at last he discovered that he was trying to read in the dark.

He struck a light and found that it was nearly seven. "I will dress," he told himself, "and dine at the club." In half an hour he was on his way to the Capucines. The streets were still crowded and the Avenue de l'Opéra in which his hô-tel was situated, vibrated as were it the main artery of the capital. As he approached the boulevard he thought that it would perhaps be wiser to dine at a restaurant; he was dis-comfited and he was not sure but that the myriad tongue of gossip might not be already busy with the cause of his discomfiture. He did not feel talkative, and were he taciturn at the club he knew that it would be remarked. Bignon's was close at hand. Why not dine there? In his indecision he halt-ed before an adjacent shop and stood for a moment looking in the window, apparently engrossed by an assortment of strass and imitation pearls. The proprietress was lounging in the doorway. *"Si Monsieur veut entrer"*—she began se-ductively, but he turned from her; as he did so, a brougham drew up before the curb and Mirette stepped from it.

Lenox, in his surprise at the unexpected, did not at first notice that a man had also alighted. He moved forward and would have spoken, but Mirette looked him straight in the eyes, as who should say *Allez vous faire lanlaire, mon cher*, and passed on into the restaurant.

Her companion had hurried a little in advance to open the door, and as he swung it aside and Mirette entered Le-nox caught a glimpse of his face. It was meaningless enough, and yet not entirely unfamiliar. "Who is the cad," he won-dered. Yet, after all, what difference did it make? He could not blame the man. As for jealousy, the word was meaning-less to him. It was his *amour propre* that suffered. He smiled a trifle grimly to himself and continued his way.

At the corner was a large picture shop. An old man wrapped in a loose fur coat stood at the window looking at the painting of a little girl. The child was alone in a coppice and seemingly much frightened at the approach of a flock of does. Unconsciously Lenox stopped also. He had been so bewildered by the suddenness of the cut that he did not notice whether he was walking or standing still.

And so it was for this, he mused, that admittance had been denied him. But why could she not have had the decency to tell him not to come instead of letting him run there like a tradesman with a small bill? Certainly he had deserved better things of her than that. It was so easy for a woman to break gracefully. A note, a word, and if the man insists a second note, a second word; after that the man, if he is decently bred, can do nothing but raise his hat and speed the parting guest. Beside, why would she want to break with him and take up with a fellow who looked like a barber from the Grand Hôtel? Who was he any way?

His eyes rested on the picture of the little girl. The representation of her childish fright almost diverted his thoughts, but all the while there was an undercurrent which in some dim way kept telling him that he had seen the man's face before. And as he groped in his memory the picture of the child faded as might a picture in a magic lantern, and in its place, vaguely at first and gradually better defined, he saw, standing in the moonlight, on a white road, a coach and four. To the rear was the terrace of a hôtel, and beyond was a shimmering bay like to that which he had seen at San Sebastian.

"My God," he cried aloud, "it's Incoul's courier!"

The old man in the fur coat looked at him nervously, and shrank away.

XV.
MAY EXPOSTULATES

That evening the Wainwarings and the Blydenburgs dined at the house in the Parc Monceau. The Blydenburgs had long since deserted Biarritz, but the return journey had been broken at Luchon, and in that resort the days had passed them by like chapters in a stupid fairy tale.

They were now on their way home; the pleasures of the Continent had begun to pall, and during the dinner, Mr. Blydenburg took occasion to express his opinion on the superiority of American institutions over those of all other lands, an opinion to which he lent additional weight by repeating from time to time that New York was quite good enough for him.

There were no other guests. Shortly before ten the Wainwarings left, and as Blydenburg was preparing to take his daughter back to the hotel, Mr. Incoul said that he would be on the boulevard later, and did he care to have him he would take him to the club, a proposition to which Blydenburg at once agreed.

"Harmon," said Maida, when they were alone, "are you to be away long?"

During dinner she had said but little. Latterly she had complained of sleeplessness, and to banish the insomnia a physician had recommended the usual bromide of potassium. As she spoke, Mr. Incoul noticed that she was pale.

"Possibly not," he answered.

She had been standing before the hearth, her bare arm resting on the velvet of the mantel, and her eyes following the flicker of the burning logs—but now she turned to him.

"Do you remember our pact?" she asked.

He looked at her but said nothing. She moved across the room to where he stood; one hand just touched his sleeve, the other she raised to his shoulder and rested it there for a second's space. Her eyes sought his own, her head was thrown back a little, from her hair came the perfume of distant oases, her lips were moist and her neck was like a jasmine.

"Harmon," she continued in a tone as low as were she speaking to herself, "we have come into our own."

And then the caress passed from his sleeve, her hand fell from his shoulder, she glided from him with the motion of a swan.

"Come to me when you return," she added. Her face had lost its pallor, it was flushed, but her voice was brave.

Yet soon, when the door closed behind him, her courage faltered. In the eyes of him whose name she bore and to whom for the first time she had made offer of her love, she had seen no answering affection—merely a look which a man might give who wins a long-contested game of chess. But presently she reassured herself. If at the avowal her husband had seemed triumphant, in very truth what was he else? She turned to a mirror that separated the windows and gazed at her own reflection. Perhaps he did think the winning a triumph. Many another would have thought so, too. She was entirely in white; her arms and neck were unjeweled. "I look like a bride," she told herself, and then, with the helplessness of regret, she remembered that brides wear orange blossoms, but she had none.

The idler in Paris is apt to find Sunday evenings dull. There are many houses open, it is true, but not infrequently the idler is disinclined to receptions, and as to the theatres, it is *bourgeois* to visit them. There is, therefore, little left save the clubs, and on this particular Sunday evening, when Mr. Incoul and Blydenburg entered the Capucines, they found it tolerably filled.

A lackey in silk knee breeches and livery of pale blue came to take their coats. It was not, however, until Blydenburg had been helped off with his that he noticed that Mr. Incoul had preferred to keep his own on.

The two men then passed out of the vestibule into a room in which was a large table littered with papers, and from there into another room where a man whom Mr. Incoul recognized as De la Dèche was dozing on a lounge, and finally a room was reached in which most of the members had assembled.

"It reminds me of a hotel," said Blydenburg.

"It is," his friend answered shortly. He seemed preoccupied as were he looking for some one or something; and presently, as they approached a green table about which a crowd was grouped, Blydenburg pulled him by the sleeve.

"That's young Leigh dealing," he exclaimed.

To this Mr. Incoul made no reply. He put his hand in a lower outside pocket of his overcoat and assured himself that a little package which he had placed there had not become disarranged.

On hearing his name, Lenox looked up from his task. A Frenchman who had just entered the room nodded affably to him and asked if he were lucky that evening.

"Lucky!" cried some one who had caught the question,

"I should say so. His luck is something insolent; he struck a match a moment ago and *it lit*."

The whole room roared. French matches are like French cigars in this, there is nothing viler. It is just possible that the parental republic has views of its own as to the injuriousness of smoking, and seeks to discourage it as it would a vice. But this is as it may be. Every one laughed and Lenox with the others. Mr. Incoul caught his eye and bowed to him across the table. Blydenburg had already smiled and bowed in the friendliest way. He did not quite care to see Mrs. Manhattan's brother dealing at baccarat, but after all, when one is at Rome—

"Do you care to play?" Mr. Incoul asked.

"Humph! I might go a louis or two for a flyer."

They had both been standing behind the croupier, but Mr. Incoul then left his companion, and passing around the table stopped at a chair which was directly on Lenox's left. In this chair a man was seated, and before him was a small pile of gold. As the cards were dealt the gold diminished, and when it dwindled utterly and at last disappeared, the man rose from his seat and Mr. Incoul dropped in it.

From the overcoat pocket, in which he had previously felt, he drew out a number of thousand-franc notes; they were all unfolded, and under them was a little package. The notes, with the package beneath them, were placed by Mr. Incoul where the pile of gold had stood. One of the notes he then threw out in the semicircle. A man seated next to him received the cards which Lenox dealt.

"I give," Lenox called in French.

"Card," the man answered.

It was a face card that he received.

"Six," Lenox announced.

Mr. Incoul's neighbor could boast of nothing. The next cards that were dealt on that end of the table went to a man beyond. Mr. Incoul knew that did that man not hold higher cards than the banker the cards in the succeeding deal would come to him.

He took a handful of notes and reached them awkwardly enough across the space from which Lenox dealt; for one second his hand rested on the talion, then he said, *"A cheval."* Which, being interpreted, means half on one side and half on the other. The croupier took the notes, and placed them in the proper position. "Nine," Lenox called; he had won at both ends of the table.

The croupier drew in the stakes with his rake. "Gentlemen," he droned, "make your game."

Mr. Incoul pushed out five thousand francs. The next cards on the left were dealt to him.

"Nine," Lenox called again.

And then a very singular thing happened. The croupier leaned forward to draw in Mr. Incoul's money, but just as the rake touched the notes, Mr. Incoul drew them away.

"Monsieur!" exclaimed the croupier.

The eyes of every one were upon him. He pushed his chair back, and stood up, holding in his hand the two cards which had been dealt him, then throwing them down on the table, he said very quietly, but in a voice that was perfectly distinct, "These cards are marked."

A moment before the silence had indeed been great, but during the moment that followed Mr. Incoul's announcement, it was so intensified that it could be felt. Then abruptly words leapt from the mouths of the players and bystanders. The croupier turned, protesting his innocence of any complicity. There may have been some who listened, but if there were any such, they were few; the entire room was sonorous with loud voices; the hubub was so great that it woke De la Dèche; he cam in at one door rubbing his eyes; at another a crowd of lackeys, startled at the uproar had suddenly assembled. And by the chair which he had pushed from him and which had fallen backwards to the ground, Mr. Incoul stood, motionless, looking down at Lennox Leigh.

In the abruptness of the accusation Lenox had not immediately understood that it was directed against him, but when he looked into the inimical faces that fronted and surrounded him, when he heard the anger of the voices, when he saw hands stretched for the cards which he dealt, and impatient eyes examining their texture, and when at last, though the entire scene was compassed in the fraction of a minute, when he heard an epithet and saw that he was regarded as a Greek, he knew that the worst that could be had been done.

He turned, still sitting, and looked his accuser in the face, and in it he read a message which to all of those present was to him alone intelligible. He bowed his head. In a vision like to that which is said to visit the last moments of a drowning man, he saw it all: the reason of Maida's unexplained departure, the coupling of Mirette with a servant, and this supreme reproach made credible by the commonest of tricks, the application of a cataplasm, a new deck of cards on those already in use. It was vengeance indeed.

He sprang from his seat. He was a handsome fellow and the pallor of his face made his dark hair seem darker and his dark eyes more brilliant. "It is a plot," he cried. He might as well have asked alms of statues. The cards had been examined, the *maquillage* was evident. "Put him out!" a hundred voices were shouting; *"a la porte!"*

Suddenly the shouting subsided and ceased. Lenox craned his neck to discover who his possible defender might be, and caught a glimpse of De la Dèche, brushing with one finger some ashes from his coat-sleeve, and looking about him with an indolent, deprecatory air.

"Gentlemen," he heard him say, "the committee will act in the matter; meanwhile, for the honor of the club, I beg you will not increase the scandal."

He turned to Lenox and said, with perfect courtesy, "Sir, do me the favor to step this way."

Through the parting crowd Lenox followed the duke. In crossing the room he looked about him. On his way he passed the Frenchman who had addressed him five minutes before. The man turned aside. He passed other acquaintances. They all seemed suddenly smitten by the disease known as *Noli me tangere.* In the doorway was May. Of him he felt almost sure, but the brute drew back. "Really," he said, "I must exp-postulate."

"Expostulate and be damned," Lenox gnashed at him, "I am as innocent as you are."

In an outer room, where he presently found himself, De la Dèche stood lighting a cigar; that difficult operation terminated, he said, slowly, with that rise and fall of the voice which is peculiar to the Parisian when he wishes to appear impressive:

"You had better go now, and if you will permit me to offer you a bit of advice, I would recommend you to send a resignation to any clubs of which you may happen to be a member."

He touched a bell; a lackey appeared.

"Maxine, get this gentleman's coat and see him to the door."

XVI.
THE BARE BODKIN

Presently Lenox found himself on the boulevard. There was a café near at hand, and he sat down at one of the tables that lined the sidewalk. He was dazed as were he in the semi-consciousness of somnambulism. He gave an order absently, and when some drink was placed before him, he took it at a gulp.

Under its influence his stupor fell from him. The necessity, the obligation of proving his innocence presented itself, but, with it, hand in hand, came the knowledge that such proof was impossible. Even his luck at play would be taken as corroboratory of the charge. Were he to say that the marked cards had been placed on the talion by Incoul, who was there outside the aisles of the insane that would listen to such a defense? To compel attention, he would be obliged to explain the act, and state its reason. And that explanation he could never give. He could not exculpate himself at the cost of a woman's fame. Which ever way he turned, dishonor stood before him. The toils into which he had fallen had been woven with a cunning so devilish in its clairvoyance that every avenue of escape was closed. He was blockaded in his own disgrace.

He rested his head in his hand, and moaned aloud. Presently, with the instinct of a hunted beast, he felt that people were looking at him. He feared that some of his former acquaintances, on leaving the club, had passed and seen him sitting there, and among them, perhaps Incoul.

He threw some money in the saucer and hurried away. There were still many people about. To avoid them he turned into a side street and walked on with rapid step. Soon he was in the Rue de la Paix. It was practically deserted. On a corner, a young ruffian in a slouch hat was humming, *"Ug-Zne, tu m'fais languir,"* and beating time to the measure with his foot. Just above the Colonne Vendome the moon rested like a vagrant, weary of its amble across the sky. But otherwise the street was solitary. Through its entire length but one shop was open, and as Lenox approached it a man came out to arrange the shutters. From the doorway a thin stream of light still filtered on the pavement. In the window were globes filled with colored liquids, and beyond at a counter a clerk was tying a parcel.

Lenox entered. "Give me a Privas," he said, and when the clerk had done so, he asked him to make up a certain prescription. But to this the man objected; he could not, he explained, without a physician's order.

"Here are several," said Lenox, and he took from his card-case a roll of azure notes.

The clerk eyed them nervously. They represented over a year's salary. He hesitated a moment, "I don't know,"—and he shook his head, as were he arguing with himself—"I don't know whether I am doing right." And at once prepared the mixture.

Ten minutes later Lenox was mounting the stair of the hotel at which he lodged. On reaching his room he put his purchases on a table, poured out a glass of absinthe, lit a cigarette, and threw himself down on a lounge. For a while his thoughts roamed among the episodes of the day, but gradually they drifted into less personal currents. He began to think of the early legends: of Chiron, the god, renouncing his immortality; of the Hyperboreans, that fabled people, famous for their felicity, who voluntarily threw themselves into the sea; of Juno bringing death to Biton and Cleobis as the highest recompense of their piety; of Agamedes and Trophonius, praying Apollo for whatever gift he deemed most advantageous, and in answer to the prayer receiving eternal sleep.

He reflected on the meaning of these legends, and, as he reflected, he remembered that the Thracians greeted birth with lamentations and death with welcoming festivals. He thought of that sage who pitied the gods because their lives were unending, and of Menander singing the early demise of the favored. He remembered how Plato had preached to the happiest people in the world the blessedness of ceaseless sleep; how the Buddha, teaching that life was but a right to suffer, had found for the recalcitrant no greater menace than that of an existence renewed through kalpas of time. Then he bethought him of the promise of that peace which passeth all understanding, and which the grave alone fulfills, and he repeated to himself Christ's significant threat, "In this life ye shall have tribulation."

And, as these things came to him, so, too, did the problem of pain. He reviewed the ravages of that ulcer which has battened on humanity since the world began. History uncoiled itself before him in a shudder. In its spasms he saw the myriads that have fought and died for dogmas that they did not understand, for invented principles of patriotism and religion, for leaders that they had never seen, for gods more helpless than themselves.

He saw, too, Nature's cruelty and her snares. The gift to man of appetites, which, in the guise of pleasure, veil immedicable pain. Poison in the richest flowers, the agony that lurks in the grape. He knew that whoso ate to his hunger, or drank to his thirst, summoned to him one or more of countless maladies—maladies which parents gave with their vices to their children, who, in turn, bring forth new generations that are smitten with all the ills to which flesh is heir. And he knew that even those who lived most temperately were defenceless from disorders that come unawares and frighten away one's nearest friends. While for those who escaped miasmas and microbes; for those who asked pleasure, not of the flesh, but of the mind; for those whose days are passed in study, who seek to learn some rhyme for the reason of things, who try to gratify the curiosity which Nature has given them; for such as they, he remembered, there is blindness, paralysis, and the asylums of the insane.

He thought of the illusions, of love, hope and ambition, illusions which make life seem a pleasant thing worth living, and which, in cheating man into a continuance of his right to suffer, make him think pain an accident and not the rule.

"Surely," he mused, "the idiot alone is content. He at least has no illusions; he expects nothing in this world and cares less for another. Nor is the stupidity of the ordinary run of men without its charm. It must be a singularly blessed thing not to be sensitive, not to know what life might be, and not to find its insufficiency a curse. But there's the rub. When the reforms of the utopists are one and all accomplished, what shall man do in his Icaria? A million years hence, perhaps, physical pain will have been vanquished. Diseases of the body will no longer exist. Laws will not oppress. Justice will be inherent. Love will be too far from Nature to know of shame. The earth will be a garden of pleasure. Industry will have enriched every home. Through an equitable division of treasures acquired without toil, each one will be on the same footing as his neighbor. Even envy will have disappeared. In place of the trials, terrors and superstitions of to-day, man will enjoy perfect peace. He will no longer labor. When he journeys it will be through the air. He will be in daily communication with Mars, he will have measured the Infinite and know the bounds of Space. And in this Eden in which there will be no forbidden fruit, no ignorance, no tempter, but where there will be larger flowers, new perfumes, and a race whose idea of beauty stands to mine as mine does to that of prehistoric man, a race whose imagination has crossed the frontiers of the impossible, who have developed new senses, who see colors to which I am blind, who hear music to which I am deaf, who speak in words of tormented polish, who have turned art into a plaything and learning into a birthright, a race that has no curiosity and who accept their wonderful existence as the rich to-day accept their wealth, in this Eden, Boredom will be King. The Hyperboreans will have their imitators. The one surcease will be in death. Yet even that may not be robbed of its grotesqueness."

A candle flickered a moment and expired in a splutter of grease. The agony of the candle aroused him from his revery. "Bah," he muttered, "I am becoming a casuist, I argue with myself."

He mixed himself another absinthe, holding the *carafe* high in the air, watching the thin stream of water coalesce with the green drug and turn with it into an opalescent milk. He toyed for a moment with the purchases that he had made in the Rue de la Paix, and presently, in answer to some query which they evoked, the soliloquy began anew.

"After what has happened there is nothing left. I might change my name. I might go to Brazil or Australia, but with what object? I could not get away from myself.

> Da me stesso
> Sempre fuggendo, avrò me sempre appresso.

Beside I don't care for transplantation. If I had an ambition it would be a different matter. If I could be a pretty woman up to thirty, a cardinal up to fifty, and after that the Anti-Christ, it might be worth while. Failing that I might occupy myself with literature. If I have not written heretofore, it is because it seems more original not to do so. But it is not too late. The manufacture of trash is easy, and it must be a pleasure to the manufacturer to know that it is trash and that it sells. It must give him a high opinion of the intellect of his contemporaries. Or when, as happens now and then, a work of enduring value is produced, and it is condemned, as such works usually are, the author must take immense delight in the reflection that the disapproval of imbeciles is the surest acknowledgment of talent, as it is also its sweetest mead of praise. For me, of course, such praise is impossible. Were I to write successful failures, it must needs be under a pseudonym. In which case I would have the consciousness of being scorned as Lenox Leigh, and admired as John Smith. Beside, what is there to write about? There is nothing to prove, there is no certainty, there is not even a criterion of truth. To-morrow contradicts yesterday, next week will contradict this. On no given subject are there two people who think and see exactly alike. The book which pleases me bores my neighbor, and *vice versâ*. One man holds to the Episcopal Church, another to the Baptist; one man is an atheist, another a Jew; one man thinks a soprano voice a delicious gift, another says it is a disease of the larynx, and whatever the divergence of opinion may be, each one is convinced that he alone is correct. Supposing, however, that through some chance I were to descend to posterity in the garb and aspect of a great man. What is a great man? The shadow of nothing. The obscurest *privat docent* in Germany could to-day give points to Newton. And even though Newton's glory may still subsist, yet such are the limitations of fame that the great majority have never heard of it or of him. The foremost conqueror of modern times, he who fell not through his defeats, but through his victories, is entombed just across the Seine. And the other day as I passed the Invalides I heard an intelligent-looking woman ask her companion who the Napoleon was that lay buried there. Her companion did not know. "But, even were glory more substantial, what is the applause of posterity to the ears of the dead? To them honor and ignominy must be alike unmeaning. No, decidedly, ambition does not tempt me. And what is there else that tempts? Love seems to me now like hunger, an unnecessary affliction, productive far more of pain than of pleasure; the most natural, the most alluring thing of all, see in what plight it has brought me. Yet it is, I have heard, the ultimate hope of those who have none. If I relinquish it, what have I left? The satisfaction of my curiosity as to what the years may hold? But I am indifferent. To revenge myself on Incoul. Certainly, I would like to cut his heart out and force it down his throat! But how would it better me? If I could be transported to the multicolored nights of other worlds, and there taste of inexperienced pleasures, move in new refinements, lose my own identity, or pursue a chimera and catch it, it might be worth while, but, as it is—"

The clock on the mantel rang out four times. Again Lenox started from his revery. He smiled cynically at himself. "If I continue in that strain," he muttered, "it must be that I am drunk."

But soon his eyes closed again in mental retrospect. "And yet," he mused, "life is pleasant; ill spent as mine has been, many times I have found it grateful. In books, I have often lost the consciousness of my own identity; now and then music has indeed had the power to take me to other worlds, to show me fresh horizons and larger life. Maida herself came to me like a revelation. She gave me a new conception of beauty. Yes, I have known very many pleasant hours. I was younger then, I fancy. After all, it is not life that is short, it is youth. When that goes, as mine seems to have done, outside of solitude there is little charm in anything. And what is death but isolation? The most perfect and impenetrable that Nature has devised. And whether that isolation come to me to-night or decades hence, what matters it? It is odd, though, how the thought of it unnerves one, and yet, to be logical, I suppose one should be as uneasy of the chaos which precedes existence as of the unknowable that follows it. The proper course, I take it, is to imitate the infant, who faces death without a tremor, and enters it without regret."

He stood up, and drawing the curtains aside, looked out into the night. From below came the rumble of a cart on its way to the Halles, but otherwise the street was silent. The houses opposite were livid. There was a faint flicker from the street lamps, and above were the trembling stars. The moon had gone, but there was yet no sign of coming dawn.

He left the window. The candles had burned down; he found fresh ones and lighted them. As he did so, he caught sight of himself in the glass. His eyes were haggard and rimmed with circles. It was owing to the position of the candles, he thought, and he raised them above his head and looked again. There was something on his forehead just above the temple, and he put the candles down to brush that something away. He looked again, it was still there. He peered into the glass and touched it with his hand. It was nothing, he found, merely a lock of hair that had turned from black to white.

He poured out more absinthe, and put the bottle down empty. Before drinking it he undid the package which he had bought from the chemist. First he took from it a box about three inches long. In it was a toy syringe, and with it two little instruments. One of these he adjusted in the projecting tube, and with his finger felt carefully of the point. It was sharp as a needle, and beneath the point was an orifice like a shark's mouth, in miniature.

Then he took from the package a phial that held a brown liquid, in which he detected a shade like to that of gold. The odor was dull and heavy. He put the phial down and stood for a moment irresolute. He had looked into the past and now he looked into the future. But in its Arcadias he saw nothing, save his own image suspended from a gibbet. He looked again almost wistfully; no, there was nothing. He threw off his coat and rolled up his sleeve. From the phial he filled the syringe, and with the point pricked the bare arm and sent the liquid spurting into the flesh. Three times he did this. He reached for the absinthe and left it untasted.

Into his veins had come an unknown, a delicious languor. He sank into a chair. The walls of the room dissolved into cataracts of light and dazzling steel. The flooring changed to running crimson, and from that to black, and back to red again. From the ceiling came flood after flood of fused, inter-mingled and oscillating colors. His eyes closed. The light be-came more intense, and burned luminous through the lids. In his ears filtered a harmony, faint as did it come from afar, and singular as were it won from some new consonance of citherns and clavichords, and suddenly it rose into tumultu-ous vibrations, striated with series of ascending scales. Then as suddenly ceased, drowned in claps of thunder.

The lights turned purple and glowed less vividly, as though veils were being lowered between him and them. But still the languor continued, sweeter ever and more en-veloping, till from very sweetness it was almost pain.

The room grew darker, the colors waned, the lights be-hind the falling veils sank dim, and dimmer, fading, one by one; a single spark lingered, it wavered a moment, and van-ished into night.

XVII.
MAIDA'S NUPTIALS

For some time after Lenox had gone there was much excitement at the Capucines. But gradually the excitement wore itself out, as excitement always does. Baccarat for that night, at least, had lost its allurement. The habitués dispersed, some to other clubs, some to their homes, and soon the great rooms were deserted by all, save one deaf man, who, undisturbed by the commotion, had given himself up to the task of memorizing Sarcey's feuilleton.

Among the earliest to leave was Mr. Incoul. "Come," he said to Blydenburg, "you have seen enough for one evening," and Blydenburg got into his coat and followed his companion to the street. They walked some distance before either of them spoke, but when they reached the hotel at which Blydenburg was stopping, that gentleman halted at an adjacent lamp-post.

"I must say, Incoul," he began, "and I hope you will take it very kindly—I must say that I think you might have left that matter for some one else to discover. Why, hang it all! Leigh is a friend of your wife's; you know all his people; to you the money was nothing. Really, Incoul, damn me if I don't think it hard-hearted. I don't care that for what those frog-eaters say; the cards you said were marked, don't weigh with me in the least; no, not an atom; it is my opinion that the young man was just as innocent as a child unborn. No, sir, you can't make me believe that he—that he—I hate to say the word—that he cheated. Why, man alive! I had my eyes on him the whole time. A better-looking fellow never breathed, and he just chucked out the cards one after another without so much as looking at them; it seemed to me that he didn't care a rap whether he won or lost. I put down a louis or two myself, and he never noticed it; he left the whole thing to the croupier, and now that I come to think of it—"

"Yes, I know," Mr. Incoul interrupted, "I am sorry myself."

"Well, then, I'll be shot if you look so. Good-night to you," and with that Blydenburg stamped up to the hotel, rang the bell, and slammed the door behind him.

Mr. Incoul walked on. The annoyance of his friend affected him like a tonic; he continued his way refreshed. Presently he reached a cab stand. The clock marked 11:50. He had other duties, and he let himself into an Urbaine and told the man to drive to the Parc Monceau. On arriving he tossed a coin to the cabby and entered the house.

In the vestibule a footman started from a nap. Mr. Incoul went up to the floor above and waited, the door ajar. For a little space he heard the man moving about, whispering to a fellow footman. But soon the whispering ceased. Evidently the men had gone. Assured of this, he opened a drawer and took from it a steel instrument, one that in certain respects resembled a key; the haft, however, was unusually large, the end was not blunt but hollow, yet fashioned like a pincer, and the projecting tongue which, in the case of an ordinary key serves to lock and unlock, was absent. This he put in his pocket. He went out in the hall and listened again. The house was very quiet. He made sure that the footmen had really gone, and walking on tip-toe to his wife's door, rapped ever so noiselessly.

"Is it you, Harmon?" he heard her ask. Had he wished he had no time to answer. A key turned in the lock, the door was opened, and before him Maida stood, smiling a silent welcome to his first visit to her room.

As he entered and closed the door her lips parted; she would have spoken, but something in his face repelled her; the smile fell from her face and the words remained unuttered.

He stood a moment rubbing his hands frigidly, as were he cold, yet the room was not chilly. There was no fire in the grate, but two gas fixtures gave out sufficient heat to warm it unassisted. Then presently he looked at her. She had thrown herself on a lounge near the hearth, and was certainly most fair to see. Her white gown had been replaced by one of looser cut; her neck and arms were no longer bare, but one foot shod in fur that the folds of the skirt left visible was stockingless and the wonder of her hair was unconfined.

He found a chair and seated himself before her. "Madame," he said at last, "I am here at your request."

The girl started as were she stung.

"You were obliging enough this evening to inform me that we had come into our own. What is it?" His eyebrows were raised and about his thin lips was just the faintest expression of contempt. "What is it into which we have come?"

Maida grew whiter than the whitest ermine; she moved her hand as would she answer, but he motioned her to be silent.

"I will tell you," he continued in his measured way, "and you will pardon me if the telling is long. Before it was my privilege to make your acquaintance I was not, as you know, a bachelor; my wife"—and he accentuated the possessive pronoun as had he had but one—"was to me very dear. When I lost her, I thought at first there was nothing left me, but with time I grew to believe that life might still be livable. It is easy for you to understand that in my misfortune I was not dogmatic. I knew that no one is perfect, and I felt that if my wife had seemed perfection to me it was because we understood and loved one another. Then, too, as years passed I found my solitude very tedious. I was, it is true, no longer young, but I was not what the world has agreed to call old; and I thought that among the gracious women whom I knew it might be possible for me to find one who would consent to dispel the solitude, and who might perhaps be able to bring me some semblance of my former happiness. It was under these conditions that I met you. You remember what followed. I saw that you were beautiful, more so, indeed, than my wife, and I imagined that you were honest and self-respecting—in fact, a girl destined to become a noble woman. It was then that I ventured to address you. You told me of your poverty; I begged you to share the money which was mine; you told me that you did not love me. I answered that I would wait. I was glad to share the money with you. I was willing to wait. I knew that you would adorn riches; I believed that I could win your love, and I felt that the winning would be pleasant. I even admired you for the agreement which you suggested. I thought it could not come from any one not wholly refined and mistress of herself. In short, believing in your frankness, I offered you what I had to give. In return what did I ask? The opportunity to be with you, the opportunity of winning your affection and therewith a little trust, a little confidence and the proper keeping of my name. Surely I was not extravagant in my demands. And you, for all your frankness, omitted to tell me the one thing essential: you omitted to tell me—"

"Do not say it," the girl wailed; "do not say it." The tears were falling, her form was rocked with sobs. She was piteous before him who knew not what pity was.

He had risen and she crouched as though she feared he had risen to strike her.

"Of your lover whom I caught to-night cheating at cards."

He had struck her indeed. She looked up through her tears astonished at the novelty of the blow, and yet still she did not seem to understand. She stared at him vacantly as though uncertain of the import of his words.

"Of your lover," he repeated; "the blackleg."

She rose from her seat. She was trembling from head to foot. To support herself she stretched a hand to the mantel and clutching it, she steadied herself. Then, still looking him in the face, she said huskily, "You tell me Lenox Leigh cheated at cards? It is not true!"

"He is your lover, then!" hissed Incoul, and into his green, dilated eyes there came a look of such hideous hate that the girl shrank back.

In her fear she held out her arms as though to shield herself from him, and screamed aloud. "You are going to kill me? " she cried.

"Be quiet," he answered, "you will wake the house."

But the order was needless. The girl fell backwards on the lounge. He stood and looked at her without moving. Presently she moaned; her eyes opened and her sobs broke out afresh. And still he gazed as though in enjoyment of a hope fulfilled.

"Now get to your bed," he said, at last.

His eyes searched the room. On a table was a pink box

labeled bromide of potassium, and filled with powders wrapped in tin foil. He opened and smelled of one and then opened another and poured the contents of both into a glass which he half filled with water.

"Drink it," he said.

She obeyed dumbly. The tears fell into the glass as she drank. But in a little while her sobs came only intermittently. "I will sleep now," she murmured, helplessly, "I think I will sleep now." Yet still he waited. Her head had fallen far back on the sofa, her hair drooped about her shoulders, her lips were gray.

He took her in his arms and carried her to the bed. One of her furred slippers dropped on the way, the other he took from her. The foot it held hardly filled his palm. He loosened her gown. He would have taken it off but he feared to awake her. Was she really asleep, he wondered. He peered down at her eyelids but they did not move. Surely she slept. A door that led to a dressing-room was open. He closed it. The chair in which he had sat he restored to its original position. Then he turned out the gas. On each of the fixtures his fingers rested the fraction of a minute longer than was necessary. He groped to the door, opened it noiselessly and listened. There was no sound. The house was still as a tomb. He closed the door behind him and drawing the nameless instrument from his pocket he inserted it carefully in the keyhole, gave it a quick turn and went to his room.

XVIII.
MR. INCOUL GOES OVER THE ACCOUNTS

There is a saying to the effect that any one who walks long enough in front of the Grand Hotel will, in the course of time, encounter all his acquaintances, past, present and to be. On the second day after the dinner in the Parc Monceau, Mr. Blydenburg crossed the boulevard. It was an unpleasant afternoon of the kind which is frequent in the early winter: the air was damp and penetrating, and the sky presented that unrelieved and cheerless pallor of which Paris is believed to be the unique possessor. Mr. Blydenburg's spirits were affected; he was ill at ease and inclined to attribute his depression to the rawness of the air and the blanched sky above him. He was to leave Paris on the morrow, and he felt that he would be glad to shake its mud from his feet. He was then on the way to his banker's to close an account, and as he trudged along, with an umbrella under his arm and his trousers turned up, in spite of the prospect of departure he was not in a contented or satisfied frame of mind.

For many hours previous he had cross-questioned himself in regard to Incoul. He knew that in speak ing out his mind he had done right, yet he could not help perceiving that right-doing and outspokenness are not always synonymous with the best breeding. Truth certainly is attractive, particularly to him who tells it, but one has to be hospitably inclined to receive it at all times as a welcome guest. Beside, he told himself, Incoul was a man to whom remonstrance was irksome, he chafed at it no matter what its supporting truths might be. Perhaps then it would have been better had he held his tongue. Incoul was his oldest friend, he could not afford to lose him; at his time of life the making of new ones was difficult. And yet did he seek him in a conciliatory mood it would be tantamount to acknowledging that Incoul had been in the right, and the more he thought the matter over the more convinced he became that Incoul was in the wrong. Leigh, he could have sworn, was innocent. The charge that had been brought against him was enough to make a mad dog blush. It was preposterous on the face of it. Then, too, the young man had been given no opportunity to defend himself. The honest-hearted gentleman did not make it plain to his own mind how Leigh could have defended himself even had the opportunity been offered, but he waived objections; his faith was firm. He was enough of a logician to understand that circumstantial evidence, however strong, is not unrebuttable proof, and he assured himself, unless the young man confessed his guilt, that he at least would never believe it.

He was not, therefore, in a contented or satisfied frame of mind; he was irresolute how to act to Incoul; he did not wish to lose an old friend and he was physically unable to be unjust to a new one. After crossing the boulevard he passed the Grand Hotel and just as he left the wide portals behind him he saw Mr. Wainwaring, with whom two days before he had dined in the Parc Monceau. He bowed and would have continued his way, but Mr. Wainwaring stopped him.

"You have heard, have you not?" he asked excitedly, "you have heard about Mrs. Incoul?"

"Heard what?"

"It appears that on going to bed on Sunday night she turned the gas on instead of turning it off. They smelled the gas in the hall and tried to get into the room, but the door was locked; finally they broke it down. They found her unconscious though still breathing; they worked over her for five hours, but it was no use."

Blydenburg grounded his umbrella on the pavement for support. "Good God!" he muttered, " Good God!"

"Yes," Mr. Wainwaring continued, "it is terrible! A sweeter girl never lived. My daughter knew her intimately; she went there this morning to see her and learned of it at the door. I have just been up there myself. I thought Incoul might see me, but he couldn't. Utterly prostrated I suppose. I can understand that. We all know how devoted he was. He will never get over it—never."

Blydenburg still held to his umbrella for support.

"I must go there," he said.

"Yes, go by all means; he will see you, of course. Poor Incoul! I am heartily sorry for him. After all, wealth is not happiness, is it?"

At this platitude Blydenburg would have gone, but Mr. Wainwaring had more news to impart. "You know about young Leigh, Mrs. Manhattan's brother, don't you? " he continued.

Blydenburg looked down at his umbrella in a weary way.

"Yes, I was there," he answered, "but I don't believe it."

"Oh, you mean that affair at the club. Well, it appears that it is true. From what I make out of the papers, he went to his hotel afterwards, and took a dose of morphine. It was his only way out of it. I couldn't bear him, could you?"

Blydenburg nodded vacantly. "He must have been guilty."

"As to that there is no doubt. De la Dèche says it is a wonder he was not caught before. Well, good-day; tell Incoul how profoundly grieved we all are. Good-day."

Presently Blydenburg found himself in a cab. He was a trifle dazed at what he had heard. He was not brilliant; he was very tiresome at times, the sort of a man that likes big words and small dictionaries, yet somehow he was lovable and more human than many far cleverer than he. To his own misfortune he had a heart, and in disasters like these it bled. He would have crossed the Continent to bring a moment's pleasure to the girl that had been asphyxiated in her bed, and he would have given his daughter to the man who had been choked down to the grave. Then, too, as nearly as he could see, he had wronged Incoul and Incoul was in great grief. As the Urbaine rolled on, his thoughts did not grow nimbler. In his head was a full, aching sensation; he felt benumbed, and raised the collar of his coat. Soon the cab stopped before the house in the Parc Monceau. He had no little set speech prepared; he wanted merely to take his friend by the hand and let him feel his sympathy unspoken, but when the footman came in answer to his ring, he was told that Mr. Incoul could see no one. He went back to his cab. It had begun to rain, but he did not notice it, and left the window open.

As the cab rolled down the street again, Mr. Incoul, who had been occupied with the morning paper, sent for the courier.

"Karl," he said, when the man appeared, "I will go over your accounts."

THE END.

MR. INCOUL'S MISADVENTURE

Other titles you may enjoy from

UNDERWORLD AMUSEMENTS
WWW.UNDERWORLDAMUSEMENTS.COM

Confessions of a Failed Egoist
And Other Essays
by Trevor Blake
5.25x8, 139 pages, $9.95
ISBN: 978-09885536-5-1

A Bible Not Borrowed from the Neighbors.
Essays and Aphorisms on Egoism
Edited by Kevin I. Slaughter
6x9, 164 pages, $14.95
ISBN: 978-0988553613

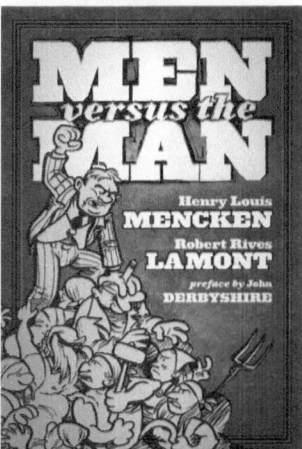

Men versus the Man
Socialism versus Individualism
by H.L. Mencken and Robert Rives La Monte
Preface by John Derbyshire
6x9, 204 pages, $15.95
ISBN: 978-0983031420

The Philosophical Writings of Edgar Saltus
*Containing the books "The Philosophy of Disen-
chantment" and "The Anatomy of Negation"*
Foreword by Chip Smith
6x9, 366 pages, $18.95

ANATHEMA!
Litanies of Negation
by Benjamin DeCasseres
Foreword by Eugene O'Neill
Afterword by Kevin I. Slaughter
6x9, 66 pages, $9.99
ISBN: 978-0988553620

IMP
The Poetry of Benjamin DeCasseres
by Benjamin DeCasseres
Introduction by Kevin I. Slaughter
6x9, 196 pages, $14.95
ISBN: 978-0983031451

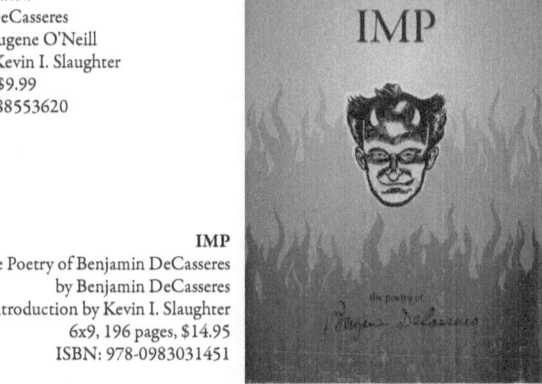